A NOVEL

Lessons
FROM THE
Gypsy Camp

ELIZABETH APPELL

Published by Scribes Valley Publishing
6824 Drybrook Lane
Knoxville, TN 37921-7312
www.scribesvalley.com

Cover and interior design: Tammy Sneath Grimes, Crescent Communications
www.tsgcrescent.com • 814.941.7447

Cover photo of 'Lolly' by Tammy Sneath Grimes, photo model Karissa Collier
Author's Photo by Allen Appell

ISBN: 0-9742652-1-7

Printed in the United States of America

First Edition

For Allen, who is everything

Acknowledgments

Thank you to Claire and Richard who gave me the courage to write the book. I also want to thank Cecilia McClellan, Karen Neureuter, and Carol Hehmeyer who slogged their way through early versions, Monica Faulkner for her guidance in fleshing out the characters, Drucilla Campbell for helping me keep the plot on track, Mark Wisniewski for assisting me in cutting those perfect seventy pages, and Mary Roby who pointed me toward the right ending. Thank you to Francie Johnson Lindsey for her friendship and for letting me use her name, and thank you to my daughters Amy and Jenner, my step-daughters Betsy and Jackie for believing in me. I also want to thank David Repsher for his enthusiasm for the work. A special thank you to Sally, our Border Collie/Lab mix, the dearest dog who has patiently listened to every version of this story.

—Elizabeth Appell, November 2003

...forty years ago you were caught by light

and fixed in that secret

place where we live, where we believe

nothing can change...

Margaret Atwood, Girl and Horse, 1928
Selected Poems, Simon & Schuster, 1976

For every life and every act

Consequence of good and evil can be shown

And as in time results of many deeds are blended

So good and evil in the end become confounded.

T.S. Eliot, Murder in the Cathedral

Lessons

FROM THE

Gypsy Camp

Chapter One

SPRING 1955

"**Y**ou can do this," Lolly whispered to her reflection in the huge antique mirror. Jittery as a wind-up toy, Lolly stood in the coolness of the marble entry hall and chewed her cuticle. "You can. Tonight's going to be different."

She whirled madly to make her lemon-yellow seersucker skirt spread like flower petals. A gift from her father last week when she turned ten, the dress had become a part of her plan. She wanted to look especially nice, except for being barefooted. She wasn't big on wearing shoes.

Excitement churned in her stomach. If she was going to get her father to take her seriously, she would have to stand up to him and state her case concisely, just as he did when he prosecuted cases in court.

Lolly opened the front door and stepped out onto the porch of the old Victorian house. Her mother always said it was a privilege to live in the Victorian, that it was a piece of history built during the days of the California Gold Rush.

She breathed the unusually warm late-afternoon air. An early summer had undulated into the Sacramento Valley, breathing fire into the orchards and rice paddies surrounding the town. Bo, her eighteen-year-old orange cat, followed her.

He curled his arthritic body on the canvas seat of the swing and lay panting.

A breeze stirring from the other side of the levee whiffled about her, tousling her sleeves and she leaned against the hand-carved railing. She raised her arms, pretending they were wings, and flew. In her mind, she soared over the gabled roof like Peter Pan.

"If I can't get him to go along with me, Bo,"—he perked up at the sound of his name—"it means he doesn't give a rat's ass and we might as well run away." She brushed her face against Bo's. "Don't worry," she said. "There's no way he won't make the deal."

The proposition she was about to make stemmed from her last visit to her occasional friend, Francie Johnson, a Protestant girl who lived down the street. It had been one of the few times that her parents allowed her to have dinner away from home.

At home, dinner meant sitting in the dark room her parents had dubbed the "add-on." In the evening, its walls flickered with light from the black-and-white television they had bought to watch the Eisenhower-Stevenson debates. Her mother rarely joined them, but stayed upstairs in the bedroom, leaving her alone with her father to pick at their tepid TV dinners. He slouched in his overstuffed lounge chair, slurred his words, and demeaned everything and everyone who appeared on the screen, except when President Eisenhower came on. Then he would sit up and shush her if she spoke. "Have you no respect?" he would say.

So it was at the Johnsons' that she realized she could eat her entire dinner without having to force food down between knots in her throat. That night, when her mother came into her bedroom to hear her prayers, Lolly knelt and made the Sign of the Cross. "In the name of the Father, and of the Son, and of the Holy Ghost. God bless Mama and Daddy and Bo and me. And God, please let us have dinners like they do at the Johnsons' and have Daddy talk to me at the table." She blessed herself and crawled into bed.

"Your daddy is who he is and nothing's going to change him." Her mother leaned over and gathered her into her arms.

Lolly twined her mother's hair around her finger and breathed in her scents of Estee Lauder and Kent cigarettes. "I don't want to change him. I just want him to talk to me."

"Don't bother with those kinds of prayers, Lolly. God made your daddy. Once the cherry pie comes out of the oven, you can't turn it into a lemon meringue."

"Do you love Daddy?" she asked.

Her mother sighed, then said, "Of course."

Lolly liked the feel of her mother's fingers combing through her unbraided hair.

"Do you think he loves you?"

Her mother said, "Yes. But there's two things I want for you, Lolly girl."

"What are they, Mama?"

"I want you to need your own approval before anyone else's, and I want you to be able to take care of yourself in case you ever have to."

"What do you mean?"

"Just that you mustn't be afraid."

"Of Daddy?"

"Of anything."

Lolly propped herself up on her elbows. She wasn't sure what her mother meant, but she felt uneasy, like she had that winter day just before last Christmas when she went to school and Sister Julie Delores, her favorite teacher, left and never came back. Some of the other fifth-graders said Sister Julie had given up convent life. Others said she was sick. Reggie Cotton, the boy who sat in front of Lolly, said aliens had abducted her.

Now, Lolly stepped back from the porch railing and smoothed the puckery seersucker of her shirt. The scent of wisteria mixed with the heavy evening and the air pressed down like a suffocating blanket.

She listened for the sound of her father's car. This year it was a slick white 1955 Lincoln Capri. Every night at precisely five o'clock, he would gun the car up the long driveway and squeal to a stop.

"Lolly."

She heard her mother calling from the bedroom window that overlooked the front garden. Her mother's voice reminded her of the clear, bright bells rung in Mass. Even when her mother was in one of her sad times, her voice sounded like music. Her mother referred to her sad times as "being in the trough." Doc Pine, who came to the house to give her mother shots and pills, called it depression. "Here you go, Clarissa, something to smooth away the rough edges." He'd give her an injection or leave a bottle of pills on her nightstand.

"I'm on the front porch, Mama." Lolly jumped down the steps to look past the overhang and up at the window. Her mother had on a mauve linen blouse the color of a bruise. In one hand she held a cigarette, the smoke snaking passed her face. Her other hand ran manicured fingers over her neck and bare shoulders as though she was trying to soothe herself. There was something about her pale, perfect skin, cheeks tinged with pink that reminded Lolly of the ladies in Grandfather Jeb's photo albums: friends of his and his dead wife Lucy's. Those women had dark hair with stiff waves pasted close to their heads, while her mother was blonde with hair that curled softly around her face and her expression was sad.

"What are you doing, Lolly girl?" her mother asked.

"Waiting for Daddy. Feeling better, Mama?"

"A little low, darling."

A breeze stirred and touched the ribbons on Lolly's auburn braids just as the deep roar of the Capri reached her from the bottom of the driveway. She flipped her braids back over her shoulders and ran her hands over her pleated skirt. Her stomach lurched. She stole a quick glance up at her mother's window. It was empty.

Back on the porch she cupped Bo's face in her hands. "Okay, Bo," she asked. "Are you ready?" She closed her eyes and breathed deeply. When she opened her eyes, the Capri had pulled up.

Chapter Two

A s the engine pinged, her father emerged lugging his bulging briefcase. Every night he hauled home stacks of work but the documents and files never left his leather attaché. Lately he had been edgier than ever. Anger had shot through his voice during the long phone conversations in his study. Lolly had picked up only bits and pieces but the issue seemed to be that someone was trying to take his job.

"Daddy!" she called even before he reached the stairs. "I have an idea..."

No, she thought, and closed her mouth. *That's no way to begin.*

Her father headed up the walk with his familiar rolling tread, his off-white suit limp and deeply creased. It was April. Early for him to wear linen, but it was too hot for wool. He took two stairs at a time and he seemed enormous, so tall that when he had reached the arbor dripping with wisteria, she half expected—as she always did—that he would have to duck. It was strange how, although he loomed large when he arrived home, by the time he went to bed, he became shrunken and small. A hank of hair fell across his brow. It was only recently that strands of gray had begun to weave through his unruly dark mane. Quick brown eyes snapped at her and a carefully trimmed mustache covered his upper lip.

"Hello, Lolly girl." His hand ran lightly over her head and down one of her braids. "You're looking mighty pretty tonight in your birthday dress. You braid your hair yourself or did your mama help you?"

She wanted to say she had done it herself, but this was no night for tall tales, just straight talk. Just like in court, because that was what he understood.

"Mama helped," she said. "But I picked out the ribbons."

He opened the screen door and held it for her. Bo jumped off the swing and slithered inside first. Dropping his briefcase on the marble floor, her father shrugged off his suit jacket and draped it over the back of one of the twin antique French chairs that sat on either side of the antique mahogany console table. Thanks to her mother, it always held a vase of fresh flow-ers. Today they were freesias.

"Where's your mama?" her father asked.

"Upstairs. She's having a head hammer."

"Is that what you call them? Head hammers?"

Lolly nodded and grabbed his hand. "Can we go into the living room?" she said trying to keep her voice strong. "I need to talk to you."

There, she thought. Her plan was in motion and she felt pleased with herself.

"I'm a tired man tonight, Lolly pie. Daddy needs a small libation and some peace. And I don't think I'm going to find either of those in the living room."

She knew his routine only too well. Straight to the kitchen, where he'd pull out a bottle of vodka and pour himself what he called "a horn of corn," knocking back the first jelly glass in three gulps, sometimes two before pouring himself a second glass and then a third. By the third horn of corn he'd be slurring his words and his eyes wouldn't snap at anyone. They'd leer, and his teeth would clamp down in a mean, desperate way. Then he'd stagger into his study to play the saxophone.

"Please," she said and tugged at his hand. Sighing, he followed her into the dim living room where heavy velvet curtains had been drawn because of the heat.

Bo had already made himself comfortable on the plush green couch, but when Lolly's father sat down beside him, loosening his tie and taking Lolly on his lap, the cat moved to the far end and curled in a circle of fur. Lolly smelled the aroma of cigar smoke that clung to her father like an invisible jacket, a reassuring smell because he smoked only when he worked and when he worked he never drank.

"So what's this all about?" He fingered her braids. "Your hair's getting longer and prettier every week."

She took a deep breath. "I want to...I want us to try and make..." Her hand brushed his loosened tie.

"Well, young lady, out with it. What's on your mind?"

She knew exactly what she wanted, knew it as completely and precisely as she knew her prayers. But her father was like a ferocious brown bear ranging through her life, and sometimes it felt like she and her mother were his only prey. Now that she was sitting on his lap, the words wouldn't come. Frustration scalded the back of her throat and seared away the words.

"I don't have all night." He nudged her off his lap, forcing her to stand.

Her lips moved, but no words came out. She should have known he wouldn't give her a chance to tell him anything. He never did.

"All right, Miss Candolin, you've had your chance. If you have something to say, put it in a memo," he said impatiently. He leaned forward to stand, but her hands came down on his shoulders with her full might and shoved him back. It wasn't her strength that kept him from rising, but surprise.

"I won't tolerate this nonsense!" He was angry now. "I've had a hell of a day, Lolly, and I need to relax!"

"I know," she whispered. The words she needed to say clanged inside her head. "I want to have dinners like they do at Francie Johnson's and I want you to..."

"Fine." He shrugged. "Talk to your mother. I'm sure she can get Ruth Johnson to share her recipes."

"No! You don't understand!" He was so smart. Why was this so difficult for him?

His eyes flickered over her. "Well, I guess I don't. But I do understand that your old daddy here needs a horn of corn, so that's my next stop."

Lolly bunched her skirt in her fists. She wanted to say, "I don't want you to drink horns of corns! I want us to sit at the table instead of in front of the television, and I want you to talk to me and not say bad words or spill your dinner or put napkins on your head!"

She felt her unspoken words hanging between. She took a step toward him but she was silent.

He leaned back against the couch. "Well?"

And then her words broke through. "If you stop drinking horns of corn, I promise I'll never cut my hair!" She buried her face in her hands. That wasn't what she had meant to say. But there it was. An ultimatum.

Her father reached out and gripped her upper arms. His hands were strong and they hurt. But then he seemed to think better of whatever he was going to do or say and, pushing himself up from the couch, walked past her into the kitchen, his shoulders slightly more stooped now, his breath a bit more labored.

She knelt beside Bo and stroked him. From the kitchen, she heard the familiar clink of the bottle connecting with the rim of the glass. Once. Twice. She knew it was vodka he was pouring.

She then heard his footsteps, one after the other, as he climbed the stairs.

Lolly's anger boiled. *It's so easy,* she thought. *All you have to do is drink milk instead of that stupid vodka. All you have to do is sit at the table and talk to me. All you have to do is...*

Then came the challenge.

I'll show you.

She sat on the couch in the darkened room contemplating her next move. The scent of cigar smoke lingered. Bo climbed into her lap and purred, a small furry motor.

She heard her parents' voices upstairs, beginning as the soft murmurings of a man and woman discussing the day and what to have for dinner, but soon the level rose. She crept to the bottom of the stairs.

"What do you expect?" It was her mother's voice.

"Goddamn it, Clarissa..."

"You can't blame her." Her mother's words came high and shrill. "Your drinking scares her!"

"Nonsense!"

"She made you an offer, Regan. Can't you at least talk to her about it?"

Lolly tiptoed up to the landing.

"You should have heard her," he said. "Barely able to get the words out of her mouth. It's time she learns that if you want to get somewhere in life, you damn well better know how to speak up."

"She's only ten!"

"I don't give a good goddamn! And then threatening to

cut her hair! I don't work myself like a jack mule all day to come home and have my daughter greet me with a take it or leave it deal at night. Who the hell does that girl think she is?"

"Don't call her 'that girl'! She's your daughter!"

Lolly clung to the banister and forced herself to breathe.

"I'll be damned if I want her to turn out a pill-popper like you!"

"That's what you always do!" her mother retorted. "Act as if I'm to blame! She just wants you to notice she's alive!"

"Look who's talking!"

Lolly fled into her room and slammed the door behind her, but her parent's voices seeped through the door like toxic gas, so she ran into her bathroom, banged that door shut, and knocked her head against the shiny-white painted wood.

I'll show you. I'll show you both!

She yanked open the medicine cabinet. Sobs hiccupped in her chest and her eyes stung. Her hands flailed at the narrow glass shelves, knocking down her toothpaste tube and toothbrush, a Noxzema jar, some baby aspirin, the lipstick she had secretly bought two weeks ago with Francie while they'd been waiting for Francie's mother to pick them up at the dime store. But what she was looking for wasn't in the cabinet. She banged the cabinet shut and riffled through the drawer under the sink.

The scissors glinted in the light.

She looked at herself in the mirror, a thin, bony kid with swollen eyelids, the rims red and raw. Her reflection reached half way up the mirror. She was a head taller than most of the other ten-year-olds in her class, a head and a half taller than Francie.

"I hate him," she said to the girl in the mirror. The reflected girl looked confused. "Isn't that a sin?"

From across the hall, the battle had resumed. She stepped

out of her room. Through their closed bedroom door she heard her father roar, "I'm sick and tired of coming home and finding you in bed."

"Maybe I wouldn't be in bed if you wouldn't anesthetize yourself every night," her mother wailed.

Lolly fled back into her bathroom. "I'll show you what's a sin," she said to the reflection staring at her. Breathless. She picked up the scissors in one hand and her left braid in the other.

Can I do this? She knew her father loved her braids. According to him they were what saved her from being ugly. She didn't care. She wanted to hurt him and this was the only way she knew.

She began hacking at the hair and finally severed the braid. Still tied to the yellow ribbon, it fell to the bathroom floor.

Her breathing came in starts and stops, and she had to blink to see through her tears. Running the back of her hand across her face, she smeared away the wetness before cutting the other braid.

Lolly looked at herself in the mirror. "Oh, dear Jesus," she whispered. "What have I done?" The scissors clattered to the floor.

"You're crazy, Clarissa!"

Lolly stormed into her parent's room just as her father flung a vial of her mother's pills across the room. The tablets made a sound like a hundred ticking clocks. Small red dots peppered the bedspread and the nightstand. Some rolled into corners and clusters landed on the overstuffed chair and under the ottoman.

Her mother had just picked up a perfume bottle and drawn back her hand when she saw Lolly in the doorway and froze.

Lolly's breath stuttered. Her face prickled and her bangs stuck to her forehead. She raised her hands and cupped them over the coarse stubs of hair where her braids had been. They felt like stalks of late-summer corn.

"Baby!" Her mother took a step toward her, her force suddenly focused.

"Don't!" Her father stepped in and blocked her path. "Stay right where you are!"

Taking Lolly by the shoulders, he shook her. She tried to pull away, but he clamped her chin with his large hands and twisted her head from side to side.

Then he said one word. "Consequences."

Pushing Lolly aside, he headed downstairs.

"He can't help himself," her mother cried, taking her in her arms. "The drinking—it's a sickness, like having a bad cold. Lolly, please..."

Wrenching herself free, Lolly ran out of the room and down the stairs, stopping dead in the kitchen doorway as she saw her father slosh vodka into his glass. He raised it, hesitated as though making a private toast, then knocked it back in one swallow. Slamming the bottle back into the cupboard, he strode out to the garage.

Lolly followed at a distance and watched him roam about the workbench, tearing open boxes, pulling out drawers.

What's he looking for?

From behind the workbench he tugged out a rough woven material: a burlap bag with a rope drawstring.

Turning, he waved it under her nose. "Consequences," he said.

Her heart pitched and her breath stopped. In the past, when his anger erupted, she had counted on the effects of the vodka to slow him and dampen his anger. This time was different. Bag in hand, he stormed back into the house toward the living room. She ran to keep up with him.

The dim room hummed with the drone of the air conditioner. For a moment, she thought his anger had died. Bo, who was still curled up in the corner of the couch, raised his head and perked up his ears in alert.

Her father stood in the coolness, staring at Bo and swaying back and forth, the bag hanging from his hands. Then Bo twisted into an instinctive crouch, ready to leap, and Lolly knew she had to get between her father and her cat. Before she could move, her father grabbed Bo by the scruff of his neck and shoved him into the bag, tied it off.

"Regan." Her mother stood in the doorway. "What are you doing?"

"Come with me, Lolly," he growled and dragged Lolly from the room, out the front door, and down the porch steps to the Capri, the burlap bag alive with the cat's struggle. Bo yowled and his claws stuck through the coarse weaving.

"Daddy, why are you doing this?"

Her mother followed behind them. "For God's sake, Regan!" she pleaded. "I'm begging you. Stop now. Don't do it!"

Regan whirled on her. "This time she's gone too far, Clarissa! Pure defiance! I'm going to damn well see she learns a goddamn lesson! Lolly, get in the car!" He opened the trunk, tossed in the bag, and slammed the lid shut.

"Don't do this," her mother pleaded. "Let the cat go. I'll discipline Lolly. I promise. I'll ground her."

"Go upstairs and take some your pills," her father sneered. He turned to Lolly. "I'll not say it again. Get in the car."

Lolly slunk around and tried to open the car door, but it was too heavy for her and it wouldn't budge.

"Damn it!" her father grunted, pulled out of the car,

tromped around and swung it open. The moment she sat down, he slammed the door as if he were punishing it.

Back in the car, her father turned the key and the engine screamed. They peeled down the driveway and out into the quiet street. Lolly twisted and saw her mother standing in the shadow of the house.

"Daddy!" she begged. "Where are we going?"

Lolly had never driven with her father when he was angry and it made her frightened. *Why would he do this?* Something bad was going to happen. *Hail, Mary, mother of God.* She pressed her hands together and huddled down into the seat.

Chapter Three

The Capri sped through the quiet, shady streets. Her father turned the wheel so abruptly that she had to grab the door handle and she realized they were heading toward the levee. He tromped on the gas pedal and they bumped up a sort of ramp that led to the top of the twenty-foot-high berm. The car jounced across the narrow dirt and gravel track that crowned the levee, then rumbled down the other side where they picked up the old highway that led east from town past the slaughterhouse and into the valley. The two-lane asphalt snaked past orchards of peaches, pears, olives, walnuts, and truck farms of tomatoes and corn. Heat hung in the air like a ghost pointing the way.

"Please, Daddy," Lolly sobbed. "I'm sorry! I'll grow my hair and I won't chew gum for a year and I'll promise to do...to do anything, just don't hurt Bo!"

From the trunk she could hear Bo yowling plaintively.

Her father kept staring at the road, gripping the wheel so hard that the veins across the back of his hands bulged. Circles of dampness spread under his armpits.

"Bo's a good cat, Daddy!"

What was her father going to do? Whatever it was, she must stop him. Bo was older than she was and sometimes so stiff he barely could jump up on the couch. He couldn't survive rough treatment.

"I'll do whatever you want. Just don't hurt him."

Without warning, her father hit the brakes and threw the car into reverse, throwing Lolly forward then thrashing her back. He came down heavy on the gas and made a squealing U-turn. The Capri took a bump, came down hard, and hurtled forward, back toward the levee where they reached the ramp, and turned onto the narrow gravel track with a tight left that sent the car fishtailing.

Lolly screamed, certain that they were going to hurtle over the embankment and die.

Instead they stopped. Dust boiled around them. Neither of them spoke. Her heart was beating in her ears. She sat for a long moment with her eyes squeezed shut. Over the car's idling she heard the soft *woo-eek* of the Valley wood ducks, the chirping whistles of the hooded orioles, the *qua-qua* of a green heron, and from the grasses, the hum made by thousands of insect legs rubbing together.

Lolly opened her eyes. The dust had settled. Her father pulled himself out of the car and she followed. Side by side, they stood on the berm and she looked out over the town. The Victorian gables of their house rose in the distance.

This was the first time she'd been up on the levee as it had been forbidden territory since she could remember. Over and over she had been warned: "Gypsies live over there and bad things happen. It's dangerous!"

She stepped closer to him. Lolly had all she could do to keep from holding her breath. She did not dare look at him, but if she was lucky he might be reconsidering.

Risking a glance, she saw that her father's hands were clenched. *Is he having second thoughts?* As long as they continued to stand together, looking out over the town, Bo was safe.

"Is this where the levee almost broke last winter?"

"Nope," he said.

"I remember you helped the other men."

"Yep."

"All night. I remember you helped them all night."

That next morning her father had told her about joining dozens of men and boys in a desperate effort to shore up the levee and how they had heaved sandbags and hay bales to bulk up the fragile areas where the water threatened to break through and flood the town.

Now Lolly squinted as she looked down on the harsh landscape. A few scrubby trees pocked the surface and through the center snaked a wide, empty gouge cut by the river that sometimes, in November and December, ran roughshod. The scene reminded her of photos of deserts she'd seen in *National Geographic*—arid with small patches of green erupting randomly, probably fed from deep underground springs. The sun had begun its descent, leaving a wake of hot molten orange that scalded the sky. Everything seemed hotter on this side.

Below them she saw a cluster of trailers huddled like desert creatures in the heat, noses down, waiting for the sun to die. She wanted to ask if that was where the gypsies lived, but before she spoke, her father had moved to the back of the car. His chin pressed down toward his chest and his eyes carried sadness. Maybe he wasn't going to hurt her cat.

Dear Jesus, don't let anything happen to Bo.

She followed him. The gravel on the road was sharp and hurt her bare feet. He opened the trunk and from inside the bag Bo let out a frightened yowl. Tears shimmered in her eyes as the bag wiggled and squirmed.

Her father reached in and took hold of the burlap.

"Daddy, please, don't!" She grappled for the bag, but he blocked her. The expression on her father's face softened and, for a long moment, it all stopped. Even Bo was quiet. In that brief rush of time, she felt as if her father was going to put Bo in her arms and together they'd drive home, him scolding her all the way for defying him.

But, he winced and hauled the bag out of the trunk. A dark patch of wet shirt stuck to his back as he walked away from the car. She had trouble keeping up with him. Bo screamed and clawed. Her father came to a spot on the embankment that overlooked the middle of the trailer camp and he ripped off the rope.

"Bo!" she screamed and her father raised the bag and flung it, one end flying open.

Bo landed with a *thunk* midway down the berm, his body now out of the bag, rolling over and over until he stopped. Dazed, he looked from one side to the other, then crawled away from the burlap and limped down through the dry, sticky levee grass and disappeared into the heart of the trailer camp.

Lolly plunged forward, wanting to get him back, but her father grabbed her and flung her over his shoulder.

"Let me down! Let me down!" she cried, kicking and flailing, but he ignored her, dumping her unceremoniously into the car. She grabbed the handle and tried to open it, but he held it closed.

"You get out of this car, Lolly Candolin, and you'll regret it."

"Daddy, please! Bo's old, he won't be able to..."

Folding his tall body into the driver's seat, he jammed the key into the ignition. The engine screamed as he turned the car around and peeled down the levee ramp. Lolly's sobs were strangled in her throat. She closed her eyes and tried to erase the image of her soft old Bo staggering down the levee, frightened, perhaps in pain.

She didn't open her eyes until the car came to an abrupt halt in front of their house, the sweet scent of wisteria and honeysuckle stirred by the warmth of the leftover day. His face looked like a clay mask and tears were running down his terracotta cheeks.

Good, Lolly thought. It was fair that he was suffering. *This time you've gone too far.*

"I had to do it, Lolly," he said, his voice low. "There are always consequences for your actions. This is a lesson you must learn and sometimes it's the hardest thing you can ever imagine."

She was grateful when he pulled himself out of the car and disappeared into the dark house.

After several moments, Lolly left the car and walked upstairs to her parent's bedroom and pushed open the door. Her mother lay on the bed, apparently sleeping, dressed only in a slip with an ice pack over her eyes. Lolly crept up to the bed.

"Mama," she whispered. "Wake up."

Her mother didn't move, but her hands twitched as though they were clawing through a deep, disturbing dream.

"Mama, he threw Bo off the levee. Can you hear me, Mama?" She squeezed her mother's arm lightly and touched her cheek, but there was no response. Finally giving up, Lolly went back downstairs, slamming the screen door behind her, and sat on the porch where the heat wrapped around her.

From the kitchen, she heard the clink of a jelly glass against the bottle. The image of Bo flying through the air flickered painfully in her memory. Then she heard her father's footsteps behind her in the doorway.

"Lolly."

She pivoted around. "I'm going to find him and bring him home," she said, then turned away. Minutes later, from deep in the house, the mournful sound of his saxophone poured out into the warm evening.

She scrambled off the porch and ran down the driveway. The closer she got to the street, the slower her steps became as she remembered. *It's a place where bad things happen.* Her foot pawed at the ground. *But don't bad things happen here too?*

She turned around and returned to the house. *Somehow I'll get you back, Bo. Somehow.*

Chapter Four

⤚⤙

Every time she closed her eyes, the dirty burlap bag flew through the air and Bo yowled as he limped down the side of the levee and into the gypsy camp. It had been just before dawn when she had finally fallen asleep.

That morning, she begged her mother to let her stay home from school. "My hair. The kids will make fun of me."

"Nonsense, my love. You look fine. Besides, it doesn't matter what they think. Put your uniform on. You're going to be late."

By noon, the heavy-handed heat pressed down on the convent school run by the Sisters of Notre Dame de Namur. Sister Theodora pushed the convent's classroom windows open as wide as they would go and when she turned, Lolly thought she was focusing on her. Sister Theodora was walleyed, which made it seem she was gazing one way when really she was looking another.

"Lolly Candolin," she barked. "Sit up straight."

Lolly bucked up in her desk, the last in the row. She had been slouching in the hopes that nobody would notice the ragged condition of her hair and had just managed to drift away from the classroom until she was sitting by the river where cool water lapped at her toes and Bo rubbed back and forth against her leg.

The moment Sister Theodora spoke, however, fifteen fifth graders in white blouses, blue skirts or pants, and brown loafers twisted around in their seats to stare at her. Small nasty snickers erupted and she heard the word "hair."

"That will be enough," Sister said and from her waistband, pulled her *clicker*, a punitive instrument as well as a pointer. It had a grip made of carved wood about five inches in length, a quarter inch around, and perfectly designed for a small hand. The grip was inserted into a bulb about an inch from the tip. Attached was a delicate piece of wood wrapped by a ribbon of suede, a leveraged splint which would click when flicked by a thumbnail. The sound it made said: *Attention children, you are to give me your attention.* And if anyone refused, the wooden knocker came down with a *thwack* on the top of the head or over the knuckles.

Lolly folded her hands on her desk and looked down at the dull linoleum tiles. Like a huge black bird, Sister Theodora flapped up and down the aisles, the wings of her habit whispering as she went.

Click.

"Take out your catechisms, children, and turn to the Angelus."

With one choreographed movement, the tops of the desks rose and hands rummaged among books and papers and secret treasures: gum, slingshots, notes that had been passed in class, marbles, a pilfered *Redbook Magazine* which, if read, insured that its reader went straight to Hell.

Click.

The class stood.

Click.

The class knelt and drew up to their hearts the prayer book

illustrated with lambs and chubby pink-cheeked babies and a Jesus with the dreamiest eyes on earth.

"*The Angel of the Lord brought Tidings unto Mary,*" Sister began.

"*And she conceived by the Holy Ghost,*" the class answered.

"*Hail, Mary full of grace, the Lord is with thee. Blessed art thou among women, and blessed is the fruit of thy womb, Jesus. Holy Mary, Mother of God, pray for us sinners, now and the hour of our death. Amen.*"

Sister Theodora inhaled a long breath and held it. Lolly counted: one...two...three...four...five...six...seven until Sister exhaled, her breath whistling out of her nose like wind through rafters.

Click.

"You're excused."

Fifteen fifth graders clambered through the door, their pent-up spirits held in check until they reached the heat of the playground which they entered with jubilant cries of freedom.

Lolly was last out of the classroom. More than anything, she wanted to climb the circular stairs up to the small white-stone chapel and pray for Bo. She loved the way the shafts of sun cut like shimmering pillars in the small nave, how the scent of flowers past their prime hung in the mote-filled air. But at the top of the stairs, she found the doors bolted. Sister Benedict had died and the chapel was being prepared for her funeral Mass. The previous Friday, her eighty-two-year-old body had fallen in such a tidy pile on the playground that, for a while, children passed by, thinking her a swatch of black wool carelessly left out.

Thinking of Bo's smiley fur face, Lolly leaned against the chapel door. He was probably thirsty and lonely and hungry and scared. *I'm coming, Bo. Hang on.* Then she thought, *Maybe*

I can slip away and go over to the levee and look for him. Did she dare? Chances were she'd get caught leaving school. Besides, she was afraid to go over there alone, even to look for Bo. She made the sign of the cross and folded her hands.

Take care of Bo, Jesus. Protect him and catch him a fat mouse.

Cringing at the image of a half-eaten rodent, she restated her prayer to ask for an opened can of tuna. Lolly blessed herself and wandered toward the back of the schoolyard, where a stone grotto housed the faded, life-sized statue of the Virgin Mary. This was where the girls from her class played Horses at recess.

Lolly would have gladly given up her dog-eared copy of Dylan Thomas' *A Child's Christmas in Wales* in exchange for these girls folding her into their group. But they didn't know who Dylan Thomas was, nor did they care, and they couldn't care less about her.

At the playground, four girls galloped wildly up to her. Sonja, a dark-haired girl with a flat face that reminded Lolly of a Persian cat, whinnied and shouted, "Hey, who nubbed your hair!"

Lolly touched the sawed off ends of what yesterday had been her braids. They felt like the bristles of her father's shaving brush.

"I think it looks neat," Christina said, running her hand through her own red Brillo curls. When the other girls groaned in disapproval, she added, "Kinda."

Vicky Clare, the tallest of the four, but not as tall as Lolly, danced around her, whipping her long blonde hair away from her face as she pranced. Vicky Clare was the thoroughbred of the herd, always chosen to place the crown of flowers on the head of the Blessed Virgin during the Spring Purification ceremony. "You need a good currying," she said. "Now your mane's a mess." The other girls laughed.

"No lie," Sabrina said, her ebony face shiny with exertion. "Wanta play?"

Lolly's heart skipped. At night, with her mother sitting heavily on the side of her bed, she'd silently launch into the most important prayer of her litany: *Please, God, make them like me and invite me to be a grotto horse. Make them want me to gallop with them.*

Sabrina trotted up to her. "Hey, nubs, wanta be a horse with us?"

"Yes," Lolly said, her voice low. *Maybe Daddy is wrong. Maybe there is a God.* "Sure."

"Okay," Vicky Clare said. "Come on!"

The four fillies sprinted for the grotto, neighing as they galloped around the smiling Virgin. "Come on!" Vicky Clare shouted. "What kind of horse do you want to be?"

Lolly chewed the cuticle of her thumb. "A small beautiful one," she said, but nobody heard her.

Sonja snorted up to her, bucking, pawing, thrashing, and knocking Lolly hard to one side. Had she done that on purpose? Maybe a misstep. "I'm an Appaloosa!" she said, and she galloped back into the circling girls.

"I'm a Thoroughbred," Vicky Clare shouted. "Christina's a Swedish Warmblood, and Sabrina's a Brumby. You can be a Quarter Horse." She whinnied and dashed away, her body bucking, and all around her the horses galloped faster.

"I want to be a whole horse!" Lolly said, but the girls didn't hear this either.

Vicky Clare snorted and trotted back to Lolly who wanted to paw at the ground with her hoof, but felt awkward. "I know," Vicky Clare snorted again. "You can be the sick horse!"

"I don't want to be sick," Lolly said, her arms swinging

around her body in shy refusal.

"Sure you do," Vicky Clare said. "If you want to play you do."

Angry at Vicky Clare's threat, Lolly's hands turned into fists. *It's my stupid hair that makes me look sick.* Maybe if she did a really good job at playing sick, they would forget about her hair. And, once in the game, they wouldn't want her to be sick anymore.

As the girls continued the trampling, Lolly entered their circle and lay down in the deep sour grass that had gone to flower. Delicate white petals bobbed at the end of each thin stem. She picked a stalk and sucked on it, the bitter juice pinching her tongue.

"Whinny in a sad way," shouted Sabrina the Brumby, trotting her heavy brown oxford hooves beside Lolly's head. "Go on!" She leaned down and tugged at Lolly's mane.

Lolly let out a soft moan.

"Louder," Sabrina said and bent down to yank even harder.

"Louder, louder!" the four horses demanded, stomping so close that Lolly saw scars on their shoes and scabs on their shins. "Louder, sicker, louder, sicker!" they chanted and their hooves pounded, kicking up dirt and pebbles.

Lolly looked up. She saw a blur of whirling flesh and behind it the smiling Virgin, her face without either judgment or compassion.

"She's a good sick horse," Christina the Warmblood said. But when the other horses didn't agree, she added, "Kinda."

"Ugly sick horse." Vicky Clare's voice was edgy, mean. The other horses joined her in a cascade of shrieking neighs and whinnies. Around and around the horses galloped, making Lolly dizzy.

"Ugly sick horse! Look at her chopped off mane! Chop, chop, chop, chop—"

Lolly couldn't tell which girl was shouting the insult. It seemed to come from them all. With her hands covering the short tufts of her hair, she raised her head and made the moaning sound.

Soon they'll say I'm well and want me to ride with them.

But the chanting only became louder as the race picked up.

"Faster, faster!" cried the Brumby and the Warmblood.

The ugly sick horse had had enough. "No more!" Lolly yelled. She jumped to her feet. The muscles in her Quarter Horse back spread and her hooves pranced, fast and sharp. Her nostrils flared, her eyes cast wild looks. She snorted.

Sonja galloped toward her. "Sick horse is up! Sick horse is up!" The Appaloosa raced full speed and knocked the Quarter Horse to the ground. The Quarter Horse stopped when a door closed at the bottom of her throat. Barely a vapor of air was left inside. It required several gulps before she could breathe again.

Lolly got up and charged the Appaloosa. "I hate you and I hope you die!" she shouted, not bothering to neigh. "I hope the worms eat your eyes and your body turns into pus until it bubbles up out of the ground!" The speed and sharpness of her words felt good, but not as good as when she hocked up a wad of saliva, aimed it at Sonja, and spit.

The next thing the Quarter Horse knew was that the great black bird was dragging her away from the Appaloosa.

"That will be enough," Sister Theodora said, pointing to a place where Lolly should go to separate herself from the herd. "Go over there and sit down." Rushing over to where the Appaloosa lay weeping in the grass, Sister pulled a cotton handkerchief from her sleeve and blotted spit off the

Appaloosa's face. When Sonja had finally settled down, Sister's attention turned to Lolly.

"It's sinful to speak that way, Lolly Candolin. And to spit at somebody is absolutely unconscionable!" Sister shook her head. "Dear child, stand up."

Lolly did and Sister touched her cheek, the hand cool and smelling of classroom paste. "Growing up isn't easy," Sister said, taking a deep breath. "For horses or for girls. Apologize to Sonja, Lolly."

Lolly looked over at the pathetic Appaloosa kneeling in the sour grass. The impassive face of Mary standing within the grotto gave her no clue what to do.

"Apologize," Sister repeated.

Lolly remained silent.

"All right," Sister said gravely. "You've given me no choice. Come with me."

Lolly sat in the one place no school child ever wanted to go. Her hands gripped the wooden arms of the upholstered chair and her head hung down.

"Lolly Candolin, what's gotten into you, child?"

Lolly raised her gaze to see Sister Superior, hands folded on her desk, her wide chest handsomely covered by the stiff white collar. Sister's quicksilver eyes did not blink. On the wall behind Sister, a small muscular Jesus was splayed painfully against a cross, a dreadful look on His face. He didn't look holy or like a martyr. More like a man very annoyed. With her.

"I'm sorry," Lolly muttered.

"That may be," Sister Superior said. "But you may not treat

another human being the way you treated Sonja. Why would you do such a thing?"

The image of Bo flying through the air replayed itself in front of Lolly.

"Well?" Sister said.

"They were making fun of my hair," Lolly said defiantly.

It wouldn't matter to Sister Superior that her father had thrown her cat off the levee, and it wouldn't matter that she had hacked her hair or how the girls had teased her. None of it mattered. She had spit in the Appaloosa's face and for that she would pay.

The thought of the Appaloosa lying in the sour grass whimpering brought forth a wave of satisfaction that broke over Lolly. That damned pony deserved it.

Bless me, Father, I confess.

"If anything like this happens again, you will write an essay," Sister Superior said. "For now all I require is that you apologize to Sonja and I will call your father and tell him about this incident. You are excused, child. And don't forget to go to confession."

Sister Superior bowed her head in dismissal.

Lolly left the office and stepped back into the chaotic games of children at play. The whitewashed walls around the convent of Notre Dame shimmered in the heat. The bell clanged. Lunch recess was over and the horses, now posing as girls, went back into the classroom where all the Quarter Horse could think about was Bo.

Chapter Five

The moment Sister Theodora dismissed the fifth-grade class, Lolly shoved her books into her plastic briefcase with the picture of Troy Donohue laminated on the sides and set out for her Grandpa's house. *Grandpa will help me find Bo and he'll help me get my hair fixed.*

A curtain of heat radiated from the sidewalks as she hopped cracks so she wouldn't break her mother's back. Sweat glued her uniform blouse to her ribs and perspiration trickled down her cheeks. As she swung her briefcase, she caught a glimpse of the picture of Troy's handsome face. He was her favorite movie star. Last year, *Silver Screen* magazine had dubbed him "America's Favorite Boy Next Door." She wished more than anyone could that he really was the boy next door. Her mother had called the briefcase cheap-looking and had refused to buy it for her, but Grandpa had stepped up and treated her.

As she approached the small clapboard house, she spotted Grandpa digging in his garden, a perfectly manicured patch of two squares separated by a stone walkway, beds of zinnias and roses along the front, tomatoes along the sides where the sun spread itself like butter. She knew by the tomato cages stacked nearby that he was adding manure to the newly turned dirt he was preparing for beefsteaks. He had a way with things that grew. They trusted him.

"How's my pretty princess?" he called to her, his stooped back pushed against his rayon shirt.

Lolly scuffed along the walkway. The paint on the face of the house had peeled and cracked, and the porch slanted to one side, making it almost impossible to play jacks on it. "How'd you know it's me without looking?"

"Eyes in the back of my head." He kept digging.

"I thought only mothers had those."

"Mostly that's true. But when your grandma died and I became daddy and mama to your mama, I had to grow 'em. It weren't easy and that's the God's truth," he said as he began to stand. "Now, first up comes the top of me, which is only twenty years old." He made the sound of a car starting. "Next comes the antique parts. Remember that my knees and legs combined are more than two hundred and fifty years old."

His rendition of rising always made Lolly laugh, but not today. She climbed to the top step of the porch and sat down. It was shady there and a degree or two cooler.

Her grandfather lumbered up the steps and sat next to her. It wasn't until he pulled out a tattered handkerchief and wiped his face, leaving stripes of dirt on the cotton, that he really looked at her.

"My, my, princess, what happened to you?" he asked, his blue eyes smiling. "You're a sight. You look like you've been in one of those thrashing machines they use in the fields."

She slipped her hand under his leg. *He's the best*, she thought.

"A little short of breath," he continued cheerfully. "Suppose fifty years of smoking doesn't help, but I've kept that promise I made when I was seventy-five to quit the habit until

I was eighty. I'm happy to say I've got one year to go."

Laughing, he pointed to an empty ashtray, then mopped at the new tributaries of sweat making their way down his forehead.

Lolly tried to smile but the hurt inflicted by the horses at school and her concern for Bo wouldn't let her. Her uniform blouse hung over her waistband, one of her shoelaces was untied, and her socks drooped around her ankles. She ran a hand ran over her chopped hair.

"I do believe you're going to have heatstroke if we don't cool you down," her grandfather said. He hitched up his sections again and shuffled into the house. "Come on. We're going to do a little fixing on you."

She followed him into the cool disorganized cave of his house. In almost every room, walls were lined with bookshelves burdened with worn volumes. The furniture was threadbare on the seats and backs. Manila envelopes filled with designs and blueprints for his inventions were piled on the living room floor. In the adjoining dining room, sketches and drawings for future paintings were scattered over the unraveling carpet. Except for just enough space for two people to sit and have lunch or dinner, the scarred mahogany dining table was also covered with sketches.

Lolly sniffed. As usual, the air was thick with the smell of oil paint. Grandpa often painted portraits, especially of his wife Lucy, although over the past year or so he'd started painting lions, cheetahs, and panthers. Leaning against the walls were canvases of cat portraits. Sometimes she'd swear she had seen a nose twitch or an eye blink.

"These paintings are the closest I'll ever get to a wild thing," he had told her several times before.

He brought out two glasses and a pitcher of lemonade, the

surface sweating deliciously. "Drink, princess," he said and, when she gulped the icy juice, added, "Not so fast."

She winced at the coldness thudding in her head.

"So," he asked. "What's with the spikes?"

She ran her fingers through her hair. "I did it myself. I was trying to hurt him."

"You mean your daddy?"

She nodded, her smile fading.

"By cutting your hair?"

She looked up at him mutely.

"Want to tell me about it?"

She shook her head and swallowed, trying to keep the sobs from taking over.

"What's the matter, love?" His wiry eyebrows drew together.

"Everything!" She tore away from the table and stormed into the living room, where she threw herself against the musty-smelling couch and began pounding its faded red brocade.

He leaned against the doorjamb and stuffed his hands, still grained with garden dirt, into his pockets.

"Bo's gone! And he's probably sick or maybe even worse." She punched a faded brocade pillow. "And every horsy kid at school makes fun of my hair, and my father's mean and drinks too much, and I look like an ugly...monster from outer space!"

"What do you mean, Bo's gone?" Grandpa's eyes narrowed.

"It's Daddy. He took Bo and..." Then she said, "Please! Take me over the levee so I can find him! You will, won't you, Grandpa?"

"A lot depends on how Bo got over there."

Lolly opened her mouth to pour out the story, but then realized that if she did, it would just make things worse. Her father had always been cranky to her grandfather. She wasn't sure why, but it probably had something to do with the fact that her grandfather had never been a very important man in the town.

She shook her head. "He's just there, that's all. And I need you to take me over the levee so I can find him!"

"I can't do that, princess."

"You have to!" she protested, but in her heart she knew that he wouldn't help her. And it was all because of Daddy again. Whatever Daddy decided, that was the way it had to be.

"Can't. Don't worry, he'll find his way home. I've heard of cats finding their way clear across the country."

"I don't believe you!" She threw a punch at one pillow, picked up another, and slammed it against the back of the couch, only to have the air come alive with hundreds of floating down feathers. Tiny birds as silent as prayers, fluttering and swirling over their heads.

"Oh, Grandpa, I'm sorry!"

His eyes crinkled as he hobbled over and plopped down beside her on the couch. "It's beautiful," he said. "Only my princess could have created something as wonderful as this."

"I'll clean it up, I promise." She squirmed, trying to dig her way out of the couch, but he pulled her back.

"No need. Not yet."

They sat without speaking until the last feather had landed on the stack of folders piled on the table in front of them.

"Lolly, I'm going to tell you a secret," he said, a slight smile surfacing on his ruddy face. "We can change most of the things that make us unhappy if we think about them in a different way."

She leaned her head against his arm and listened.

"Let's take those horsy kids at school. Fact is, most horses are dumb. Tiny brains lodged in great big heads. So if they're doing something that makes you feel sad, it's because they're stupid. As far as your daddy goes, the vodka he drinks is like medicine. He takes it for what ails him."

"But what ails him, Grandpa?"

"He's a bundle of ailments. Always has been. And now the talk is that he's got a battle on his hands at work."

He paused, then stood and dug behind the couch. With every movement, feathers stirred. "And as far as you thinking you're ugly, let me show you something."

Grunting and huffing, he finally tugged out a photo album, his knees barking as he sat back down beside her. He placed the book on his lap and opened it. Lolly had seen many of his albums before but never this one filled with photographs so faded that she could not make some of them out. With his index finger splattered with green oil paint, Grandpa pointed to a hand-tinted photo of a small girl. She was fat and her hair was cut ruler-straight across her forehead and bluntly down each side of her face, chopped off right at the level of her ear-lobes.

"What do you see?" he asked Lolly.

"A funny-looking kid," she answered. The small hitch of a leftover sob forced itself up her throat. "Kind of weird-looking."

"Yep." The skin under his eyes crinkled. "Kind of weird. You know who that is?"

Lolly shook her head.

"Your grandmother. When she was about your age. Maybe a year younger."

"Grandmother Lucy?"

"Yes, ma'am. Grandmother Lucy."

"But she was beautiful! Like Mama!"

"True," he said. "She was a beauty. But to get there,

princess, she had to start from here."

Lolly thought fast. *If he thinks I'm anything like my grand-mother, maybe he'll help me.*

"Grandpa," she said hopefully, "do you still go to that hair-cutter lady down the street? Because I want her to trim my hair. Mama tried to smooth out the ragged ends, but she just made it looked worse."

Grandpa leaned forward and rubbed his gnarled hands together. "I'd like to do that, princess, but you know what your daddy's like. If an idea isn't his, well, then it's no good."

"But I look awful!"

"Not awful. Just a little unraveled."

"I'll pay you back." She wondered why she pushed her Grandpa so hard because she knew he wouldn't help. He could-n't. Not with her daddy making the rules.

"It's not the money. What provoked you to cut off your braids?"

"I don't know."

"You can tell me when you're ready," he said.

The two of them sat silently on the couch drinking lemon-ade. She was about to go against her better judgment and tell him all about her parents' fight and what her father had done to Bo, thinking he'd feel sorry for her and help her get the hair trimmed, but then the door opened and her mother stepped into the living room. The feathers erupted into a swirl. Looking beautiful as usual, her mother wore a pale green, full skirt with a stiff petticoat.

"When you didn't come home, I knew where to find you," her mother said to Lolly. Then she looked around. "What hap-pened here?"

"Magic," Grandpa said. "Want some lemonade?"

"Please," her mother said, trying futilely to gather up

feathers. "Lolly, did you do this?"

"I'm going to clean it up."

"You certainly are. I think you've caused enough trouble for a while." Her mother pulled a cigarette from her purse, but changed her mind and put it back.

"Lolly wants to get her hair trimmed." Grandpa handed her mother a glass of lemonade. "I have a friend down the street who's pretty good with hair."

Her mother took a sip and put down the glass. "I know," her mother said impatiently. "But we can't unless Regan says so. He's furious that she cut her braids." Her mother left the room. "Come on, Lolly, let's clean up this mess. Are you still keeping the vacuum cleaner in the closet, Daddy?"

"But, Mama, the kids at school call me nubs!"

"My princess does look a bit shaggy."

Her mother returned with the vacuum. "Your father will have a fit unless he has a say."

"Would Regan even notice?" Grandpa asked. "He's consumed with those durn downtown politics."

"No trim!" her mother said and switched on the vacuum. The machine choked as it began sucking up the feathers.

"I'll do that later," Grandpa shouted over the noise and pulled the plug.

"Please, Mama, give me the money," Lolly pleaded. "I'll set the table every night for a year to pay you back. Please, please!"

"No! Your father will have a fit."

"I don't care. I'll go by myself. You and Grandpa don't have to have anything to do with it."

"Lolly, I think we'd better be getting home," her mother said, again pulling a cigarette out of her purse. This time she put it in her mouth and lit it. As she walked toward the door, her full skirt whipped around her slim legs.

"It's not fair. The kids are punishing me, not you or Daddy."

Her mother stopped, found the ashtray, and stubbed out the cigarette.

Lolly continued, "You told me not to be afraid of anybody. You're afraid of him, but I'm not!"

Her mother raised her chin. The muscles in her jaw worked. Finally she turned around and looked at Lolly. "You're right," she whispered. She dug into her purse and pulled out some bills. "Go on." Her voice was strained. "But hurry. I'll wait here."

Lolly snatched the money and pecked her mother's cheek. "Thanks. I'll be back before you know I've been gone." She dashed across the room, the feathers drifting in her wake.

Chapter Six

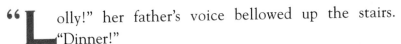

"Lolly!" her father's voice bellowed up the stairs. "Dinner!"

Lolly had stretched out on her bed and was reading *A Child's Christmas in Wales*. Her intention was to linger upstairs as long as possible because she knew that when she went down and her father saw her hair, he would hate it. And her.

He's going to kill me.

"Lolly!"

"Coming, Daddy."

After the haircut, she and her mother had come straight home. As they entered the house, the color drained from her mother's cheeks.

"You okay, Mama?"

"No. I'm going to take a smoothie. But your hair, it looks nice. The bangs emphasize your eyes. I think you're even prettier, my darling, with it short."

Lolly watched her mother make her way upstairs to her bedroom and silently close the door before going to her own room where Troy Donohue smiled down at her from the poster over her bed. Going into the bathroom, she took her hand mirror, and studied the reflection of her new haircut in the vanity.

Grandpa's friend Mattie had clucked like a chicken as she

had trimmed her hair. "We're going to fix you right up, young lady," Mattie had said. "Just you wait and see."

Mattie shampooed her hair with gentle hands and then, after a brief towel-dry, started the trim, handling the scissors with ease and confidence until Lolly's hair had become a wavy, stylish cap.

Now Lolly cocked the mirror to see the back. *I look pretty,* she thought. And then she added, *Is that possible?*

"Lolly, get down here, goddamn it!"

She pulled at the twigs of hair that fringed out above her ears and over her eyes, crept down the stairs, and saw her father lurch into the television room as he did almost every night, carrying two TV-dinners, their usual fare.

When she stepped into the add-on room he was already in his lounge chair, his dinner on an enameled TV table in front of him. With the blinds drawn, the room was dark except for the flicker of the television. Music blared and an Alka-Seltzer tablet danced, the little figure's delicate arms and legs moving to the rhythm of the jingle.

Lolly slipped into her chair, a few feet in front of his, and peered down at the aluminum tray of pallid food. A chicken leg, mashed potatoes, applesauce. The skin of the chicken looked like her hands when she stayed in the bathtub too long. She bit into the meat that was tough and cold in the center.

"Where's that goddamn woman?" Her father's words slurred over the jingle coming from the television.

"Mama's got a head hammer," Lolly said, picking at the gluey mashed potatoes.

Thank you, God, for the dark. If I eat quickly, maybe I can get out of here without him noticing my hair.

"Let's play *What's My Line!*" John Daly said. His face filled the television screen. "Meet tonight's panel: Arlene Francis,

Desi Arnaz, Bennett Cerf, Deborah Kerr, and Robert Q. Lewis." The black and white figures flickered on the screen.

Though her mouth was full, Lolly tried to smile like Deborah Kerr. "What do you think the Q stands for in Robert Q. Lewis?" she asked, trying to make conversation.

"Quack. How the hell do I know?" her father replied. He draped his linen napkin over his head.

"Daddy, why do you do that?" It was something he did only if he'd had a third horn of corn.

"It's funny," he answered, growling at the television. Then he shouted, "That damned Robert Q. Showoff! You're a goddamn quack! You couldn't hold a candle next to me in a courtroom!"

She hated his angry language, the fights he'd pick with the faces on the screen, the mess he made of his dinner. But what revolted her most was when he sat slumped, eyes glazed, and his napkin draped over his head. She wanted to find the place where they made fathers so she could exchange him for a new one.

"Go get your mother," he said.

"She's not feeling well."

"I don't care! Go get her!"

She slid out of her chair, crawled under the tray, and sidled toward the door.

"Your Sister Superior called me today."

She stopped.

"Why in hell did you spit at some girl?"

She turned around and faced him. Her right foot scratched her left calf and, to avoid his eyes, she examined her short ragged nails in the flickering light of the television screen.

"Well?"

She inspected her cuticle.

He slammed his fork down on the aluminum tray. "Answer me!" Food flew in every direction, lumps of potatoes hitting the silk lampshade, applesauce landing on the front of his shirt.

"I don't know," she said. She bobbed back and forth, toes to heels. *I felt like it, and I feel like spitting now.*

"What do you mean you don't know? You think you're a llama? You know why you did it. Don't lie to me."

Tears stung her eyes. "They made fun of my..."

Don't bring up your hair, she thought. *Say anything, but don't talk about your hair.* "They made me be the sick horse."

"I don't know what you're talking about," he said. "Sister said you spit at Sonja Somebody. If she was giving you a hard time, why didn't you poke her in the nose?"

She looked up at him and a tear escaped down her cheek. She wiped it away. "I didn't think of it."

"Well, why not? If you're going to threaten somebody, don't do it half way for Christ's sake."

She returned to the nail inspection.

"I don't like my daughter getting hauled off to the principal's office." His eyes opened wide then narrowed as if he were trying to focus. "If you're going to fight somebody, scare the piss out of them so they won't turn you in. Understand?"

He picked up his tray and tried to lunge out of the chair but stumbled and fell back into the chair.

"So you got caught," he continued, breathing heavily. "That's your problem. Now you got to do what the nuns say." He teetered on the edge of the seat. "I don't pay good money to send you to those mackerel snappers for nothing."

"But it wasn't the nuns who..."

"I don't care who it was. You got caught, so you do what they say."

Then he was up, with his arms out, as though he were trying to stand in a rocking boat. He leaned toward her, his face too close in the animated shadows.

"If you think you're doing the right thing, then fighting doesn't bother me. Were you doing the right thing?"

She looked away.

"Always do what you think is right," he mumbled, wheeling away from her. "Yes, that's it. Do what you think is right." He staggered on past her, almost pinning her against the wall.

Static lines cut through Robert Q. Lewis' face. "Do you drive in your job?" he asked the contestant.

The contestant, a man with the biggest nose she had ever seen, said, "No."

"Does your occupation require you to walk?" Arlene Francis asked.

Big Nose said, "Yes."

Bennett Cerf screwed up his pear face. "In this job, do you have to walk quickly?"

"No," Big Nose said.

Desi Arnaz chimed in. "Do you walk in order to..."

Lolly shut off the television.

Her father banged into the downstairs bathroom. She put her hands over her ears to block out the sound of his urine streaming into the toilet.

I hate him! I hate that medicine he takes!

As Lolly dumped her TV tray into the garbage under the sink, her father appeared. He steadied himself by grabbing the counter. His eyes narrowed.

"Your hair," he said.

Her hands flew to her head and ran over the new trim.

"Cutting your braids," he mumbled. "They were so...so thick and...beautiful." He swayed forward, but straightened himself at the last moment. "So beautiful..."

Don't say anything, she told herself. She drew the dishtowel off its rack and pressed it over her mouth. *Keep quiet.* She put the towel back and edged away from him. "I have homework."

"You look different," he muttered. "Your hair. It looks different." He lurched toward her. She stepped back. "What'd you do to it?"

"Nothing," she said. So far she hadn't violated the Ninth Commandment: she hadn't done anything to her hair. Mattie had.

"Don't 'nothing' me!" he snarled. "Somebody's fooled with your hair. Who?" He took another step toward her.

Lolly backed away through the kitchen into the breakfast nook, which was large enough for a Formica table and four plastic upholstered chairs. She got on one side, putting the oval table between them.

"Who?" He slammed his hand down hard on the table.

"I got it trimmed!" she said. Tears began running down her face.

"I told you before, don't lie to me!"

"I'm not!"

"Who trimmed your hair? Nobody touches my daughter's hair without my permission!" He hit the table again. "Who?"

"A lady," Lolly said. "And she barely did anything."

He circled the table, knocking a chair out of the way and into the wall. She moved again, keeping the table between them, but he kept coming. "Who trimmed your hair?" He knocked a chair down. "Stay where you are. Don't you dare move!"

"Daddy, it was a lady I don't know. I've never seen her before."

He pointed at her, a signal meaning she better not move. "Okay, Lolly, I'll play the game. Where was she? Where was she, goddamn it?"

"Near Grandpa's," she said.

He sucked in his breath and clamped down his teeth. "So Jeb put you up to this," he said. "I should have known. Was your mother there?"

She couldn't speak.

"Of course she was," he sneered and headed for the stairs, drawing himself up the bannister, hand over hand.

Lolly inched along behind him as he flung open the bedroom door and staggered over to her where mother was lying on the bed, her favorite silk shawl pulled over her.

"Why do you always go against me?" he roared.

Her mother's eyelashes fluttered.

"Can't you keep your nose out of things?" he demanded. "You're ruining her! If you keep stepping in, she'll never learn that actions carry consequences!" Wrapping his hand around her mother's wrist, he yanked her upright. She was wearing a slip, one strap slipped down over her shoulder.

"Regan," she protested. "She's just a little girl, you're too hard on her."

"When I make a rule, you know I don't want you undermining it," he told her. He was steadier now. Anger had sobered him as it so often did. "I don't want you sneaking around and doing things without my approval."

"It's not her fault!" Lolly screamed. "It was all my idea! Mine! I can do things all by myself! And you can't stop me! Nobody can stop me!"

Lolly shoved past them and into their bathroom, where she grabbed her father's razor from his shaving cup. With one hand she snatched a handful of her hair and hacked it off. White scalp appeared and a small nick that raised a bead of blood. Next, she tugged at the hair just above her forehead and more crimson speckles welled. She shaved and shaved, creating pads of bare scalp all over her head.

In the mirror, she saw her parents. Her mother stood in the doorway, her hands clapped over her mouth. Behind her, her father stood frozen, his arms dangling at his sides.

"I hate me!" Lolly shouted as she hacked. "I hate everyone!"

"Stop!" Her mother, weeping, took a step into the bathroom, but her father put out his arm and blocked her as Lolly slashed away and more pads of scalp appeared. Finally, the razor clattered into the sink. Clumps of hair dotted the floor. She heard her mother groan.

Her father folded his arms. He seemed to have grown even larger. Her eyes met his in the mirror. He shook his head—but then, for a moment, she saw the man whose face could break into a bright-eyed, unfamiliar smile. He stood behind her and rested his hands on her head. They were warm.

"Why?" he asked. He closed his eyes, and when he opened them his hands had become vices. "Okay, Lolly, more consequences." He left the bathroom.

"Why, baby?" her mother said. "Why must you do these things?"

But before she could answer, her father returned and shoved a navy-blue wool watch cap under her nose.

"You'll wear this to cover the mess you've made." He seized her hand and made her take the cap. "Put it on!"

Lolly ran her fingers across a bleeding spot of scalp. It had already dried and the skin felt tender. Inside, her head was buzzing.

"Now!" he snapped, his voice quavering.

She pulled open the cap and tugged it over her head. The stitching was rough and it smelled of mothballs.

"Regan, I don't think this is right." Her mother rushed over and put her arms around her. "The child is bleeding."

"She's not bleeding. This is the way it's going to be." He pried her mother away and stepped between them. "You'll wear it until your hair grows back. And next time you decide to do something, you'll ask me first. Are we clear?"

"It's too hot," Lolly said, and she glared at him.

"Are we clear?"

"But do I have to wear it to school?"

"Everywhere. I don't want to see you without it. Ever."

Her breath shuddered.

"Got it?"

"Yes," she said.

The wool made her head sweat and her scalp was starting to itch. Schemes to get around the rule flashed through her mind. Surely she'd be able to get away with not wearing it when he wasn't around.

"Mark my words, Lolly. If I *ever* catch you without it on..." Then came the true consequence, the weighty and terrible consequence: "I'll shave your mother's head."

"Regan, for God's sake! Why must you be so brutal?"

He bit down in that angry way he did when he drank. "I swear to God I will. Come on, Clarissa. The girl's got some thinking to do." He staggered over to her mother and grabbed her arm, but his weight was too much and when they went through, they knocked against the doorjamb.

She stepped toward them wanting to scream "I'd die before I would let you touch my mother's hair!" but she remained quiet. As soon as they were gone, Lolly took off the cap and looked at herself in the mirror. *You're a creep. A big, ugly creep.*

But even when she said this to herself, she knew it wasn't true. The ugliness of her father's behavior was far uglier than she ever would be.

Chapter Seven

~

She lay on her back under the giant weeping willow tree. Its graceful tendrils spread cool patterns of shade over the grass, coloring it deep green and, in some places, almost purple. In the sun the blades glowed, shining as though they'd been polished. One of her father's legal pads lay next to her, a pencil behind her ear under the watch cap. As punishment for her latest breach in playground etiquette, Sister Superior had ordered her to write an essay on why anger is a sin.

Plenty of ideas about anger filled her head but none emerged about why anger was a sin. She began drawing circles, one inside the other until she had reached the dark center. From time to time, she slipped her fingers under the hat to scratch her head.

She was wordless and tired. That morning at school, the horses had amused themselves by galloping around, grazing her, pawing and whinnying and flinging their manes. Vicky Clare had begun the chant, "Sick horse is wearing a hat!" Then the Thoroughbred had galloped up and ripped the cap off her head. The moment the horses got a glimpse of her raggedly shaved patches of scalp, they had hooted and whooped, "Hairless horse! Hairless horse!"

It wasn't the humiliation that had pricked at her most, but

the fear: all she saw was the vision of her father shaving her mother's head.

She had stifled the rage coursing through her horse nature and had done something she'd never done before. She'd begged. "Please, please give me the cap back."

Christina the Brumby pawed the ground. "Give it to her," she whinnied. "She looks so weird. Give it to her." The Thoroughbred flung the cap at Lolly. Lolly caught it and scrunched it down over her ears.

Out of nowhere the Appaloosa bucked forward and bumped hard into her, causing Lolly to stumble backwards and fall hard on her bottom.

You! she thought. *I'll show you.*

The Quarter Horse got to her feet, rearing back, head high, her front legs beating the air as she let loose a terrible mad whinny and slammed into the Appaloosa, hitting its white chest hard. Then she drew back her arm, knotted her hand into a fist and aimed for the horse's muzzle. At the last minute the horse jogged and instead of hitting her in the mouth, Lolly's fist met the Appaloosa's eye square on. Now it was the Appaloosa's turn to reel backward, off-balance, taking little steps, trying to stop the fall before toppling to the ground. The Quarter Horse didn't stop. *If you're going to threaten somebody, don't do it half way.*

She threw herself on the Appaloosa, pummeling and kicking with her hooves until the Appaloosa cried out, "Make her stop, make her stop!"

Sonja lay in the sour grass whimpering, blood gushing from her nose, her eye swelling like that of a prize fighter.

This time Lolly's father might approve of something she had done. *It has been one week since my last confession and these are my sins.*

The hot blue sky burned through the quivering weeping willow branches. Lolly pressed the pencil against the yellow pad and found herself drawing a primitive outline of a cat. Two days had passed and Bo hadn't found his way home. She longed to go over to the other side of the levee but she didn't dare. Not now. One misstep and her father might make good on his threat. She shuddered at the image of him shaving her mother's head.

In a careful cursive hand, she slowly formed the letters *The Virtue of Not Being Angry*, then continued with the essay. "One reason for not being angry is that you might go to hell where it is hot all the time and flames burn your feet and you breathe terrible gases. Not being angry is one of God's rules."

Is this a rule made by the God who loves me? she wondered.

Then she wrote, "God and Daddy are very much alike." She wrinkled her nose and underlined the last three words.

The Capri roared up the driveway in front of the house. Perspiration slid from her head down the back of her neck and she gave the hat an extra tug over her ears.

"Lolly, daddy's home," her mother called from upstairs.

Maybe tonight things will be different, Lolly thought, and this burble of hope accompanied her inside.

She walked into the cool house, through the laundry, and into the kitchen to the open French doors that divided the dining room from the marbled entry.

"Where're my girls?" her father's voice boomed, unusually cheerful. His briefcase thudded to the floor of the entryway and she saw his shadow as he tugged at his tie and shrugged off his jacket. "Hello!" he called and she heard her mother's footsteps on the stairs.

"Regan, you're home early," her mother said. Lolly peeked around the corner. Her mother wore pale gray silk slacks, a sleeveless white top, and choker pearls at her neck, an aura of soapy scent surrounding her. She had pulled the sides of her hair high and secured them with white combs and the back was pulled into a ponytail and tied with a white ribbon. She looked beautiful.

"Where's Lolly?" her father asked.

"Around here somewhere," her mother said. "Lolly?"

"I've got a surprise for you two," he said.

"A surprise? Well, that's nice. Lolly?" Her mother's voice had a bright, artificial quality.

Lolly made her way out of the dining room and into the entryway. Her father squatted down until they were eye-to-eye. He was smiling and his eyes were clear.

"Pick a hand," he said.

She hated this game. Never in all her life had she picked the correct one.

"Left," she said anyway. His hands came around and he was holding two small stuffed cats with zigzagged black thread for mouths and shining glass ovals for eyes. *Stupid toys*, she thought. "Thank you," she said.

"Aren't they nice?" her mother said and Lolly saw that her eyes were full of tears.

Her father rose to his feet.

"And for you, Mrs. Candolin. Follow me."

Sitting in front of the house was a 1955 forest green Ford station wagon with paneling on the sides that looked exactly like wood.

"Where's the Capri?" her mother asked.

"One of the girls at the office will bring it," he said. "This is for you, Clarissa. It's yours. Do you like it?" He trotted down the porch stairs, a set of keys jingling from his fingers. "Come on, take it for a spin!"

"For me?" her mother exclaimed. "But there's nothing wrong with my car. It's fine."

"Fine is not good enough for Mrs. Regan Candolin. I want you to have the best. This is the newest model. I thought a station wagon would be good for you to haul your art projects around in. It has all the bells and whistles. Go on. Drive it!"

"But, Regan..."

"No buts. Here. Take the keys."

Lolly stood on the porch clutching the stuffed cats.

Her mother turned to her. "Come with me?"

"Sure, Lolly, go with your mother. I'm going to change my clothes, relax a little. I'll see you girls when you get back. You like it, Clarissa? If you don't, I'll take it back and get another model."

"No," her mother said. "It's...it's fine."

"How about the color? Want a different color? They have a metallic red, but I thought it was a little too flashy."

"No, Regan," she said. "The color's lovely. It's a lovely car." Opening the car door, she ran her hand over the upholstery. Then she stood on her tiptoes and kissed his cheek. "Thank you very much."

She got into the car and put the key into the ignition. "Come on, Lolly," she said.

Still clasping the stuffed cats, Lolly ran down the porch stairs and got into the passenger seat. Her mother turned on the ignition, released the clutch, and put her foot on the gas. The car jerked twice and off they drove, down the long driveway, and onto the street. Lolly looked back. Her father was standing with his hand raised. She raised hers.

They turned left then left again. "Where should we go?" her mother asked.

Lolly felt confused. They drove down the street. Ahead

was the road that led up to the crown of the levee.

"Let's go up on the levee," she said. "Maybe I can find Bo."

"I don't think that we should do that," her mother said, but she gunned the motor and they chugged onto the gravel road at the top of the berm.

"I've never driven up here," her mother said. "There's no traffic. Maybe this is a good place to get used to the car."

Lolly peered out at the forbidden landscape of the river bottom. Rolling down the window, she inhaled the smell of hot grasses and baked dirt. "Why do you stay with him?" she asked her mother. "I mean, I know some kids whose parents are divorced."

"They're not Catholic like us. Catholics don't get divorced. It's a sin."

Lolly gazed intensely out the window, looking for any sign of Bo. The car spit rocks as it drove over the rugged levee road. From this vantage point, she could look down and see St. Joseph's, the church where she and her mother went to Mass on Sundays. Across the street from the church was the convent. She even saw the grotto within the convent grounds. The horses had gone home.

"Besides," her mother said. "You take what you get out of this life. Sometimes it's a tongue-lashing or worse. Sometimes it's a new car."

Mama's face is coated with sweat, or is it sadness? "Maybe you should tell him to take a flying leap."

"Do you think so?" her mother asked, an edge to her voice.

"No," Lolly said. *But if he were my husband I would tell him, but maybe I wouldn't have to because I'm never going to have a husband.*

Though the road was gravelly and rutted, her mother guided the car expertly. They had driven around the entire town on the levee's track and were almost back to where they had begun when Lolly spotted the dingy trailers a few hundred feet in front of them.

"The gypsies," she said.

"Not gypsies in the true sense," her mother said. "More like forsaken people."

"Daddy says they're trash."

"He would," her mother replied. "The town's been trying to get rid of them for years. When the river rises they're forced to leave, but they always come back. They're like weeds."

"Why?"

"Why do they come back?"

"No, why is the town trying to get rid of them?"

"Oh," her mother said in her vague way. "I guess because they're...rough people. Yes, I think it's because they're rough."

"If I lived over here, I'd be rough too," Lolly said. "Can you stop? This is the place, I think. I want to look for Bo."

"No, darling. I can't let you go down there."

Lolly got on her knees, leaned out the window, and squinted into the sun. Most of the trailers were rusted and scarred. Tattered awnings hung over some of their front doors in a feeble attempt to create shade. Here and there abandoned cars, some without wheels, some stripped of their engines, lay like the bones of dead animals. Twenty, maybe thirty, trailers clustered close together, but for the most part they sprawled across the flat river bottom as though their inhabitants had a faint desire for privacy.

They drifted, her mother driving slower now, past the outskirts of the trailer community until they came to a colony of boxy structures.

"Look at those!" Lolly exclaimed as her mother stopped the car. "Houses made of cardboard."

Her mother craned across the seat to see. "Shameful," she sighed. "And to think there are children who live there."

At that instant, a girl appeared at the top of the levee. She was about Lolly's own age, with pale skin and dark red hair that corkscrewed into tight bright ringlets. She ran down the gravel road toward them.

"Oh my," her mother said and cranked the handle, winding up her window. "Sit down, Lolly. Pull your head into the car."

The girl ran toward them, arms flailing. Behind her, the sun ignited a shimmery aura. She reached them, breathless and panting, and drew her finger down the length of the car over the slick green paint.

"We should go," her mother said.

"Wait," Lolly said.

"Careful," Mother whispered. "Better roll up your window."

Instead, Lolly rolled her window all the way down. The girl, only inches away, smelled musty, like dried grass, her eyes a muddy green. Her lashes and eyebrows were the same dark red as her hair.

"Hi," Lolly said.

The girl stared at them curiously. She was wearing faded blue shorts and a sky blue halter-top, the stitching lightened from being washed. She clutched the side of the open window with dirt encrusted fingers.

"I'm looking for my cat," Lolly said.

The girl surveyed the car from one end to the other. Then she peered inside and sniffed.

"He's orange with white smile lines," Lolly said. "His name is Bo. Have you seen him?"

The girl raised her right hand and licked it three times

starting at her wrist up to the tips of her fingers. Then she pressed her hand against the windshield. When she lifted it, a smudged print was left on the glass. Her eyes narrowed and again she pushed her head in through the open window. "I know secrets about cats," she said.

Her mother jammed the car into gear and they sped off, leaving the girl standing in the center of a dust devil.

I'd give my seat in hell to find out the secrets that girl knows.

Chapter Eight

That evening Lolly waited on the porch for her grandfather to arrive. He didn't come often. She figured it was because her father was so hard on him, just as he was with everyone, except maybe Doc Pine.

Finally hearing his car rattle up the driveway, she rushed down the porch steps scattered with wisteria petals and waited for him to park.

Getting out of his old Ford, he spread out his ropy arms and she jumped into them. "Grandpa!"

"What's with the cap?" he asked as he set her down.

She stretched the collar of the hat out so her grandfather could peek under.

"Uh," he grunted. "Very chic. What does your daddy think of it?" He released her. "Or does his opinion have something to do with why you're wearing the cap."

She nodded. "I wish somebody could talk to him so I wouldn't have to wear this thing."

"You know as well as I do there's not much chance of that," he said, eyes sparkling. "But I've got two pieces of good news for you. The first is hair grows back faster than a falling star."

She smiled. "And the second?"

"Second is you look as cute as a bug in that cloche." He put his arm around her shoulders and leaned on her as they ascended the stairs.

"Hi, Daddy," her mother said, sweeping into the foyer, her full, silky skirts rustling as she entered and embraced her father. "Want to see the car now or after dinner? I've made your favorite: Freddy Marzetti."

"Hot doggie," Grandpa said. "Spect I can wait until after dinner." He turned to Lolly and in a loud whisper said, "What in tarnation is Freddy Marzetti?"

She laughed and bounced on her toes. "Casserole. I named it."

"Come on in where it's cool," her mother said, leading them into the living room.

"I've got something to tell you, Grandpa," Lolly said. "Yesterday, Mama and I were up on the levee and..."

"Hello there, Jeb." Interrupting, her father looked up from his newspaper, his tone riddled with dislike. "Read about this new U-2 plane?"

"Nope, can't say that I have."

Her father folded up the paper and went to the wet bar. "How's it going?"

"Good, Regan. No complaints. Course if somebody offered to turn the clock back a few decades, I'd most likely accept, and that's the God's truth."

"But then you wouldn't be my grandfather," Lolly said.

"By golly, you're right," Grandpa said, raising his eyebrows in genuine concern. "You're a smart little dickens. Cancel that last request. Think I'll stay right where I am. I may be old but I'm still a handsome dog, right, princess?"

"Right," Lolly said. And then she brought up the elevator story. She always brought up the elevator story when her father and grandfather were together because she figured it reminded her father why her grandfather was important.

"Tell me about that day!"

Her grandfather looked over to her father as though asking for permission. That was always the way it went. Her father nodded, poured a shot, and tossed it back.

"Tell me the story again, Grandpa!" she begged.

Her grandfather laughed and shook his head. "You mother and daddy met in my elevator," he said smiling. Your mother had stopped by to bring me some lunch. She did that sometimes. When she did, she'd always take the round trip ride with me, sometimes a couple of times. That day, your father got on. I think it was the second floor."

"It was the fifth," her father said. "It was the top floor."

"Right," Grandpa said. "The top floor. Anyway, he got on and took one look at your mama and I knew something very important had happened and when I looked around to take a peek at my baby, I was positive. A month later your daddy rode down with me for the last trip of the day. We were alone in the car."

Grandpa drew himself up, becoming taller and attempted to make his voice sound like her father's.

"'Would you mind stopping between the second and first floor, Mr. Hitchcock? I've got something to ask you.' That's when your daddy asked me for your mama's hand."

Lolly grinned and looked over at her mother, who smiled faintly and lit a cigarette.

"Horn of corn, Jeb?" her father asked.

Grandpa nodded and sat down. "But make it light. This old man can't hold his liquor like he used to."

Her mother cocked her head to one side and looked at her father, then she said, "Dinner will be ready in about ten minutes." She left the room.

Her father turned away. Lolly wanted him to turn around and talk to Grandpa. She wanted him to be nice.

Finally, Grandpa spoke: "How's life treating you, Regan?"

Her father didn't reply.

"That old river keeps a rolling along," Grandpa said to fill the conversational gap. "Met a nice woman. Real nice. Might bring her over one of these Sundays to meet the family."

Her father handed her grandfather a drink before knocking back another vodka. "Real nice," Lolly's grandfather went on, leaning back in his chair. He sipped his drink. "She's really something. Retired now. Used to be a doctor. Quite a feat in her time. Thinking about painting her. Might ask her to sit for me. Light shines from that woman's face."

Her grandfather winked at her. "She's real interesting," he said, tapping his lip with his finger. "Course there'll never be anybody like my Lucy."

Lolly traced a large blue vein that burrowed through her grandfather's flesh like a worm. She wanted to tell him about the girl she had seen on the levee.

Just then, her father said, "You never know when to quit, do you, Jeb? Don't you know by now that all women are trouble?"

"Daddy just got mama a new car," Lolly said. "But I don't think it was because she's trouble."

Her father pulled her onto his lap. "Your mother deserves it," he said and then he immediately scooted her off.

"And you, Regan," Grandpa said. "How's it going? You putting the bad guys away?"

"Goddamn election's coming up, and the rumor mill reports that Drake Halliday's going to try and unseat me."

"He shouldn't be any trouble for you," Grandpa said.

"Not so sure. If you've been paying attention, I've lost my

last two cases. Thaddeus Edmunds has been giving me quite a negative run."

"Who's Thaddeus Edmunds?" Lolly asked.

"The judge. There was a lot of publicity on both cases. Bad news is not good news."

Lolly noticed her father was beginning to slur his words.

"You can't win 'em all," Grandpa said. "I doubt the town expects that."

"They expect me to get the riff raff put away, that's what they expect." Her father's voice was edgy. "It wouldn't hurt my reputation any if I could get rid of the gypsy trash heap on the other side of the levee."

He poured more vodka into his glass.

"Isn't that enough medicine, Daddy?" Lolly asked in a small voice.

"Watch your mouth, youngster," her father flared.

"She didn't mean anything, Regan," Grandpa said. "With the election coming up, you might consider going easy on the sauce, know what I mean? This is a small town and people love to talk."

Her mother came to the door. She had tied on an apron and her cheeks were flushed from the heat of the stove. "Dinner's almost ready," she told them.

"People love to talk? What're you saying, Jeb?"

"I'm not saying anything. Just that you're hitting it maybe a mite much."

Lolly took her grandpa's hand. "Let's go out and see the new car," she said.

"A mite much?" Her father eyes were like dark slits. "Do you have any idea the pressure I'm under? Of course you don't. You've never taken a risk in your entire life."

"Regan, please." Her mother clung to the doorway.

"Now, Regan, I'm not criticizing," her grandfather said. "It's just that it would probably be..."

"You've lived from hand to mouth your entire life," her father told him. "Running that goddamn elevator and before that, I don't know what."

"Please, Grandpa," Lolly said and tugged more insistently. "Let's go outside."

"I had a good business before I took over the elevator. Electrical." His tone was defiant.

"You barely could keep your head above water," Regan snarled.

Her mother stepped into the room. "Don't do this, Regan."

"When I met you," her father continued, ignoring her mother, "you were on your way to bankruptcy, for Christ's sake. If you hadn't gotten the elevator job, I don't know what you would have done."

"Stop!" Lolly cried. She hated to see that expression on her grandfather's face, angry and sad at the same time. She pulled harder on his hand and he put down his drink and followed her outside.

"I thought we were going to see the car," Grandpa said. He grunted as he pulled one leg up through the hole and onto the platform of the tree house. He had built it for her almost three years earlier in the maple at the far end of the yard.

"We'll see it, but first I want to talk to you, and this is the best place."

Her grandfather pulled up his second leg. "My, my, princess, it's getting tough for this old man to get up here."

"Don't pay any attention to Daddy. He's had too much medicine."

"Yep, that's for sure." Her grandfather reached over and pulled the cap off her head.

"Please, Grandpa," she said. "I have to wear it." She tugged the hat back on.

"It's so hot, princess."

"It's okay," she said as her grandfather wiped the perspiration trailing down her cheek with the back of his hand. "Bo hasn't come home yet."

"That doesn't mean he won't."

"Have you ever been over the levee where the gypsies live?"

"Not for a long time. Why?"

"I've been over there," she said.

"I know you want Bo home, but you mustn't hang around those trailers. It's not a good idea."

"I was with Daddy. A couple of days ago. That's where he threw Bo down the levee."

"I had an inkling that old cat didn't leave home on his own," Grandpa said.

"And yesterday Mama drove up there when she was getting used to the new car. It's dry over there and not very nice. But a girl came up to our car. She was real pretty and she said she knew secrets."

Her grandfather frowned. "The people who live there are strange, Lolly. They do things that some folks don't understand."

"I know," she said. "Come see this."

She scrambled down through the hole of the tree house and used the boards nailed across the trunk as steps. Grandpa followed and jumped from the last rung to the ground. "Damn this knee. It's worthless."

"Are you all right, Grandpa?"

"Fine, fine. Just a crabby joint."

"Come on," she said and she took his hand and pulled him around to the garage. They went through a side door into the cool, dim room. She flipped on the light switch. The new station wagon gleamed.

Her grandfather whistled. "Holy smokes! That's a beauty. Your daddy must have been bad as week-old meat to buy this baby. Guilts are powerful motivators." He clucked his tongue. "Poor man. I don't think he means to do what he does."

"Look, Grandpa." She led him to the passenger side of the windshield where the handprint of the redheaded girl was still smudged on the glass.

"What's this?" Grandpa asked.

"It's from the gypsy girl," she said. Cautiously she placed her hand over the print. Her fingers and palm matched that of the girl's. She pulled her hand away.

"What's the matter?" he asked.

I must be imagining things, she thought. *Nobody can leave a print like this, unless they're magic.* "It feels hot," she said. "Hotter than a pancake!"

Chapter Nine

"I love you, Grandpa," she said, standing on her tiptoes to place a good-bye kiss on his stubbled white chin. She was sorry he hadn't stayed for dinner, but after the flak he'd taken from her father, she understood. She watched her grandfather's Ford belch its way down the driveway before falling into the squeaky couch swing on the porch. One leg touching the floor, she pushed herself back and forth, squeezing out a high metallic note with every pass.

Early twilight stretched over the valley. The garden had recently been sprinkled and the dampness released the musky smells of earth and the sweetness of the vines. Back and forth, rocking, she thought about what her grandfather had said.

I don't think he means to do what he does.

She could hear her parents' voices arguing from the second floor: "Why must you humiliate him like that? Especially in front of Lolly. Daddy's never claimed to be anything but what he is, a good man with a big heart. He doesn't deserve that kind of treatment."

"He's such a wind bag." Her father's words sounded lazy and thick. "I don't want Lolly to grow up to be deluded like him."

"How could that possibly happen with you riding her at

every turn? You're on her all the time. Just once, couldn't you tell her she's pretty or smart?"

"Don't tell me how to handle my daughter!"

"The way you're going, you won't have a daughter!"

The sound of the slap was sharp and painful. The swing shimmied and stopped and Lolly curled into herself like a potato bug. She pressed her hands over her ears, but even then the sound of her mother's sobs reached her. They were big and gulpy, and they went on and on.

"Stop this, Clarissa, or I'll have to call Doc!"

"Call him!" her mother cried. "Give me the shot! Put me out! I want to sleep forever!"

She heard her father's voice on the telephone and soon headlights blended with the gathering nightfall as Doc Pine's 1955 Buick roared up the driveway and stopped. Every year, each of her father's friends bought new cars.

Lolly sat straight up in the swing as Doc Pine, black bag in hand, climbed the porch steps. He reminded her of the skeletons in store windows at Halloween. He was tall and gangly, and his dangling arms and legs moved separately from each other, his forehead bulging out like a small wall. His eyes were crayon blue, but they were so deeply set that they looked empty. A bright pink bow tie set off his sparkling white short sleeve shirt and he wore long khaki golf shorts.

"Evening, Lolly" he said brightly. "What're you doing out here by yourself?"

"Nothing," she said. "You going to give Mama a shot?"

"We'll see," Doc said. "She upstairs?"

Lolly nodded.

"Why don't you come on inside?" Doc said. "The mosquitoes are pretty bad. They usually don't start spraying for them until July, but it's my bet they're going to set on them earlier this year. At my house those critters are attacking like B-29 bombers." He opened the screen door and she scooted off the swing and followed him into the house.

"I'll tell them you're here," she said.

"What's with the hat?" he asked.

"I have fleas," she said. "It keeps them in." She scrambled up the stairs, motioning for Doc to come up. She sat on the steps and thought hard. *This is a man who fixes bodies*, she thought. She had an idea and decided to ask Doc about it after he was finished with her mother.

Soon the doctor came out of her parents' bedroom and stopped on the step above her. "How come you're not watching *Superman*?" he asked her. "He's on just about now. My daughter Pamela is hooked."

"I don't like television," she said.

"You don't?" His knees clicked as he sat beside her. "What do you like to do?"

"Read," she said.

"I'm trying to get Pamela to read. Maybe I could borrow a couple of your favorite books for her."

"Sure," she said.

"Which one would you suggest?"

"I'd start her with *The Sign of the Twisted Candles*. Nancy Drew. She won't be able to put it down." She didn't give him an opportunity to say another word. "I have a question."

"Shoot," Doc said.

Her father called from the landing, "Doc? Golf game this weekend?"

"Sure," Doc said. "But let's start early. So dang hot these days. Now. What was your question, Lolly?"

"Nothing," she said, looking up at the two men who stood over her like towering redwoods.

"Well, I've got to go," Doc said.

"Thanks for coming," her father said. "Sorry to drag you out this late for one of Clarissa's hysterical fits."

"Not a problem," Doc said. "Got a couple more house calls to make anyway. Across the levee."

"Tonight?" her father said. "You got to go there tonight?"

"Ever since last summer and that gypsy woman and her baby died, we've had to handle those people like egg shells. You remember the fuss they made?"

"A baby died?" Lolly asked.

"That white trash stirred things up something terrible," Doc said. "Nothing they'd like better than take one of us town folk to the cleaners, and as far as they're concerned, it might as well be me."

"What baby?" Lolly asked again.

"Sooner or later we're going to clear the whole bunch of them out of there, and I predict it'll be sooner," her father said. "Did you hear about the new committee I'm heading? We're sending in a social worker to do evaluations of the ones with kids. If they don't meet the standards, we'll put their kids into foster homes. That'll make them think twice about staying."

"Sounds like a good plan," Doc said.

Doc and her father shook hands, and Doc hurried down the porch stairs. Lolly followed him. "Doc Pine?" she called as he tossed his bag into the back seat. "What baby were you talking about?"

"Is that what you want to ask me about?"

"No." She bit her nail. "I want to ask you something else."

Her father suddenly burst through the screen door and trotted down the steps. "Seven-thirty okay, Doc? I'll call the club for a tee time."

Doc nodded, then cocked his head toward Lolly. "Fleas you

said?"

She looked from her father to Doc, then ran back into the house.

"She's an interesting one," she heard Doc say and her father mumbled something in reply. Doc shot her father a salute and soon his car purred down the driveway.

I have to talk to him about finding Daddy some different medicine, Lolly thought. *If Doc knew about how Daddy acts, he'd do something.* She knew if she called his office, her mama might hear. And if she went there she didn't know how to explain to the nurse that she wanted to talk to Doc privately. Lolly gnawed on her nail.

She stood on the landing outside her parents' bedroom and listened to her mother breathing deeply. Whatever Doc had given her had probably put her out for the night, as it usually did. Her father was downstairs in his study playing his saxophone now. Long, mournful notes lazed up the stairs like seagulls. A session like this often would go on for over an hour.

Lolly's throat tightened and her stomach lurched. But she had no choice, she thought. She had to go now. If she hurried, she could meet Doc on the other side of the levee and get back without anyone knowing she'd been gone. And while she was there, she could look for Bo.

She put on her brown school oxfords, tugged the cap down over her ears, and made her way through the house. If she moved fast enough, she'd be home before the evening light had faded. She tiptoed down the back steps, skipped out the backyard gate, and ran toward the levee.

The first house she passed was the Remington's where Mr. Remington sat in the living room illuminated by the flickering light of a television. Next door was the Berkeley's huge ranch style house with a Spanish fountain set smack in the middle of manicured grass. Lolly could smell garlic coming from Mrs. Berkeley's kitchen.

Lolly ran faster, her knee socks falling down around her ankles. Within minutes she found herself at the base of the looming levee. Her mouth was dry and her heart was beating fast like the white pet mouse's she used to have. A narrow path, made by dogs or raccoons she guessed, had been worn down the side of the levee. It was steep and dried grasses grew on either side. Knowing that if she came home covered with foxtails, her parents would be suspicious, she looked around for another and easier way. Finding none, she began the climb, occasionally having to use her hands to haul herself up until finally she stepped up onto the road that ran along the top of the levee. She stopped to let her breath catch up with her.

A huge white moon hung over the dry river bottom. A lonely howl came from far away. And then, from behind her, the sound of a whisper scared her and she whirled around. Nobody. It must have been the wind playing through the grasses.

Making her way over the gravel track, she came to a point where she could look down on the gypsy encampment on the river bottom. *We're neighbors*, she thought. *These people live as close to us as some of the most important people in town.*

Indecipherable voices tumbled like water in a stream. A woman laughed raucously and a dog barked. Lolly scrunched her eyes shut. *Please, God, let me find Bo.*

Inching along the crown of the road, she looked down on several clusters of trailers. Doc's car was parked in front of a small van, which was not connected to a car or truck, but its nose was propped up on a metal foot, and it heeled to one side. There was a light in its windows. Was that where Doc's patient was? In the van?

Lolly walked on, looking for a path down. Not only was there no trail, but the far side of the levee was covered with bushes and trees, some taller than she was.

She stepped into the thicket. Branches broke as she forced her way down and sharp limbs clawed at her. Thistles scratched at her legs and nettles bit at her ankles. Finally, she made it off the levee and stepped quietly toward Doc's car.

The door of the trailer opened. Silhouetted by the light from behind, Doc himself emerged, walked to his car, and slipped a key into the lock.

"Doc," Lolly called. "*Pssst!*"

Doc turned. He sputtered, "Lolly! What the hell? This is no place for you! Get in the car. I have a couple more people to see—if I can find them in this jungle. Then I'll take you home."

"I need to ask you something." Doc had always been kind to her and now, here in this place, surely he would help her.

"On the way home. I want to finish these calls."

"Please!" she said.

Doc looked at her out of his shadowy deep-set eyes.

"It's about my daddy."

"What about him?"

Why did she even have to ask these questions? Didn't Doc know her father drank medicine every night? How was it that he didn't know that the medicine transforms people into mean, staggering idiots? Doctors were supposed to know these things.

"Speak up, Lolly. I haven't got all night."

"He needs a different kind of medicine. To make him better. I mean something besides the horns of corns."

Doc's eyebrows rose. Then he drew his mouth to one side. "Lolly Candolin, you skeedadle into my car. This is not the time or place for that conversation."

"Do you know of something that will help him?"

"Girl, I'm not sure what you mean. And even if I did, your daddy's a grown man and there's plenty in the world you don't understand."

"Would you promise to think about it?"

I need Doc to talk to me now! How am I going to get him to understand?

"Lolly, get into the car!"

Doc opened his car door, waiting for her. She knew it was no use. Impatient and angry that Doc hadn't helped her, she stood her ground.

"Don't tell him that you saw me," she said.

"I won't lie to your father, Lolly."

"Don't lie. Just don't tell. Please!"

"Get into my car," he repeated.

If Doc took her home, how would she explain to her father how she'd met up with Doc, or why he'd brought her home? Her father would know she'd been in the gypsy camp and he would skin her alive. She had to return on her own.

She turned and ran.

"Wait!" Doc shouted. "You shouldn't be out here!"

"I'm all right!" she yelled over her shoulder. "I can get home by myself."

She darted behind a trailer.

"Lolly Candolin, come back here!" he called, and she could hear him stumbling after her. "Lolly, please, answer me. You must come now." He was close, but he passed. He called again, "Lolly, please." He waited, then his breath stuttered out. "Dang kid. Where'd she go?" He stopped and listened. "Lolly, this is not a good idea." Sweat made its way down the side of her face. "Lordy, child," he muttered and turned away. Moonlight slashed across his shoulders as he made his way back to his car.

Lolly watched as his Buick started with a sigh and rocked over the rutted road toward his next patient, knowing that he'd call her house as soon as he got home to see if she had arrived safely. She'd have to move quickly.

"*Haram infata cum,*" a woman's voice chanted.

Lolly raised her head.

"*Lo epoodo sonesta tum. Ray deponda slatin fey. Zezapito trudo hay.*"

Lolly crept around to the window of the trailer, put her foot on the tire, and hoisted herself up to look in.

Three people glowed in the flickering light of more candles than a Christmas Eve midnight Mass.

"*Ithic noto slumta na, presa masa nedhem pa…*"

The chanting woman had flashing dark eyes and dark blonde hair burnt with auburn streaks. Her pedal pushers were like hot pink skin and a strapless top hugged her slim waist and accentuated her smallish breasts. She looked to Lolly like a movie star. An unlighted cigarette bobbed from her mouth as she chanted with fierce intensity. In her hand she held up a bracelet of beads.

"*Lehem nathra penito to signum straum brthra sho.*"

Two people hovered close to her, a man with skin so white it looked like paper and strands of yellowed hair that appeared to have been painted across his bald head. He wore a Hawaiian shirt. The second was a tall woman stuffed into a blue print cotton shift with a neckline so low that it exposed a fleshy shoulder. Muscles roped along the sides of her neck, and her face was oily with heavy, bright make-up. The chanting stopped, and the three people clasped hands.

"Please cleanse Andrea of the infection and let her be pure and whole," the woman in the hot pink said. "Make her clean and free of all that can harm her."

They dropped hands and the woman in hot pink slipped a bracelet over the wrist of her big shouldered companion, who broke into silent tears.

A rustle came from behind. Lolly turned.

"*Ahhhiii!*" A demon raced toward her, a papery brown face and clawing hands. Gasping, she fell off the trailer tire. The creature growled and flung its arms wide. Lolly opened her mouth to scream, but nothing came out.

Oh, Blessed Mary, help me.

She inched back on her behind, but the monster kept coming. She found a rough stanchion to pull herself up with and, not looking back, she dashed through the maze of trailers to the foot of the levee and started the climb, fighting through brush and flailing through spiky sharp limbs, their crooked arms and hands hooking her, scraping her skin.

Fear pulled her up the side of the berm. *They were right,* she thought. *Terrible and strange things do live in the gypsy camp.*

Now on the levee, she panted, filling her lungs, desperate for air. Only then did she dare to look back. Dark swatches of inky shadows hid whatever had threatened her. Gasping, she crossed the road, and searched for the path she had used. In the distance, a low howl sent her sprinting down the town side of the levee, down to the safe, tidy streets where damp summer lawns lay in front of large houses and porch swings complained in the breeze. Running past the Berkeley's, then the Remington's, she finally came to her own driveway. She slipped through the back door and took the stairs two at a time up to her room.

She closed the door and leaned against it, breathing in the safe darkness. Before going into the bathroom she switched on the light. In the mirror, she saw her face heated to a ripe scarlet, an ugly scratch over her ear. Though she'd stopped crying, terror quivered at the corners of her mouth. She leaned over the basin and splashed cold water onto her face. Her skin stung, but she was snug in the fact that she was home, away from a danger outside that seemed bigger than anything she'd ever faced before.

Somewhere in the house, the phone rang.

The image of the demon she'd seen was replaced with that of Bo's paws scrambling at the mouth of the burlap bag. Bile gathered in the back of her throat.

A knock sounded at her door.

"Lolly?"

It was her father, his voice hollow, a familiar sound after he had spent an evening with horns of corn.

"Doc Pine's on the line," he said. "He wants to know if you can talk to him. Something about an answer he has for you regarding your science project."

Lolly let go of a big breath. "Thanks, Daddy," she said. "I'm in the bathroom. Could you ask if I can talk to him another time?"

"Righto," her father said. His footsteps receded as he shuffled back into his bedroom and closed the door.

She slumped. Fear still remained at her side. She wished she could tell her father what she'd seen in the gypsy camp, but he would punish her if she admitted where she'd been. There were times, when her father was sober, that he might listen to her story and soothe her fears. But in the condition he was now, he wouldn't care if she'd seen a man from Mars.

She closed her eyes. The face of the demon loomed in front of her, and she heard its deep, throaty growls. Was God punishing her for punching the Appaloosa in the nose? Maybe the devil was attacking her because she hadn't gone to confession.

She fell to her knees and closed her eyes.

"Bless me God, I confess," she prayed. "It's been two weeks since my last confession, and these are my sins. I'm truly sorry for what I did to Sonja, and I won't do it again. If you keep the devil away from me, I promise never to want to be a grotto horse again. Dear, God, please—"

Something trickled down her cheek.

Dear sweet, Jesus. Oh, my dearest sweetest, Jesus.

She placed her hands on the bathroom sink, and pulled herself up. She opened her eyes and looked into the mirror.

Her bare head, patchy and ugly, shone in the bathroom light and the scratch above her ear was weeping. She then realized the cap was gone. It must have been torn off during her wild climb.

Go back, she thought. *Tonight. Go back tonight and find the cap.*

Chapter Ten

She stood on the landing outside her parents' room and listened to the silence. Downstairs, the antique Waltham chimed ten o'clock.

Heart hammering, she took a step down. The stair creaked. She froze. The maple tree tapped at a downstairs window. She waited and took another step, which was silent. As was the next. Then another and another.

Suddenly, she heard coughing. It was her father, which meant that he might burst from the bedroom and weave his way downstairs for water or juice since it was past the horn of corn hour. She waited. Finally came the familiar groan followed by creaks from the bed straining under his weight. She unlocked the back door, inched it silently open, and slipped out.

Clouds were moving across the bright moon. She retraced her steps to the levee, passing the Remington's, which was entirely dark, and then the Berkeley's, where their fountain was dry and silent.

At the base of the levee, she found the animal path she'd taken before and made the climb, piling three large rocks to make a marker so she could find the trail later. Crossing the road, Lolly hunted for the rough parting she had carved through the limbs, squinted and peered into shadows, trying to find the cap.

About halfway down, on the river side of the levee, a condensed piece of blackness caught her eye. Assuming this was what she was looking for, she ducked and twisted through spikey low trees and bushes, and found that it was only a cluster of leaves caught in a tangle of limbs.

She continued to creep down the levee, looking from side to side. Just as she reached the bottom, a cloud drifted across the moon and she shuddered.

I should have brought a flashlight.

She would have to find the trailer Doc had visited and work her way back from it. Shuffling forward, she moved closer to the lighted windows of the parked vans. She heard voices murmuring and smelled cigarettes and bacon on the warm easterly breeze.

Something rustled behind her. She whirled. Nothing. All she heard were voices sounding like laugh tracks on a television.

Again something rustled. The hair on her arms stood up. Somebody or something had followed her. With breath clotted, she took two steps forward. Whatever was behind her followed. She counted to three, whirled, and saw a ragged canvas attached to a trailer flapping innocently in the rising breeze. Breathing again, she proceeded through the maze of trailers. Which trailer had Doc been in? They all looked alike.

From behind her came a growl.

Dear God, help me!

Something tapped her shoulder and, whirling around, she saw the same raspy-faced demon she had seen before pressing its ugliness toward her, expressionless, smelling of stale sweat and dirty clothing. As she backed away, heart pounding, she tripped over a braided wire running from a van's porch and landed flat on the ground.

Lolly's mouth opened, but her throat was too constricted for her to make a sound. The demon let out a shout and ripped off its face. "You came back for them secrets, didn't you?" Peering down at Lolly was the redheaded girl.

Dragging herself to her feet, Lolly turned and ran for the levee, arms and legs far out of sync. Footsteps dogged her, so she ran faster until her pursuer grabbed her wrist and brought her to a dead stop. Now they were face to face.

"I ain't gonna hurt you!" the girl said, her grip tightening. "I want you to stay!"

"Let go of me," Lolly said. When the girl released her, she backed away rubbing her shoulder.

"I guess I sceered you." The girl held up the demon face with two holes cut for eyes. "Sorry."

In the moonlight, Lolly could see that it was a grocery bag from Tony's Market on the other side of the levee.

"How come you're bald?" the girl asked.

Lolly ran her hand over her scalp. "Fleas."

"Fleas don't do that! Least, no fleas I know."

The girl reached out and ran her fingers over the patches of hair. "Neato," she said, her green eyes staring from an impassive face. "My name's Tick. It's a play name. Sometimes my mama calls me Angel Snoot or Pookers. My truest name is Teresa. Mama says a kid who's really loved has a bunch of names. You got a lot of names?"

"No," Lolly said. "I'm just Lolly. Lolly's my true name."

It was strange, but she didn't feel frightened by this dirty, wild girl.

"Don't sound so true to me," Tick said. Another long silence. "Sure it ain't Lolita or Lorissa or somethin' like that?

What's you doin' here so late?"

Lolly chewed her cuticle, biting off a splinter of skin. She'd never thought about it before, but if having different names was a way of judging how much you're loved, she wasn't so bad off. Her grandfather called her princess, and often her mother called her darling. "Looking for a cap," Lolly said.

"What'da you mean 'cap'?"

"A hat. Dark blue knit and I can't go home without it."

A hot ache pulsed in the back of Lolly's throat. She didn't want to cry in front of this girl, but if she wasn't able to find the cap soon and get back home, she wasn't sure what would happen. Her mother wouldn't wake up until morning. That's what Doc Pine's shot did. But there was no telling about her father. The medicine made him dry and he might get up for water again and find her gone.

"You lost it somewheres here?"

Lolly nodded.

"Yippee," Tick crowed. "A treasure hunt. Let's go!" She scampered off into another strip of moonlight. Lolly didn't move. "What's you waitin' for?" Tick said. "Come on! Ain't no way we can have a hunt at night with no flashlight."

Tick skipped off into the shadows and Lolly followed her into the heart of this strange place, jogging to catch up with Tick as she took two right turns and then a left before stopping in front of one of the larger trailers. In the weak light coming from the shabbily curtained windows, Lolly could see a sculpture of twisted coat hangers in the shape of a unicorn hanging by the door.

"Mama, we're havin' a visitor!"

Through the open door, candles flickered and shadows danced on the walls. Even from where she stood outside the trailer, Lolly smelled paraffin, which reminded her of the candles burning in the small, white chapel at the convent school.

Then a woman stood in the doorway, unmistakable in her hot pink pants.

"Hello, there, pretty little ragged head," she said in a breathy voice. "Come in."

Lolly stayed out on the porch.

She was sure this was the same person she had spied on earlier, the one chanting the strange words.

Maybe I shouldn't go inside. I don't know these people.

"You're as pretty as they come," the woman told her. "That a new hair style? Shaving your head in sections? You want to do that Tick, shave your head in sections?"

"This here's Lolly." Tick threw her arms around the woman's waist. "We need a flashlight."

"Back room, darlin'. Second drawer down to the right under the box holdin' the diamonds." The woman turned back toward Lolly. "I'm Sophie, Tick's mama. She's my only baby by my fourth husband. That don't mean I have babies with other husbands, but it means she's my *only* baby and I love her more than I love my thumbs. Try to do somethin' without usin' your thumbs. It's close to impossible. Ever been married, Lolly?"

Lolly's eyes felt big as ping-pong balls. She'd never met anyone who talked like this before. Certainly she wasn't like any of her mother's friends. "N-no," she stammered.

Laughing, Sophie flexed her long neck like a movie star waiting for a vampire to take a bite. Her fingers were tipped with frosted nails and a dozen beaded-bracelets clicked on both wrists.

"You hungry, Lolly? How about a chocolate cookie? They say chocolate makes for calm and it appears to me that you've got a might of agitation goin' on."

"No thank you, Mrs., ah, Mrs...."

"Sophie. Just Sophie. Come on in."

Lolly hesitated. She wasn't supposed to speak to strangers, let alone go into their trailers, but Sophie seemed so nice. She took a deep breath, stepped inside, and looked around curiously. The narrow room had a built-in couch covered in a worn nubby material the color of dead grass, and there was only one chair, the kind that had a lever that raised a footrest. On a table stood four frames, each holding pictures of different old men cut from newspapers.

"Them's my make-believe grandpas," Tick said, popping between them, flashlight in hand. She carefully repositioned each frame.

"It's true," Sophie said. "Tick'd take a grandpa before a chance for free ice cream."

In the center of the trailer there was a small kitchen with something rich and aromatic bubbling on a two-burner stove.

Sophie took a step toward Lolly. "What's wrong, child? Why you got such sadness in them big, brown eyes?"

Sophie's eyes were gray and placed far apart under carefully tweezed eyebrows. Her pink lips were full and they shined, and her porcelain skin reminded Lolly of the hand-touched photographs in Grandpa's picture albums. Sophie shrugged dark blonde hair out of her face and lit a cigarette, her mouth forming an O around the gold tip.

"You going to tell Sophie what's wrong?" she asked softly.

Lolly shook her head. "Nothing," she said. "I just need to find my cap."

"We're goin' on a cap hunt, Mama!" Tick announced. "Tell us where we should look?"

Sophie closed her eyes. Her blonde head nodded slightly to one side and then to the other.

"Try the dead cottonwood tree about three feet up the

levee next to Andrea and Charlie's trailer," she said in a dreamy voice. "I'd bet a Saturday night's worth of beer at the Chiseler's Inn it's there."

A momentary wave of relief swept over Lolly. She was going to get the cap back. Then logic took over. *This is nonsense*.

"Come on," Tick said.

Lolly hesitated, but she had nothing to lose. "Thank you, Sophie," she said, feeling strange calling this girl's mother by her first name.

Sophie held out a bracelet, a strand of blue-green moons threaded on a silver chain. "Put this on, child. Aquamarines. They encourage truth and service to the world and might help you learn the lessons you need to know."

Lolly held out her right wrist and Sophie slipped on the bracelet, which felt like a ring of fire.

"It feels warm," Lolly said.

Sophie smiled. "It's different for everybody," she said. "It'll do for you what it needs to do."

"Come on!" Tick pulled at Lolly's hand.

"Thank you," Lolly told Sophie and followed Tick out into the night.

"I hope you come back some time," Tick said, and she turned on the flashlight. "I get lonely."

"Aren't there any other kids that live over here?" Lolly asked.

"Nope," Tick said.

"How come?"

"There used to be when I was young. Mama says we're a dying breed."

"Oh," Lolly said, although she didn't understand "dying breed" at all.

The moonlight was even brighter now, causing the white trailers to glow. After three turns they came to a small van.

"This is where Andrea and Charlie live," Tick said. "They're kinda different." She cast the flashlight around the trailer's hitch and over to the cottonwood tree, running the beam up its gray bare limbs.

"Is that it?" she asked.

Hooked on a gnarled finger was a cap. Lolly unhooked it, and tugged it down over her ears. "How'd she do it?" she asked. "How'd she know?"

"My mama's different," Tick said proudly. "She says if you stop and think about it, we're all different in our own way and she ain't talkin' about ears and noses."

"What then?" Lolly asked.

"I'm not sure," Tick said. "I think it has something to do with hearts." Tick slashed the beam through the darkness. When it slid under the trailer, Lolly caught sight of something.

"Over there!" she cried and took Tick's hand in both of hers. The girls moved closer and, even before she picked it up, Lolly knew what it was: the burlap bag.

She looked around and called for Bo, her stomach flopping. *Please, Jesus. Please.* "Have you seen an orange cat with stripes on his face?" she asked.

"Maybe," Tick said.

"Where?"

"Round here abouts somewheres. Reminded me of a cougar."

"A what?"

"Nothin'," Tick said.

"If you see him, would you let me know? He's my cat. His name is Bo."

Lolly called again and listened for the little bell attached to Bo's collar. She heard nothing.

"I'd better be going," Lolly said. For the first time since her father had flung Bo into the trailer camp she felt hopeful. More than anything she wanted to come back across the levee again. Bo had to be nearby, and in this world she felt different. She felt safe. "Thanks for helping me."

"If you come back, maybe I'll show you our secret." Tick walked her to the base of the levee and, with the beam of the flashlight, pointed out the path.

"Can't you show me now?" Lolly asked.

"Nope," Tick said. "You gotta come back." The flashlight snapped off and darkness engulfed them.

"Tick?" Lolly whispered, but it was as though Tick, too, had been extinguished with the flip of the flashlight switch. All Lolly heard were the sounds from the camp and the cicada hum of the premature summer.

Holding the cap on her head, she climbed. She didn't take her hand off the cap until she passed the Berkeley's silent fountain. Tick's secret itched like a mosquito bite.

Chapter Eleven

Sister Theodora stood at the back of the brightly lit classroom. "All right, class," she said briskly, "we're going to listen to Lolly's essay." She thrust her hands into opposite sleeves and nodded a signal to begin.

Slowly, Lolly unfolded the long piece of yellow legal paper. Perspiration ran down her ribs as she pressed her elbows tightly against her uniform blouse, her scalp itching under the cap, knowing that fourteen sets of eyes were mocking her. How she wished for a miracle that would allow her to disappear. Deciding it was best to get it over with as quickly as possible, she cleared her throat.

"The Virtue of Not Being Angry," her voice trembled, "by Lolly Candolin."

She stole a glance at the faces of her classmates. Sonja Hyatt, the Appaloosa, pretended to pick her nose and flick the dried snot at her. Christina Triplet, the Warmblood, stuck out her tongue. Vicky Clare Couvillaud, the Thoroughbred, held up a badly drawn picture of a horse with its legs stuck straight up in the air. Sabrina Albert peered at her out from under her dark African eyes.

"Anger is a sin, and it can make you go to hell where you will burn forever and your skin gets black and icky and cracks like the skin of hot dogs when you roast them over a fire. If you get angry for a good reason, then it is not a sin."

"Excuse me, Lolly," Sister said. She stepped into the aisle and Vicky Clare folded the horse drawing and tucked it under her book. "The assignment was to write about the virtue of not being angry."

"I'm getting to that part," Lolly said.

Sister's brow furrowed, but she stepped back and nodded.

Lolly squirmed. "It is a sin to unjustly punish someone for being angry if they are angry for a good reason. Injustice is a sin. Not doing what is right is a sin."

"Lolly!" Sister said in a loud voice. "What are you saying?"

"I'm saying that I think anger is okay when you're angry for a good reason," Lolly told her defiantly. "When it's real and for a real good reason."

"What do you mean 'real'?" Sister's hands worked beneath the sleeves like trapped animals.

"What I mean," Lolly said, "is if somebody does something bad to you and you don't get angry and stand up for yourself, then that's a sin. And if somebody punishes you for getting angry when you *should* get angry ... well, then they're the sinner."

Sister's hands escaped. One gripped the clicker but Lolly was already reading the next line: "Sister Theodora is unjust, and that is a sin and unless she goes to confession, she will end up an overcooked hot dog after she dies."

The class broke into laughter.

"Silence!" Sister bellowed. The hilarity ceased. Brandishing the clicker, Sister flapped up the aisle to the front of the classroom, causing a breeze as she passed.

"How dare you, Lolly Candolin?" she demanded. "You have no respect for anyone. You're going to regret this impudence, child. That I guarantee!"

The herd reacted. Vicky Clare's face turned pink, Sonja did a thumbs up while Sabrina's eyes flicked back and forth in confusion and Christina had to bury her face in her hands to stifle snorts of laughter.

All this made Lolly smile until Sister rapped her head with the clicker. Then Sister gripped Lolly by her ear, hauled her out of the classroom, and down the hall to Sister Superior's office where she exploded in angry explanation.

"Thank you, Sister," Sister Superior said. She folded her hands on her desk. "I'll take it from here."

Sister Theodora nibbled at her lips, her hands fluttering over her black skirts. She opened her mouth for one more rebuke, but Sister Superior cocked her head toward the door, and Sister Theodora slunk out.

Sister Superior surveyed Lolly for a long time in silence with an expression that said, *What have I done, Lord, to deserve this?* Then she said, "Let me see your essay."

Lolly handed over the crumpled sheet of paper and watched Sister Superior unfold and read it.

"Where did you get your definition of injustice? Did you father help you with this?"

"No, Sister. Daddy hasn't seen it."

"You are a thinker, Lolly," Sister Superior said after a thoughtful pause. "And for that I admire you. But you've missed the point, child. The harm you did to Sonja the other day was an act of misplaced aggression. Your anger was not appropriate. Do you understand?"

"That's not the way it was."

"Thou shall not kill. Granted, you did not kill anyone, but striking a person is a step on that path. Violence stalks us and definitely carries Satan's fingerprints. That means we must be alert to all our negative thoughts, words, and deeds. Physically striking a person is a sin, Lolly, and it will not be tolerated here."

Lolly looked at the pint-sized Jesus on the cross behind Sister. His expression hadn't changed since the last time she'd been here. He was still annoyed. *Sacrificing myself wasn't enough? What do I have to do to get you to behave?*

"I thought it was important to tell the truth," she said to Jesus.

"Ah, the truth," Sister said. "It's tricky, dear child. To really tell the truth, you must stare yourself in the face. Most of us turn away, as you have done."

She picked up the telephone and dialed.

"Sorry to bother you, Mr. Candolin. I know you have many pressing issues today, but we've had another incident involving Lolly. I regret having to report that she's impertinent and blatantly rude. Can you offer any insight as to why her behavior has deteriorated lately? Anything going on at home that would upset the child? I'm extremely concerned."

Sister's face registered approval as she listened, and Lolly knew Sister Superior would never have guessed the advice her father had given her after their last confrontation: *If you're going to fight somebody, scare the piss out of them.*

"I see," Sister said. "Well, we'll stay in touch. Good-bye, Mr. Candolin." She hung up. "Your father's a very smart man, Lolly. He'll know how to handle this. When you go home rewrite your essay. Have you been to confession?"

"I'm going this afternoon."

"Good." Sister looked through the windows cocked open to the playground as the bell rang for the end of recess. "Remember, Lolly. Anger is a sin. Go back to your classroom. I'll join you there. You will apologize to Sister Theodora in front of the other students."

It was all she could do to hold back the torrent of words in defense of herself that were damning up in her throat. *This is unjust,* she thought bitterly. *Maybe Sister Superior should write the essay.*

"One more thing," Sister Superior said. "That woolen hat. It seems superfluous in this heat. Why do you insist on wearing it?"

"Ask my daddy."

Lolly left Sister Superior's dark cave and entered the hot glare of the playground. She felt badly about the rude way she had answered Sister Superior. Moreover, she regretted that she had connected the cap to her father. *What if Sister calls and asks about the cap? Won't that stir the pot even more?*

She wandered toward the back of the playground, near the stone wall surrounding the school where the horses were galloping their last round at the grotto before returning to the classroom.

You keep the devil away from me, Lolly prayed, *and I'll never again ask to gallop with the grotto horses.*

Then the Appaloosa caught sight of her and signaled the others. A cold shiver grabbed Lolly's spine as the herd circled her at a fast trot. The Warmblood spotted the bracelet sparkling on her wrist.

"Whoa," Christina said, and reigned herself in. "Where'd you get that? It's pretty."

"It's cheesy," snorted the Thoroughbred. "Looks like it came from the CYO thrift shop!" She whinnied as she ran.

"Well, I think it's kinda pretty," the Warmblood insisted.

The herd kicked up a ring of white playground dust just as Sabrina, the Brumby, made a grab for the cap. But Lolly saw her coming and raised her arm in time to smack at the grabbing hand. The herd's gait slowed, but still they circled. Lolly waited for the Warmblood to pass in front of her, then shoved her wrist up close to the horse's face.

"It's a magic bracelet," she said, her voice pitched high. "Beware of its power." Lowering her voice, she circled in the opposite direction from the ponies, rotated the bracelet on her arm, and chanted:

"*Haram infata cum. Lo epoodo sonesta tum. Ray deponda slatin fey. Zezapito trudo hay.*"

The ponies stopped and went silent. A smile pricked at the corners of Lolly's mouth, but she resisted the urge to grin as she glared at the Thoroughbred.

"This bracelet encourages truth, and the truth is, none of you are nice horses. Do you know what I can do with this bracelet?"

Eyes bulged.

"I can make you sick!" The ring of dust that had eddied around them settled. "Sick horses!"

Vicky Clare was the first to turn. She signaled and the others backed off. In a tight group, they walked toward the classroom. Christina broke away from them, stopped, and looked back at Lolly.

"I think the bracelet's neato," she said. And then she added, "Kinda."

Chapter Twelve

After the apology to Sister Theodora, and after classes let out, Lolly crossed the street, leaving the convent school behind and climbed the long flight of steps up to St. Joseph's.

Dipping her finger in the holy water font, she made the sign of the cross and knelt next to the confessional, hearing Father O'Connor's unmistakable Irish lilt coming from within the curtained stall. Occasionally, she also heard the voice of a woman who sounded as though she were crying. Two minutes later the woman stumbled out of the confessional, rushed up to the altar rail, and knelt.

"Next."

Lolly took a deep breath and, drawing back the heavy velvet curtain, stepped in and knelt. The flowery scent of shaving lotion filled the small space. The priest said, "Yes, child. Proceed."

"Bless me father, I confess," she began. "It's been one week since my last confession and these are my sins." Her mouth was dry.

"Go on," Father said.

Lolly clamped her eyes shut and tight red worms crawled across her vision.

"Well?"

"I have not..." She turned Sophie's bracelet around and around on her wrist.

"Get on with it, dear," Father O'Connor said. "There are others waiting."

She swallowed. "I have not...I have not..."

"Yes?" Father O'Connor said again.

She exhaled a puff. "I have not sinned!" she declared more loudly than she intended.

Silence came from the other side. *I should have lied*, Lolly thought.

Opening her mouth to amend her confession, she was interrupted by Father O'Connor who said, "Pray for *me* then, child."

In nomine Patris, et Filii, et Spiritus Sancti. Amen.

Lolly shot out of the confessional and ran from the church into the heat of the afternoon.

Hail Mary, full of grace, the Lord is with thee.

When she got home, the house was empty and silent except for the hum of the air conditioner. The pungent smell of Freon hung in the rooms and her mother's presence was everywhere. The light scent of Estee Lauder even laced the kitchen. A magnet in the shape of an artist's palette held a note to the refrigerator door:

*Apples and cheese snacks in the refrigerator. I'm
at the art club if you need me. Sherwood 7-5790.
I've talked with your father. Rewrite your essay.
I'll be home by five.*

Love, Mama

Lolly bit into a chilled apple quarter and checked the clock. Almost three-thirty, an hour and a half before her mother got home. Quickly, she changed out of her uniform into shorts and tennis shoes, dashed out the back door, and started jogging toward the levee. When she passed the Remington house, Mrs. Remington, pruning roses in front, raised her clippers in a wave.

"Where you going in such a hurry, Miss Lolly?" she asked her.

"Nowhere," Lolly said without breaking stride. She was going so fast that when she got to the base of the levee, her chest burned. But still she hurried to scramble up the steep path.

This'll give me something to confess.

She reached the top of the levee, crossed the road, and started down the other side, cutting back and forth through the brambles until she reached the dry river bed.

At the bottom of the berm, she peered at the surroundings. In the daytime the gypsy camp looked different, the trailers bigger, and the thirsty land spreading in front of her more alien. It was hot and the earth was so dry and cracked that only a few tufts of grass survived.

There wasn't a person in sight. *The gypsies must be trying to stay cool,* Lolly thought. In every trailer there was lodged a cooler that hummed a sleepy, monotonous song.

Lolly nosed her way into the camp, trying to remember the route to Tick's trailer. After a couple of missteps, she saw the unicorn hanging next to a door.

She mounted the steps and peered through the trailer's screen door. Inside, Sophie sat at a Formica table, her back straight, a canary-yellow halter pressing her breasts together. Her pants today were lime-green, and her dark-blonde hair was pulled into a high ponytail. Her long neck stretched forward as she bent over beads, stringing one after another.

Lolly cleared her throat, and Sophie looked up.

"Look who's here! Hey, Lolly. Come on in." Sophie cocked her head to the back of the trailer and called, "Tick, Baby. There's a surprise out here for you."

Like a jackrabbit, Tick hopped out from the rear of the trailer, wearing cut-offs, a grimy short-sleeved shirt, and the same sandals she wore the night she had appeared as the demon. Pushing the screen door, she threw it open. "Hey, Lolly!"

Lolly stepped into the trailer. Tick stared at her, then brushed grimy fingers across her cheek.

"Ain't she pretty, Mama?" Lolly felt her eyes fill and her heart squeezed. Never had she felt so welcomed.

"You girls want lemonade or crackers?" Sophie asked, chin cupped in her hand. "Looks to me like Lolly Pop here would prefer lunch in Paris, France. Ever been to Paris, France, Lolly?"

"Oh, no," Lolly said. "Why?"

"Because you wear that cap. Strictly high fashion. So high, there ain't no possibility that me or Tick can compete with you."

Lolly smiled and then tugged her cap down even further. For the first time since her father had made her wear it, she didn't feel so much like the ugly monster she imagined herself to be.

"They have fleas in Paris, France?" Tick asked.

"I believe they do," Sophie said. "In Paris, France there are flea markets. It's where all the fleas go to shop!"

The girls giggled and Tick crossed her ankles, then twisted and jumped so that her feet ended up side by side.

"Wanta come with me?" she asked.

"Where?" Lolly asked.

"To meet a giant." Tick performed a shaky arabesque and leaped through the doorway, the screen slamming behind her.

Lolly turned to Sophie. She felt somehow as though she should be asking for permission.

"Go on," Sophie said. She motioned with her head. "Tick's got all kind of things to show you."

She put her hand on Lolly's arm and smiled. Her moist mouth was the color of strawberry ice cream, and her hand as soft as cotton. She looked like she belonged on the cover of *Modern Screen*.

Lolly had no trouble following Tick, whose scuffles and skips sent up rooster tails of dust. She stopped at a trailer further down, its sides ablaze with crudely painted pink and orange flowers that reminded Lolly of an Italian wall on the postcard her Auntie Gillian had sent from Naples. She waited at the bottom of the steps while Tick hopped up two at a time and banged on the door of the trailer.

A woman appeared, the same tall, broad-shouldered woman Lolly had seen crying that first night in Sophie's trailer. Her make-up was lurid with greasy brown eyebrows crawling like worms across her forehead, gashes of frosted blue eye shadow on her lids, rouge smudged on her cheeks, and bright orange lipstick on her lips.

"How're ya feelin' today, Andrea?" Tick asked.

"Havin' a good day, thank the Lord. 'Course I know if he gives me a good one today, likely he'll give me a bad one tomorrow. But we take what we can get, don't we, child?"

"Yes'um," Tick said.

"So I say thank you, Lord, for today. Who's that in the divine cap?" Andrea pushed her face forward.

"My friend Lolly. From the other side."

"Hello, Lolly. I don't know too many little girls who cross over. 'Course, crossing over is my specialty. We all know that, don't we, child?"

"Yes'um," Tick said again. "Is Charlie home? I want him to meet Lolly, too."

"He's on the throne, child. Likely to be there a while, I'd say. Where you headed? Don't tell me. You gonna share the secret. Well that's fine. This Lolly person don't look like she's gonna cause no trouble. Maybe when Charlie finishes his business, we'll see you over there." Andrea winked and closed the door.

Tick smiled. "Andrea used to be a man. Had an operation and became a woman."

"That's impossible," Lolly said, though she was beginning to think that anything was possible on the other side of the levee.

"It's true," Tick assured her, grinning. "She used to be Andrew. She and Charlie got married couple of months ago. They love each other. Charlie's gonna be real sad when Andrea kicks the bucket."

"Kicks the bucket?" Lolly asked.

"God's gonna take Andrea. Mama says it's not because she changed into a woman. It's because she's such a good person that God needs her in heaven to be His helper."

Lolly looked at the flowers peeling off the face of the trailer. She'd never thought about God needing anybody. What would Father O'Connor say about that?

"Tick, what is Charlie king of?" she asked.

"Charlie ain't no king!" Tick said.

"Then why was he sitting on a throne?"

Tick rocked with laughter. "The throne is the pot!" she

snorted.

"Oh." Lolly flushed with embarrassment.

"Come on," Tick said, and she skipped up the stairs of another trailer, this one with swatches of rust slashed across its face. She knocked. "Mr. David Robinson Crocker!" she called. "It's Tick! I want you to meet my friend Lolly."

The door creaked as it opened, and standing in the doorway was a man so old and thin that Lolly thought she saw bones through his skin. His eyes burned like coal on fire.

"Howdy, Miss Tick. Now, I know why you're here. You want me to tell you how in the deep winter of '46 I came over the Sierras with the Donner party and survived. A young tike I was, but I made it. Yesiree, I made it. I'm happy to tell you the tale from beginning to end, but it's gonna hafta be another time."

"Yes, sir," Tick said. Then she turned to Lolly. "This is my friend."

"Hello, Miss Friend," David Robinson Crocker said. "Miss Tick going to show you the secret?"

Lolly was unable to take her eyes off the old man with his string tie and hand-carved cane. He looked as if he'd stepped out of a different time.

"Well, if she doesn't, you come back and I'll take you. Yes, Miss Friend, I'd be most happy to show you the secret." He chuckled and gently closed the door.

Tick put an arm around Lolly's shoulders and whispered, "Mama says Mr. David Robinson Crocker only *thinks* he came over with the Donner party. Mama says if he actually had, he'd now be something like a hundred and nine years-old."

"He looks pretty old," Lolly suggested, wondering if she had left the earth and landed in another world.

"Mama says he'll never die until he tells his story, and

somehow he never gets around to spittin' it out."

"What's the secret?" Lolly asked.

"You'll see," Tick said. "Come on." She flew around the corner of the trailer, Lolly following. Somehow Tick dodged an old lady who appeared suddenly, but Lolly ran smack into her.

"I'm sorry, ma'am," Lolly said.

"Don't you know that young ladies don't run?" the woman asked her. She looked like a dried rose, beautiful in a faded way. When she spoke, her teeth clicked.

"Miss Berg, we didn't see ya. You all right?" Tick asked.

"I'm fine. Oh, dear, where was I going?"

"I ain't sure, Miss Berg. Miss Berg, this is my friend Lolly. Lolly, this is Miss Hattie Berg."

Miss Berg nodded. "Pray tell, Tick, what's your hurry that you must go so fast you run over an old lady?"

The old woman's long white dress was gathered at the bodice with small pink satin roses nestled in the pleats at the shoulders and her sparse white hair was scooped up into a high bun, strands of fine curls around her face.

"Blankenship will be serving tea this afternoon promptly at five. Will you young ladies join me?"

"Thanky, Miss Berg. We'll sure fire do our best," Tick said.

Lolly elbowed Tick. "I can't. I have to..."

Tick nudged her back. "We'll be there, Miss Berg. Your tea parties are dang fine."

"We're having eclairs today. Cook has outdone herself. They are light and delectable."

"Thank you, ma'am," Tick said. She grabbed Lolly by the sleeve and tugged her off.

"I'll inform Blankenship," Miss Berg called.

When they'd disappeared around the corner of another trailer, Lolly turned to Tick. "Who's Blankenship?"

"The butler," Tick said.

"Butler!"

"There ain't no butler and there ain't no eclairs." Tick tapped her finger on her temple. "Mama says Miss Hattie Berg lives in another world. It's a rule around here to always accept her invitations to tea. It makes her happy."

Suddenly, out of the corner of her eye, Lolly saw something flying toward them. She yelped and pulled Tick aside as a bean pot whizzed over their heads. It had come from a window of the trailer in front of them.

"That was close," Lolly said. Nibbling on her cuticle, she glanced back toward the levee. All she had to do was scramble up and over the berm and she would be back where things were familiar.

Tick yelled, "Hey, Maltilda and Ducky! I want you to meet my friend Lolly."

Two faces appeared at the window. Both were pale, creased with accordion folds, and capped with faded brown hair. It was, Lolly thought, like looking at twins.

"You tell your friend that tonight I'm going to kill Ducky by taking a knife from the top of his sternum right down to his pee-pee, and then I'm going to paint the trailer red with his blood! You tell your friend that!" Matilda announced, smiling in a disconcertingly self-satisfied way.

"Let's get out of here," Lolly said, but Tick didn't budge.

"That's nothing!" Ducky replied. "Tonight I'm going to chop off Matilda's hands and feet and string them up on the clothesline. Then I'll cut off her head and dry it out, take it to town, and use it for a bowling ball. Tell your friend that!"

That's it. These people are too different.

"I'm leaving," Lolly said.

Tick grabbed her shirt collar and dragged her back. "Wow,

Matilda and Ducky, those are both really good stories," she said. "There ain't no way I could pick the better."

"Lord, girl, you never can," Matilda lamented. "One of these days I'm gonna quit on you, Tick."

"Me, too," Ducky said. Together, they slammed their window shut.

Lolly frowned at Tick.

"They do this every day," Tick said, releasing her collar. "We had an anniversary party for them last year. Forty years married. And right in the middle of everything, just when Miss Berg was about to serve cake, they had a contest to see who hated the other the most."

"Who won?" Lolly asked.

"Neither," Tick said. "They were both so obnoxious, the giant carried them both back to their trailer and made them stay inside until the doings was over."

"'The giant'?"

"Come on," Tick said, and she dashed off in a straight line to a small trailer, blackened and scarred with time, parked in the dappled shade of a gnarled cottonwood. "This here's where the giant lives," she said breathlessly.

On one side of the trailer was a smoldering pit layered with soot and charcoal from dozens of fires. Beside it, a scratched stainless steel basin sat in the sun holding less than an inch of soapy water. A clothesline, from which hung two plaid shirts as big as tablecloths and a pair of under shorts the size of a small tent, sagged from the trailer to the tree. Around the trailer, the rusted parts of abandoned machines lay like bones.

"Bob Bob!" Tick called. "Come out and meet Lolly."

No voice came from inside, but the trailer rocked slightly.

"I don't believe in giants," Lolly whispered.

Tick bounced from her toes to her heels. "You'll see."

Again she called, "Bob Bob!"

The trailer rocked harder. Lolly cocked her head. Giants only exist in stories, but the hair on her arms was rising. She scuffed her sandal over the dried earth. "What about the secret?" she asked. "Maybe you could..."

Four fingers the size of Polish sausages wrapped themselves around the edge of the door.

"Here he comes," Tick announced proudly.

From the darkness of the trailer emerged a large balding head, its remaining hair pulled tight into a clump at the nape.

Lolly reached for her new friend's hand.

"Don't be afeared," Tick said.

The big head was connected to a pair of shoulders so wide that the man had to lower one and twist the other to get himself through the door. Following the shoulders was a massive torso with a stomach like a potbelly stove, and legs that were columns of muscular flesh bulging out of khaki shorts. He was wearing the largest tennis shoes she had ever seen.

When he had finally squeezed his entire body out of the trailer, he put his hands on the small of his back and stretched, expanding his massive chest, and rotating his head back and forth, side to side.

"He *is* a giant," Lolly said, awestruck.

Tick dashed toward him and threw her arms around one of his legs. "Hi, Bob Bob," she said. "Were you sleepin'?"

Bob Bob bent over and scooped up Tick as though she were a doll. "Yeah, Bob Bob's been sleepin'," he said. "How've you been, my friend Tick?"

"Good, Bob Bob, real good. That's Lolly." Tick pointed down.

Bob Bob crouched and gently deposited Tick back onto the ground. His face was the size of a basketball while his nose looked like a soft mound of clay, and his cheeks had as many potholes as the road up to the levee.

He offered his hand. Lolly placed her palm on his. His sausage fingers closed. Her hand disappeared.

"Nice to meet you, my friend Lolly." His voice was surprisingly soft for such a big man.

"Want to come with us to show Lolly the secret?" Tick asked.

"Sure," Bob Bob said. "Bob Bob likes to go anywhere my friend Tick goes."

Bob Bob scratched under a yellowed tee shirt that sported a faded bull's-eye design with *Chiseler's Inn* printed around it in old fashioned script.

Tick raised her hand and slipped it into his, skipping three times for every one of his steps.

"Come on, Lolly," Tick said, flinging her head. "We're going to see the secret."

"What time is it?" Lolly asked.

"Time to be with your friends," Bob Bob suggested with a hint of sadness in his voice.

Lolly knew that half an hour had passed easily and that she had to be home by the time her mother arrived. But Tick was going to let her in on the secret and that was one thing she didn't want to miss. She gave the cap a quick tug down, then ran after Tick and her gigantic companion.

Crack!

The sound came from the back of a large trailer parked about fifty feet from Bob Bob's.

Crack!

A gunshot!

"I catch you stealin' from me again..." A gruff voice boomed from behind the trailer.

Crack!

"...you can bet that gold tooth in your worthless head that I'll cut off your hand!"

Tick let go of Bob Bob's hand and skipped back to her. "Don't worry. That's just Sam. He's kind of the mayor around here."

"Does he cut off people's hands?" Lolly asked.

"Naw, not too often," Tick said, glee flaming in her dark green eyes. "He's just settling somethin'. That's how things are done in Cougarville."

Tick flung herself at Bob Bob, who picked her up. Together, they disappeared behind the trailer.

Lolly swallowed hard. She was alone and she didn't know her way back to the levee. A crow flapped overhead, then dove, flying so near she could hear the whoosh of its wings.

"Tick!" she called out, running after them and colliding with a man wearing pants so worn she could see the leathery skin on his knees. He quickly regained his balance and straightened his ragged jacket that had only one button.

"Upon my grandma's grave I swear, I ain't no angel," he said, spittle flying, "and Sam's in his rights. That's for durn sure."

He nodded at Lolly as if he expected her to agree and held up both hands.

"Well, blessin's be," he declared, looking backward. "I still got 'em both!"

With that, he cut a hell-bent path toward the main camp, his coat flapping as he ran.

Laughter broke out behind the trailer. Lolly felt foolish and tired and dirty and knew she had to get home. Tick popped around the trailer. "You comin' or not?"

The sun hung low in the sky. Lolly knew what would happen if she were late getting home. "I'm coming," she said and, pressing her hands against the side of the trailer, peered around the corner.

"In the name of the Father, and of the Son and of the Holy Ghost!"

Chapter Thirteen

In a cage at least twenty feet in diameter, lay the biggest cat Lolly had ever seen. The moment she stepped around the trailer, the cat sniffed in her direction. His eyes blinked slowly and his nose twitched. Then he stretched out his front paws and kneaded dirt and straw.

The cage was constructed of steel rails three-inches wide and seven feet tall, sunk three feet apart into the dry river bottom soil. Cyclone fencing stretched from rail to rail and over the top.

The cat's muscles rippled as he rose from his haunches and limped around the cage. Then he sat and licked his paw, running it over his face exactly as Bo had done. The big cat was tawny, also like Bo. His great, luminous eyes were outlined with black as if someone had taken a charcoal pencil and drawn around the edges. His face was broad with a white muzzle and his constantly whipping tail was striped.

Never had Lolly been so close to such a big cat, or one so beautiful. Even though he was in a cage, he seemed proud and confident. His cage smelled of fresh hay and strong pee, reminding her of fruit fermenting in the orchards in late summer.

"What do you think?" In one outlandish leap, Tick came

to stand next to her.

"What's his name?" Lolly managed to ask.

"We call him Survie."

"Survie? What kind of name is that?"

"It's short for 'Survivor,'" Tick told her. "Sam found him in a trap. Poor Survie practically chewed off his foot tryin' to get free. He was a baby."

"How old is he now?"

"Older 'n me! Sam says livin' in the wild ain't so good for Survie no more. That's why Survie loves Sam. He gives him food and everything. Sam's got himself a picture of him when he was a baby. Survie had spots then, but he's grown out of 'em."

"Who's Sam?" she asked.

Crack!

The arm of a bullwhip flicked within inches of Lolly, wrapped itself around a small wooden stool, picked it up, and flung it aside.

"That's Sam," Tick said, and she smiled.

A tall, rangy man winding a whip into a coil stepped out of the shadows into the light. He had eyes the color of a cold blue ocean, and he wore a blood red cowboy shirt with gray piping on the grimy collar and sleeves that had once been white. He snapped his wrist, flung the leather tendril out, and fired off another shot.

Crack!

Lolly cringed and hid behind Tick.

"Don't be afeard," Tick said. "It's just Sam's way of saying hello. Mama says what he's really doin' is crackin' at his sadness. Hey, Sam! This is my friend Lolly."

Sam looked at Lolly with his cold eyes and she held her breath and put her hands behind her back so he wouldn't be able to cut them off.

"Hey, Tick," Sam said, merely nodding at Lolly. "How you be?" His voice sounded like sandpaper.

"She good," Bob Bob said, swaying from one foot to the other like a huge pendulum. "She so good, Sam."

"Glad to hear that, Bob Bob," Sam replied. "What's your mama up to these days, Tick? I've been doin' a lot of drivin' lately, so I'm out of the loop."

"Workin'," Tick told him, thoughtfully. "Last week she sold some bracelets to the department store in town."

Lolly brought her right arm from behind her and held it out to display what Sophie had given her.

"Lookie there," Sam said. "Your friend here's a walkin' advertisement for your mama's handiwork."

Lolly had never seen a man that looked quite like Sam. His eyes peered out of skin so brown and worn, it might have been cut from a saddle. His hair was dull brown and there was a big dent where his nose met his eyebrows. He was thin and wiry, but she figured he was strong.

"You new in Cougarville, Lolly?" he asked.

"Naw," Tick said. "She lives on the other side of the levee. She's just visitin'. She has fleas. That's why she wears the hat."

"That true?" Sam asked. He squatted down again, this time in front of her and she saw well into his shadowed eyes. Maybe it was the way they softened when he crouched down to her level, or maybe it was the respect in his voice when he spoke to her. Whatever it was, she wanted to tell him exactly why she wore the cap. She'd bet he would never drink horns of corns, or wear napkins on his head, or send Bo flying off the levee. When she spoke, the strength of her voice surprised her. "That sure is a neat belt."

"Gen-u-ine snakeskin," Sam said. He unbuckled it and

whipped it out of its keepers. "Ever seen a rattlesnake before?"

"No, sir," Lolly said. He took her hand and placed the belt in her palm. Fear flashed through her. It was smooth and beautiful, but what if it came alive?

"It's swell," she said and she handed the belt back.

Something clanked in the cage. They all turned to see Survie rubbing himself against the chain links, his collar meeting the metal. He favored the badly maimed front paw as he moved about the cage. He went around once, then came to a halt in front of them, pressing up against the fencing.

"Hey, boy," Sam cooed, stringing his belt back through the loops of his jeans, then pushed his fingers between the chain links and scratched the big cat's pelt.

"Hey, boy," echoed Bob Bob. "Hey, boy."

"Can we pet Cougar?" Tick asked.

"Sure," Sam said. "Right here's one of his favorite spots." He dug into the animal's shoulder.

"No, I mean *inside* the cage," Tick said.

"You want to go in?"

Tick bounced up and down. "Oh, yes. Please, Sam, please!"

"Yeah, Sam," Bob Bob joined in. "Please."

"I guess it's okay. What do you think, Bob Bob? You been in the cage since I've been gone?"

"Sure, Sam," Bob Bob said, a little smile twitched at the corners of his mouth. "I've been in the cage."

Sam turned to Lolly. "Bob Bob takes care of the cougar for me when I'm drivin' semis. He's good at it, too, ain't you, Bob Bob?"

"Yeah, Sam. I'm good at it."

"Tell Lolly the rules, Tick," Sam said. He pulled a key chain from his pocket, inserted a small key into the padlock, and opened the cage door.

Tick put both her dirt encrusted hands on Lolly's shoulders. "The cougar's our secret," she said. "You can't tell no one in town about him. Promise?"

Lolly held up her hand. "Promise."

"Cross it," Tick demanded.

"Cross what?" Lolly asked.

"Your heart, for Christ's sake," Tick said.

"Watch your language, young lady!" Sam said.

"Cross it," Tick repeated.

Lolly crossed her heart. "I promise."

Sam stepped in and whispered to the big cat. His voice sounded so kind that Lolly thought he might be capable of soothing even Sister Theodora.

"Hey there, boy," Sam said. "How's my big beautiful boy? How's my best friend?"

Bob Bob swayed back and forth. "Beautiful boy," he said, repeating Sam's words in his thick and simple manner. "How's my best friend?"

Sam scratched the cougar behind his ears just as Lolly had done a thousand times to Bo. When he ran his hand down the back flanks, the cat's skin rippled.

Tick chuckled. "Ain't he beautiful? Can I come in now, Sam?"

"Come on," Sam said. "Just no sudden moves."

Lolly grabbed Tick by the arm. "Don't go in there!"

"It's okay," Tick said. "I've been in the cage lots of times."

Tick stepped in and stretched out her hand as she approached the cougar. After he sniffed her, she began stroking his nose and running her fingers down the cat's back. "You come on in," she said to Lolly.

"No, thanks," Lolly said. "I'll pet him from out here." She stuck a finger through the chain fence. The animal's fur felt thick and coarse.

"Bob Bob'll bring you in," the giant told her, and before Lolly could open her mouth to refuse, Bob Bob had taken her hand in his and ducked inside the cage. "My friend Survie ain't gonna hurt you," Bob Bob said as Lolly pulled back. "Survie's good and kind and likes Bob Bob. Come on, Lolly."

Lolly put one foot into the cage. The cougar panted in the heat as Sam and Tick ran their hands down his back. He closed his eyes contentedly. Bob Bob tugged again and Lolly allowed her second foot inside.

She felt a rustle from the other side of the cage. A small audience had gathered: Andrea, a man Lolly figured to be Charlie, David Robinson Crocker, Hattie Berg, and Matilda and Ducky. Smiles lighted their faces and they stepped closer.

"Survie's been in this cage since he was itty bitty," Sam said. "Ain't never been hunted or hurt by nobody, 'cept when he was caught in the trap. I don't think he connects that to us, though, 'cause he don't view us as his enemy. Don't get me wrong, I ain't sayin' you shouldn't be careful. This animal's still wild."

Lolly clung to Bob Bob's arm. Surely he could protect her.

"One important rule," Sam said. "Nobody goes into Survie's cage when I ain't here. 'Cept for Bob Bob, that is."

The cat got up and Lolly quickly stepped behind Bob Bob.

"That's exactly what you can't do," Sam said. "Showing fear to an animal is like showing him fresh blood. It ain't a good idea."

Lolly nodded, but stayed behind Bob Bob.

"Ain't a good idea," Bob Bob repeated.

"He's sweet," Tick said, nuzzling her face into the cat's neck. "And he smells good."

Suddenly, the cougar stretched and fell in a heap on the

hay-strewn floor.

"Come on, Lolly," Tick prodded. "Pet Survie. He's lookin'
at you and wonderin' why ain't that girl payin' me no attention?"

"It's okay if'n you don't," Sam said. His eyes changed from
icy to deep blue. "But if you decide to, you might be surprised.
Facin' the things that scare you ain't such bad medicine. Fact
is, courage can be down right tasty."

She peeked at the cougar from behind Bob Bob.

"Courage," Bob Bob said, as if he wasn't sure what the
word meant.

"Come on," Tick prodded. "Once you feel his fur, you'll
think you're in heaven."

With one hand on Bob Bob's shoulder and one foot touching his worn sneaker, Lolly leaned forward and felt the back of
the cougar's head. His ear twitched and she jumped.

Ticked giggled. "This here's Lolly," she whispered into the
cougar's ear. "She's my friend."

The cougar's paws kneaded the warm dirt. When Bo used
to do that, Lolly had known he was heading for a nap. She
inched forward and pressed her palm against the cougar's muscular neck. The thick pelt was luxurious, the muscles hard.
When she ran her hand down over his shoulder, the cougar
raised his head and tried to rub it against her.

"He's smiling," Tick said. "He likes you."

Having the safety of the giant, Lolly stepped slowly around
to face the cougar. She stopped breathing as the animal's hot
breath whispered over her face and down her arm to her hand.
Tentatively, she placed her fingers on the cougar's muzzle and
scratched.

When the cougar's eyes closed in contentment, Lolly
scratched even harder until she was gripping his pelt in big

handfuls, exactly as she had done with Bo.

"I'll be darned," Sam said. "He's purrin'!"

"Never done that for me," Tick said softly. Her eyes crinkled in pride. "Only for my friend, Lolly."

As her hands moved away from the cougar's face and down his body, Lolly felt something inside her shift. It was as though, in the presence of the huge cat, everything was possible. She felt transported to a place where she was beautiful like her mama and smart like her daddy. The blazing heat, the great purring cat, the jigging dances of the redheaded girl, the edginess of the man with the snakeskin belt, and the kindness of the simple giant combined into one overriding certainty: there in the cougar's cage, she was learning something she would never learn in school.

The deeper she dug into the cougar's jowls, the louder he purred.

"Cougars don't roar," Sam said. "When they're mad they open their mouths and a scary kind of hiss comes from the backs of their throats, a hackin', fearful scornful sound. But they sure can purr. Not often, mind you. This is somethin'."

Finally, Sam said that the petting time was over. Reluctantly, Lolly gave the cougar a last stroke. Strange how she could feel lighter and at the same time, more closely connected to the earth. Sam was right. Courage was tasty.

Lolly stepped out of the cage to a patter of applause from the bystanders. She turned to them and smiled so fully that she thought the edges of her mouth might tear. On impulse, she bowed, pulled the cap from her head, and flung it wildly into the air, only to have a sunburned hand reach out and snatched it before it touched the ground.

"My bet is," Sam said, twirling the woolen cap on his finger, "you better not arrive home without this."

"I hate it!" Lolly protested, her new found courage suddenly evaporating. She wished she could confront her daddy and tell him she wouldn't wear it, but the threat he had made about shaving her mother's hair loomed great. "It's hot and stupid and the kids at school make fun of me!"

"Anybody here make fun of you?" Sam asked.

"No," she admitted. "But I still hate it. I hate it more than anything in my whole life."

Sam grinned and nodded. "Sometimes you do things, not because you want to do them, but because they're the right thing to do. Besides, I suspect there'd be a ferocious consequence if you go home without this cap on your head."

"Ferocious," Lolly agreed. Somehow, Sam had understood without her going into a long explanation.

"Yep," Sam exhaled. "Sometimes we do the right thing because it's good for somebody else."

Sam stood beside her like an old pine tree. *How did he know these things?* Lolly angrily took the hat from him and pulled it on. The wool itched against the shaved patches. She yanked it off again and threw it in the dirt.

"I don't hate that hat! I hate *him!*" She fell to her knees and tears began pouring down her cheeks.

Tick rushed over and bent down in front of her. "Your tears are making dirty roads down your face." She pulled a grimy handkerchief from her pocket and dabbed at Lolly's face.

"Who do you hate, young lady?" Sam asked.

"My daddy!" she said. "I hate my daddy. All he does is work and drink horns of corns!"

"What does he do for a living?" Sam said.

"He goes to court and puts bad people in jail."

"He's a lawyer?"

"Uh huh."

"What's his name?"

"Regan Candolin."

"Your daddy's the county prosecutor?"

"Yep. I think that's what they call him."

Bob Bob spoke up, "Ain't he the guy who's wantin' to move the kid out of Cougarville or somethin'?"

"Not exactly," Sam said quickly.

"But ain't he the guy?"

"Drop it for now," Sam said.

Bob Bob's eyes opened wide. "You know Moose Perry, Lolly?"

Lolly looked up at the giant. His fleshy face had become bleached and blotchy, like it had gone through a washing machine and he had begun to pace. "He's the sheriff and he and my dad..."

"Would you shake his hand?" Bob Bob interrupted her, still pacing.

"I suppose. I mean if he came to my house and my daddy made me. You know, manners and stuff."

Bob Bob stopped. "Then I can't be your friend. I'm sorry. Good-bye, Lolly." He turned and walked away, his gigantic shoulders hunched, his gait slow. The other residents had already drifted away.

"What'd I do?" Lolly asked.

"Yeah, what'd she do?" Tick turned to Sam.

"Come on, kids," Sam said. He walked away from the cage and around to the front of his trailer. Lolly and Tick followed, but Lolly noticed that Bob Bob hovered nearby, watching her.

The girls sat in the shade of the awning attached to Sam's rusted trailer and Sam brought them icy bottles of Coca Colas. The soda tasted so sweet that it set Lolly humming. Her mother wouldn't let her drink soft drinks.

Sam took the hat out of his pocket and tossed it to her.

"Can Bob Bob have a drink?" Lolly asked.

"Sure he can," Sam said. "Hey, old buddy, want a Coke?"

Bob Bob didn't move.

"Bob Bob's story is a long one," Sam said, and chugged his Cola. "You see Bob Bob's mama left him when he weren't nothin' but a tyke smaller than a June bug."

Maybe it was because Bob Bob heard his name, or maybe it was just the telling of the story, but as Sam spoke, he shuffled closer.

"His daddy raised him," Sam went on, "but Dennis, bless his sweet heart, was even more simple than Bob Bob and one day Dennis was arrested for takin' a bag of groceries from the Pay 'n Pack."

"Daddy just didn't understand!" Bob Bob roared. "The rights and wrongs weren't so easy for him."

Though he was standing directly in sunlight, he trembled as if he were freezing, and sweat ran down his face.

"It weren't never clear to Daddy he had to pay! Damn! Old Moose Perry knew my daddy weren't all there. That weren't no secret to anybody!"

"Calm down, Bob Bob," Sam said.

Bob Bob stormed over to Lolly, who pulled away in fear. Tick patted her hand as if to say, *Don't worry.*

"How'd you feel if someone did somethin' bad to your daddy?" Bob Bob asked. His eyes were like huge platters, brown and flat. "I went into the jail and told the sheriff. I told Moose to let my daddy go."

"True," Sam said, "but you made the mistake of takin' a gun with you."

"Weren't no mistake, Sam," Bob Bob said in a low voice.

Lolly looked from Bob Bob to Sam and she knew by the

way Sam stood that he was on alert. Bob Bob paced in a small circle, his hands turning in and out of each other.

"Easy does it, there," Sam said.

"You tell it, Sam. You tell it." Bob Bob's voice quavered.

"All right, Bob Bob, I'll tell it." Sam put his hand on Bob Bob's shoulder. "You let me know if I get off track. You see, Lolly, Moose Perry wouldn't listen to Bob Bob, so Bob Bob figured out how to get him to listen. Right?"

Bob Bob nodded vigorously. His eyes focused on something in the distance, as though he was watching the scene all over again.

"Bob Bob walked into the sheriff's office just as calm as you please."

As he listened to the story, Bob Bob turned his hand into a gun and began making vicious shooting sounds with his mouth, his hand jerking with the kick of the make believe gun.

"That's right," Sam said. "You shot up the office, didn't you?"

"Weren't tryin' to hurt nobody, Sam," the giant of a man protested, his voice cracking. "That's the God's truth. But I needed for Moose—needed for Moose Perry to know that..."

Bob Bob fell to his knees and began to cry, great choking sounds erupting from his chest. The back of Lolly's throat closed and her breath almost stopped and she could feel Bob Bob's wrenching sobs in her own chest.

"That's enough for now," Sam said, his hand on Bob Bob's shoulder.

"Finish the story," Bob Bob said between sobs. "You got to finish the story."

Sam raised his hand and touched Bob Bob's shaggy head like a priest giving absolution.

"In the spray of bullets, Moose Perry caught lead in a thigh and lost a finger tip," Sam said. "Your daddy was on the case, Lolly, and got Bob Bob three years in the hoosegow. His daddy died during that time and Bob Bob blames Moose. Figures that since he weren't around to remind his daddy to eat and sleep, old Dennis just plain forgot to breathe and died."

Lolly no longer wanted to drink her Coca-Cola. For a long time, the only sound to be heard was the calling of the crows and the giant's lessening sobs.

"I don't like Moose Perry," Bob Bob said, wiping at his face with his hands. "I don't like him one bit."

After that story, I guess I don't much like him either, Lolly thought. "I have to go home," she said, and scooted off the box.

"You're scarin' these girls, Bob Bob," Sam said. "Go to your trailer and rock a little. Calm down."

"I'm not scared. It's just that I really do have to go," Lolly said. "Thanks for everything."

Tugging down the cap onto her head, she ran for the levee as fast as she could. In the distance she heard Tick's voice calling. "Come back soon, Lolly, ya hear? Real soon."

Chapter Fourteen

olly ran through the gypsy camp, zigzagging through the trailers, then scrambled up and over the levee and made for home. She dashed up the driveway just as her mother pulled up in the new Ford. Hoping she hadn't been seen, Lolly went around to the back door, stomped through the kitchen, and into the hall. When her foot hit the first riser of the stairs, a hand pressed down on her shoulder.

"Lolly Candolin, where have you been?"

Yikes, Lolly thought. *How am I going to explain this?* Her heated face pulsed and her clothes, grimy with river bottom dirt, stuck to her skin. Her mind flipped through a range of ideas that might provide a diversion. "Mama, what does the county prosecutor do?"

"Never mind about that," her mother retorted. She had been working at the art club and was wearing a paint-spattered apron over tailored pants and a lank of her blonde hair fell over one eye. "What have you been up to? You're a sight. Take off that cap. You're as red as a ripe peach!"

Lolly pulled off the cap and ran her hand over her sweaty stubble.

"Where have you been?" Her mother looked directly into her eyes. "And you'd better tell me, Lolly, or it's the confessional for you, young lady."

"Mama, I promise you it's better we don't talk about it. Better for you and better for me."

Her mother looked at her watch. "Your father's going to drive up in twenty-one minutes. I suggest we have this settled before he walks through that door."

"Do you trust me, Mama?"

Her mother let out a frustrated sigh. "Of course, I trust you. All right, but for goodness sake, go to your room and clean yourself up. And give me that cap. It needs a good freshening."

Lolly did a little hop that reminded her of Tick and scrambled up the stairs. At the top of the stairs, she called down. "Thank you."

"Lolly."

"Yes, Mama?"

"You're not involved with anything that could get you hurt?"

"No, Mama."

"Sure?"

"I'm sure."

"Because you know..." Her mother's eyes swam in tears.

"I know, Mama," she said. "Don't worry."

Minutes before her father's Capri pulled up, she showered and put on her seersucker shorts dotted with strawberries and her halter top with gathered half sleeves.

His footsteps fell heavy as he walked up the front stairs and slammed the door behind him. Next she heard the briefcase thud to the hallway floor, followed by his measured steps into the kitchen, and finally the familiar clink of the vodka bottle against the rim of the jelly glass.

Talk to him before he has another horn of corn.

Standing in the doorway to the kitchen, she chewed her cuticle. "What does a prosecutor do?" she asked him as he started to pour a second drink.

"And good day to you, Miss Lolly. Aren't those nuns teaching you anything in the way of manners?"

"Good evening, father," Lolly said. "How was your day?"

"Brutal, Miss Lolly. Your *father*, as you choose to address me tonight, is bushed. I need to relax and put aside the burdens of my position." He reached for the glass. "Ready to show me that essay you've rewritten?"

"No, sir," she said.

"Putting the last polishing touches on it?"

"Well, I..."

He ran his hand over her cheek. Two of his fingers traced a shaved patch on her head. "It'll grow back," he said. "Where's your cap?"

"Mama's freshening it," she said. "It gets pretty stinky in this heat."

"Put it on." He poured a shot. "I don't want to look at that mess you made of your hair."

"Yes, sir," she said. Several steps out of the kitchen, she paused and turned back. "Does the prosecutor put people in jail?"

"If the crime warrants it." He raised his glass to his lips.

"Don't drink that!" Lolly sprang forward and bumped his arm. Vodka spattered over the linoleum floor.

"Drat you, child. What'd you do that for?"

"Sorry," she said, grabbing a towel from the sideboard and mopping up the spill. "But what if you put a person in jail who doesn't belong in jail?"

"You mean somebody who isn't guilty?" He narrowed his eyes.

"I mean somebody who really isn't bad."

"The law doesn't recognize the good or bad nature of people. It's more a matter of guilt." He poured another drink.

"What if you made a mistake and put somebody in jail who shouldn't be there?"

"I don't make mistakes," he said, knocking back the entire glass in one gulp.

Lolly edged toward the vodka bottle. "How can you be so sure?" An impulse to empty its contents down the sink griped her so suddenly that she thrust her hands into her pockets.

"Because my mistress, the law, has contingencies for every action."

"What if a man did something angry, but not bad, but it looked bad and you put him into jail? What would you do to make it right for him?"

"Does this have something to do with your essay?"

"What would you do?" she persisted.

"It's not an issue because I don't put people in jail who don't belong there. Currently, the issue is one of *not* putting people in jail."

Her mother appeared wearing dusty green shorts and a pale pink linen blouse, her scent soapy and clean. She slipped into a green apron with her art club insignia on the bodice.

"Now what are you two going on about?" she said with an uncommon cheerfulness. "Set the TV tables, would you, darling?"

The fact that her mother was cooking tonight indicated that she must be feeling better. Happily, Lolly pulled out the silverware drawer.

"What if an old man is arrested and put in jail for stealing," she said. "And what if someone does something kind of bad, not trying to hurt anyone but because they're mad about the way the old man is treated. Should the someone go to jail too?"

"How in hell did you come up with that scenario?" her father asked.

"Would you put the someone in jail?"

"Are we verging on a discussion regarding the virtue of anger?" her father asked. "You know, Sister Superior called and we spoke about your behavior at school. She wants me to make it perfectly clear to you that anger is disruptive as well as destructive."

"Isn't anger sometimes good?" Lolly asked. "If bad things happen and you don't get angry at them, that means your bad, doesn't it? So the someone shouldn't go to jail."

He knocked back another drink. His eyes glazed and his lower jaw jetted out, a signal that he was aggravated.

"I'm too tired to debate this," he told her. "Set the trays for dinner, then get that essay written!"

Lolly clutched the silverware in her hand. "Can I set dinner at the table instead of the trays? Can we eat dinner at the table like at the Johnsons?"

"No." He started for the door.

"Regan, don't be so hard on her," her mother said. "We could eat at the table."

"I said no!"

"Maybe we can turn this incident at school into a positive thing."

He turned on Clarissa. "Don't tell me how to handle this girl!"

"But, Daddy, don't you think..."

"Not another word out of you! I don't want to hear any

more stories. Go up to your room and do what the damn nuns told you to do! Rewrite the essay!"

"Regan," her mother said. "Please don't..."

"Please don't," he said in a high, feminine voice. "Please don't. Please don't do what, Clarissa? Don't discipline the little darling? Let her run roughshod over her parents like she's a gypsy kid?"

"There's nothing wrong with being a gypsy kid!" Lolly snapped.

Her mother turned toward her and Lolly saw an expression that might be one of recognition. *She knows*, Lolly thought. *She knows about me going to Cougarville!*

"What do you know about gypsy kids?" her father demanded. "You get everything laid out for you on a silver platter. Nice house, plenty to eat, two parents here for you every single day of your life. You don't know what it's like being little and one day seeing your daddy leave the house and never come back."

She stepped away from her father and her mother put a hand on his arm. "Regan, don't."

Blinded by whatever was boiling inside, he slapped her mother away, knocking her against the counter as though she were a gnat. Lolly rushed over.

"Mama, your nose is bleeding."

"You don't know what it's like to get a call that your father's dead," Her father continued. "You're sixteen and you have to go down to the goddamn morgue, walk into the stinking place, and identify your father. And not because you know what he looks like." He brought the bottle down hard on the counter, shattering it, liquor flooding the tiled surface.

"You don't know what he looks like because he's been gone so goddamn long you wouldn't recognize him if he sneezed on you. But your mother tells you to look for a scar carved down the side of his left cheek."

Whimpering, Lolly pressed into her mother, trying to hide from her father's blast.

"And you stand there alone trying not to breathe the smell of rot and chemicals and death because they stink and because you know you'll smell them for the rest of your life."

With trembling hands, he rifled through the cupboard, causing glasses to clatter, and pulled out a new bottle of vodka. He twisted the cap, poured a drink, and gulped it down.

"And then the doctor asks you if you're the next of kin, and you say yes, and he says, 'Sorry, son, but your father drowned in a sea of rum.'"

Her father's words ricocheted around the kitchen as if the three of them were standing in a deep cavern. Somehow, Lolly knew then that she would always remember the rage ignited in her father's eyes tonight and his trembling hands.

"Daddy," she whispered, stepping toward him.

"Get out of my sight, you impudent child, before I knock that disrespect right out of you!" he bellowed. "And I want to see that essay in less than an hour!"

Lolly knew that he would be too drunk to stand in an hour, let alone read. Five minutes ago, she'd wanted to tell him to go to hell. Now she just wanted to get away from him. His need for medicine rode him as if he was a bull and he would drain jelly glass after jelly glass until he was so full of alcohol there was no more room for memories.

"Daddy." She had to tell him about Bob Bob and his father, and that she wanted to somehow make it all right for them.

"Go to your room!"

"But, Daddy..."

"No 'but Daddy.' Just do it!"

He lunged for her, and she whipped away from her mother and shot up the stairs. From the top, she heard their voices, her mother's speech tremulous and high-pitched.

Suddenly he emerged from the kitchen and lurched to the bottom of the stairs. Hanging on to the banister for support, he blinked as though trying to focus his eyes.

"I'm not going to tell you again to put that goddamn hat on or I'll make good on my promise." He gripped the railing and pulled up one step. "You hear me?"

"I hear you," she said. Lolly fled to her room and closed the door.

She lay on her bed for a long time thinking about Bo and the cougar and Tick. She hadn't eaten dinner and was quite sure that neither had Mama, and surely not her father. When she felt the familiar weight sink onto her bed and smelled her mother's cigarette, she knew her father had passed out and the bad part of the evening was over. Her mother had brought up a tray of food.

Through her bedroom window, she watched the evening sky fade from a salmon tint to darkness. A sliver moon rose and hung there like a drawing in a child's storybook. A solitary heaviness drifted around both of them sitting on the bed. They did this often. Sometimes they talked, but most of the time Lolly just fell asleep, content with the knowledge that her beautiful, lonely mother was nearby.

"Are you all right, Mama?" she finally asked.

"Fine," her mother whispered. "Just fine." She let out a sigh. "Lolly, you're playing with fire when you argue with your father like that."

"I just wanted to know what he does."

"I know, but don't push. It's not a good idea." Her mother massaged her temples. "I'm so tired."

"A head hammer?" Lolly asked.

Her mother nodded. "At night in bed I pray to God to either make me or the headaches go away."

Lolly sat up, rolled the bracelet Sophie had given her off her wrist, and undid the delicate clasp.

"Put this on," she said. "Maybe it'll help."

Her mother took the bracelet in her slender fingers and lifted it up to catch the light from the dim April moon. "It's lovely. Where'd you get it?"

"Put it on," Lolly said. Her mother held out her wrist for Lolly to do the clasp. Then she lifted her arm and studied the stones.

"Aquamarines, if I'm not mistaken. It's strange and you're going to think I'm crazy, but I think I feel something like a current pulsing round my wrist."

Lolly smiled. "It's different for each of us."

"Thank you, darling." Her mother kissed her on the forehead. "Good night."

She watched her mother leave the room, disrupting the layers of cigarette smoke still eddying in the heavy, warm air.

Lolly wondered what the people in Cougarville were doing at that moment and felt a yearning, mixed with a little fear, to be with them.

Chapter Fifteen

The next day after school, instead of going home, Lolly crossed the levee. *There's time*, she assured herself. Her mother was working at the art club to get ready for the annual luncheon and would be there at least a couple of hours. Lolly wanted to find out more about Tick and Sam, and she longed to pet the cougar again.

She knocked on the door of Tick's trailer.

"Hey, Lolly," Tick said. "Come on in."

Lolly slipped through the door. "Where's Sophie?"

"In town selling bracelets."

"Oh," she said. "Can we go see the cougar?"

"I don't know."

Tick didn't turn or hop a hop or jig a jig. Her red hair lay flat and lifeless. Awkwardly, she scuffed her sandal back and forth across the worn carpet, not meeting Lolly's eyes.

"What's the matter?" Lolly asked.

"I found something," Tick said.

"What?"

"It might make you sad."

Lolly sat down on the built-in couch. "It's Bo, isn't it?" A pain the size of a boulder filled her stomach. "Where'd you find him?"

"Underneath the trailer," Tick said. "But maybe he ain't yours."

"When did you find him?" Lolly asked.

"Last night. No use in puttin' it off. Let's take a looksee."

Lolly followed Tick around to the back of the trailer. In the shadow of the van, there lay a cat, his legs stretched as if reaching for cat-sprawl comfort. His eyes were closed and he was smiling a cat smile.

Lolly shook her head and turned away. It wasn't Bo. It couldn't be Bo. He wouldn't just give up and die without letting her find him. That would be selfish and Bo was anything but selfish.

She wanted to walk away, to forget the little body that Tick had found. "Just ignore it and the dead cat will go away," said a voice in her head. "But it won't," said another. "You have to do this."

She turned back and knelt beside the body, tears burning at the back of her throat. "It's Bo," she said and ran her hands over his fur. She pulled quickly away. "He feels different." Sobs threatened to close off her throat. "He was strong. I don't know why he died. He must have suffered a broken heart."

Tick flung herself down next to Lolly. "Mama says that when we die, we hang our bodies up in the closet like an old dress and our spirits go shoppin' for a new one. So this ain't really Bo. It's just his old dress."

"I'm s-sorry, Bo," Lolly said, stuttering through the wracking sobs. "I-I should h-have been able to save you."

Tick took tears from Lolly's face and rubbed them onto Bo's cheek. In the coolness under the trailer, they sat and stared at the dead cat. In the distance a woman laughed.

"What do you want to do with his old dress?" Tick finally asked.

Lolly drew up. "If it weren't for him, Bo'd still be alive! He killed Bo. He killed him!"

"Who?"

"My stupid father! I'd give anything to go to an old, ugly morgue to see *him dead!*"

Tick clapped her hand over Lolly's mouth. "Careful," she said. "Mama says words have power."

"Good," Lolly said. "Maybe I can make him dead by saying it. You're dead! You're dead! You're dead!"

"Come on," Tick said, shifting uncomfortably. "We have to care for Bo's old dress. Do you want to take it to the other side?"

"No!" Lolly said. "I want him here with you and Sophie and Bob Bob and Sam. I want him here!"

"I know a great place," Tick said. "You stay with Bo. I'll be back in a jiffy."

When Tick had jogged off, Lolly lay her head on Bo and nuzzled his fur. "My baby Bo. My sweet old Bo. Don't forget me, Bo, because I'll never forget you. And if you need me, come to me in my dreams. Can you do that?"

She closed her eyes and listened. Insects churred a hum and a radio played in one of the nearby trailers, but no words came from Bo.

Tick returned with a small plaid blanket. "We'll wrap him in this and take him to the stand of cottonwood trees down by where the river runs in the winter time. When the rains come, the river will fill and take Bo's old dress with it."

"Where will it take it?"

"I ain't sure, but I think it's back to where they make dresses. Some place where they'll use it again. Mama says it don't make sense to waste anything."

Lolly nodded. Fatigue weighed her down, and her eyes burned. Her cheeks felt hot and swollen. Tenderly, she picked up Bo, shocked at how stiff he was, and laid him on the blanket. He was still beautiful even though his tawny fur was dirty and matted. He'd left a handsome old dress, that was for sure.

She folded the wool over Bo and, with great solemnity, they walked through the camp, she cradling Bo, Tick shouldering a small shovel.

As they passed through the camp, Andrea thrust her square chin out the door, her raccoon eyes flicking back and forth over them before she and Charlie, dressed in a bright flowered Hawaiian shirt, joined them. As he walked, he spit on his fingers and pasted strands of hair across his shiny scalp.

Next they came to David Robinson Crocker's trailer. The old man was sitting on his porch, fumbling with paper and pencil. He raised his head and squinted at them through watery eyes. Tick nudged Lolly. "He's been writin' his story. Calls it My Sierra Memoirs. What are memoirs?"

Lolly felt so sad that she had no energy to answer the question.

"A procession!" David Robinson Crocker said. "That means a ceremony, and a ceremony means the need for insight and reflection, and reflection calls for a story. Yesiree! There's a likelihood you'll want me to tell about my coming across the Sierras. Yesiree." He grabbed his cane.

When Hattie Berg joined the small band, she looked like a fine lady from a long time ago, toddling after them in a white skirt, which she held up delicately with both hands. "Tea at my house afterward," she said. "Tea and eclairs. I've told Blankenship to alert Cook."

By the time they'd reached the cottonwoods, even Matilda and Ducky had joined them. "When I do you in Ducky, you can be damn sure they'll not be a soul around who'll take the time to bury you," Matilda grumbled, fanning herself with a Silver

Screen Magazine.

"That's a laugh," Ducky hissed back. "When I finish you off, I'm going to toss you in the river. Nobody'll even notice you're gone!"

Finally, the group arrived at the stand of six majestic cottonwood trees, several of which had girths of more than five feet and reached more than a hundred feet into the hot blue sky. Seedpods floated in the air around them and sunlight filtered through the scalloped leaves, creating flickering shadows on the ground like water boiling in a pot.

"Who died?" David Robinson Crocker asked. "Anybody I know?"

"Don't be rude," Hattie Berg elbowed him. "It's not important who. It's just matters that we're here to say so long."

"Hattie, did I ever tell you about crossing the Sierras in the dead of winter?" the old man began.

"Hush," Andrea said.

Lolly lay Bo down gently and Tick began digging a hole, but the summer earth was hard.

"Hey there, my friend Tick," said a deep voice. Bob Bob appeared from behind one of the huge trees. "Let Bob Bob help." He took the shovel from her and, within minutes, had dug a deep and beautiful grave.

"Thank you, Bob Bob," Lolly said, and the giant shyly nodded.

Lolly knelt down. She pulled back a corner of the blanket, kissed the fury face sleeping in her arms, and placed Bo down into the grave.

Looking up at the group surrounding her, she saw tears in their eyes and she tried to speak, but her voice was somewhere in the hole with Bo.

"Today we're putting away an old dress," Tick said. "It

belonged to Lolly's cat, Bo."

"Amen," Andrea said, and sniffed. Charlie put his arm around her shoulders. "Oh, Charlie," Andrea dabbed at the black rivers of mascara flowing down her cheeks, "it's so hard to say good-bye."

"I know, Doll Face," Charlie said. "I know."

"I can say a few words about dying," David Robinson Crocker said. "I know a little bit about it. That winter of forty-six was a doozie and we..."

"Not now," Hattie Berg said. "After tea maybe."

"This ain't easy for Lolly," Tick interjected. "I think we should let her be alone with her cat."

Everybody nodded and before wandering back to their trailers, they patted and hugged her. Bob Bob was the last to leave.

"I'm sorry, my friend Lolly," he said, clearing his throat as his eyes darted back and forth between her and Tick. "Sam would be here, but he's drivin'. I ain't mad at you no more about your daddy," he added, his voice thick. "Cats are good."

"You're right, Bob Bob," she said. "Cats are good."

As Bob Bob shuffled away, Tick turned to follow him.

"Stay," Lolly said. "Please. I want to do a ceremony of some sort."

"Neato," Tick said, excitedly. "What do you want to do?"

"I don't know. Maybe we can hold hands over the grave."

The two girls clasped their hands and bridged the dark gap. The crows barked mean calls from the trees. In the distance a scrub jay nagged.

Lolly began the chant:

"Haram infata cum, Lo epoodo sonesta tum—"

Tick jerked her hands free. "Where'd you get that gobble-de-gook?"

"Your mama," Lolly said. "I heard her one night. She was saying it over a bracelet that she gave to Andrea. Those are powerful words."

Laughter tumbled out of Tick like small pebbles into a pond. "Those words don't mean nothin'!"

"Do too."

"Do not. My mama makes that stuff up. Says if you believe things, they'll happen. Andrea's sick. Mama makes up things for Andrea to believe, like the bracelet's magic and words have power and stuff. It don't matter if they do or don't. It only matters if Andrea believes they do."

"Well," Lolly said, pushing the mounds of loose dirt into Bo's grave, "I believe these words have power. And I happen to have proof. They worked with the grotto horses."

"What are grotto horses?" Tick asked.

"Never mind. The important thing is the words work. So now I want Bo to be safe wherever he's going, so I want you to say these words with me."

"Okay," Tick said. "I guess."

In the shade of the cottonwood trees, in the presence of the squawking birds and the click of the tiny wings of sizzling insects, Lolly shoveled dirt and sang out the mysterious chant, and Tick repeated it. Soon the small grave was filled.

"One more time," Lolly said. "We need to do the chant one more time."

"Aw, gosh," Tick said. "I feel like a rat-faced fool doin' that again."

"Please."

"All right," Tick said. "Once more and that's it."

"And this time, do what I do."

"Okay, okay, but let's get this over with."

Lolly made the sign of the cross and so did Tick, but

instead of touching her left shoulder first, she touched her right. Lolly considered correcting her, but then decided against it. God wouldn't mind, especially seeing that it was the first time Tick had ever blessed herself. Then Lolly raised her arms up to the sky. Tick followed suit. Overriding the competing squawks of the crows and jays, Lolly sang out the chant: "Haram infata cum."

"Haram infata cum," Tick repeated.

"Lo epoodo sonesta tum." As Lolly sang, she whirled in a big circle, her arms reeling loosely around her. Tick spread out her arms, copying her every movement. "Lo epoo..."

Suddenly, Tick froze.

Lolly followed her gaze to a woman standing just outside the border of the cottonwood shade. The sun reflected off her black hair, making it glint like a nylon hood. Her face was pale, but her thin lips were painted heavily with red lipstick. She wore a dark blue suit with buttons of matching fabric that ran the length of the jacket, clear up to her neck. Black patent high heels gleamed, and she carried a briefcase — thin, but important looking.

"Hello," the woman said.

"Hey," Tick said.

"I'm looking for Teresa Peckinpaw. A gentleman in one of the trailers said I might find her here." Her gaze paused on Lolly, shifted to Tick, then returned to Lolly.

Something's wrong, Lolly thought.

"I'm Teresa Peckinpaw," Tick said. "My mama ain't home and I'm not suppose to talk to strangers."

"How long will your mother be away?" the woman asked.

"Don't know," Tick said.

"Does she leave you alone often?"

Lolly stepped in front of Tick. "No," she said, protectively spreading her arms. "Almost never. Sophie almost never leaves Tick alone."

"Well, that ain't exactly..." Tick started.

Lolly stepped backwards and tramped hard on Tick's foot. "And when she *is* away, there are plenty of people here who watch out for...Teresa."

"I see," the woman said. "And who are you?"

"My name's Lolly."

"Do you have a last name, Lolly?" The woman looked up at the sun, then moved into the shade. In the absence of the glare, her glossiness dimmed.

"Candolin," Lolly said.

"Any relation to Regan Candolin?" the woman asked.

This was not good. Definitely not good. "He's my father," she said.

"I only asked because he's on the committee that asked me to..." A cacophony of river critters sang their song while the woman chewed her lip nervously.

"What committee?" Lolly asked.

The woman touched her helmet of black hair and shifted from one shiny foot to the other. "That's not important," she said, narrowing her eyes. "What were you girls doing here?"

"None of your goddamn business," Tick said.

Lolly tramped on Tick's foot again.

"We were having a little ceremony. My, ah, Tick's cat died and we buried him."

"Ain't my..."

"Teresa's very upset about her cat," Lolly said quickly, nudging Tick with her elbow. "She can't talk now."

"Sorry about your cat, Teresa," the woman said. "But I'm afraid it's important that I talk with you and your mother today. Do you think we can go to your trailer and wait for her?"

"She ain't—I mean, Tick *isn't* suppose to talk to strangers," Lolly said.

A blur of hot pink streaked toward them from the camp. Sophie entered the shade, panting and flushed, to gather Tick up in a tight hug.

"I'm Sophie Peckinpaw, Tick's mother. I heard you were here. I was just gone for a jiffy. Workin'. I had business in town. Important business. Selling my bracelets."

"Nadia Greenberg," the woman said, and extended her hand, which Sophie took hesitantly. "I represent the Child Welfare League and I'd like to talk to you about Teresa."

Sophie pulled Tick closer. "All right. We should go to our trailer. Come on, Lolly. You come with us."

Placing a glass of lemonade in front of Nadia Greenberg, Sophie sat down and began stringing a bracelet. Her hands were trembling so much, however, she couldn't thread the beads on the string.

"Mrs. Peckinpaw," Nadia Greenberg began. "I want to ask you some questions in regards to Teresa. Is that all right with you?"

"Sure," Sophie said. "Shoot."

"Let's see." Nadia Greenberg rifled through a stack of papers. Lolly didn't think anything good could come from that many papers. "Yes, here we are," she said, licking her thin lips. "Let's get some of the housekeeping info out of the way."

"I keep a good, clean house," Sophie exclaimed.

Nadia Greenberg glanced around and pursed her lips. "What I meant, Mrs. Peckinpaw, is that I need to gather some basic information. For example, who is Teresa's pediatrician?" When Sophie hesitated, she added, "Her doctor?"

"Well, I don't really..."

"Isn't it Doc Pine?" Lolly asked. "Wasn't that what you told me?"

"That's right!" Sophie said. "Doctor Pine."

"Very well," Nadia Greenberg said. "I assume you'll have no objection if I call him and talk to him about Teresa's medical history?"

"Oh." Sophie twisted around to look at Lolly. "He ain't her doctor at the moment. But the girl ain't sick at the moment, is she?" Sophie's mouth stretched into a quivery smile.

Nadia Greenberg returned the smile with her lips only, her dark eyes remained cold and lifeless. "Do you make meals for Teresa, Mrs. Peckinpaw?"

"Of course I do. Good food. Healthy. Not an ounce of junk food for this girl. Over my dead body will you find a cotton candy in this house."

Nadia Greenberg pursed her lips again. "And what is your employment?"

"Like I told you. I make jewelry." Sophie held up a couple of bracelets. "Here, let me give you one. The green would be a nice complement to your colorin'."

"No, thank you." Nadia Greenberg pulled out a notebook and scribbled intently, her pencil noisily scratching across the page.

"So, Mrs. Peckinpaw," she said authoritatively, "you're self-employed."

"Yeah," Sophie said. "That's right." She sat up straight as if a worm of pride had crawled up her back. "Self-employed."

"And Mr. Peckinpaw? What does he do?"

When Sophie didn't answer, Nadia Greenbe

her eyes alert.

"Sorry," Sophie said frowning, "there ain't no Mr. Peckinpaw. Tick's—I mean Teresa's—father left before she was born. Haven't got a clue where the bastard is now. Heard he was six feet under, but it don't matter whether he is or not because the two of us do real good, don't we, baby?"

Tick wrapped her arms around her mother. "Real good." She bounced over to the picture frames of old men. "Besides, I've got a whole herd of grandpas. And I could have more if I wanted."

Just then the trailer door tore open and Andrea plunged in. She wore a leopard-patterned sarong with matching turban. Her eyelids sparkled with gold glitter, and she had drawn a huge beauty mark to the right of her mouth.

"Sophie, darlin', I need some of your magic," she said in her falsetto voice. "I'm havin' a hell of a day. I do declare that God Himself has got a hard-on for me!"

Nadia Greenberg's eyes widened. Lolly watched her take in this huge, ungainly woman, who was sweating so profusely.

"Oh dear, Andrea," Sophie said, staring pointedly in the direction of Nadia Greenberg. "Sweetie, this ain't a good time. How about as soon as we finish here?"

"Sorry to intrude," Andrea said, awkwardly, aware that she'd walked into something serious.

Nadia Greenberg wrote ferociously while Andrea made her departure. "Mrs. Peckinpaw, I've checked and it appears that Teresa isn't enrolled in school."

"I don't like her crossing over," Sophie explained earnestly.

"Crossing over?" Nadia Greenberg cocked her head.

"Over the levee," Sophie said. "She's better here with me. I'm her teacher. Tick's smart as they come. I'll put her up against any kid, except maybe Lolly here. Lolly's sharp as a bee's stinger. But Tick—I mean Teresa—is special."

"It's always my recommendation that children go to regular school," Nadia Greenberg said, glancing at Sophie in between scribbles.

"No!" Sophie said. "I want my baby here. Not over there. She's not missin' nothin' by not goin' to town."

"Can you read, Teresa?" Nadia Greenberg's eyelids fluttered.

"Yes, ma'am," Tick said.

"And can you add and subtract and do your times tables?"

"Yes, ma'am."

Sophie straightened even more in her chair. That pride worm was wiggling like crazy.

"Well, we'll see," Nadia Greenberg said. She made a few more notes before clapping the notebook shut. "You should know, Mrs. Peckinpaw, that my agency has concerns about neglect."

"Neglect," Sophie repeated. "I'd die for this girl!"

"Please, Mrs. Peckinpaw. Understand that I'm only interested in Teresa's welfare. I'm sure together we'll come up with what's best for her." Nadia Greenberg stuffed her notebook into her briefcase. "I'll be back in a couple of weeks to test her."

"Test?" Sophie stood. "What kind of test?"

"We'll see how Teresa's reading, vocabulary, and math scores stack up against scores of students attending school in town. Plus, the committee requires that I write up a report regarding Teresa's environment, home influences, and role models, people like your—er, friends. My review will be part of the recommendation. Foster care might be something we should consider."

"You mean you want my baby to live with strangers?"

Sophie demanded, clearly astonished at the idea. "Never! I'd fight to my death for that not to happen. She'll ace your test. You'll see!" Sophie shoved her hand toward Nadia Greenberg, who had no choice but to take it.

"Thank you for coming, Miss Greenberg," Lolly said, extending her hand, as well, in order to force Sophie to let go of Nadia Greenberg. "I'll tell my father you were here."

As a small furrow rippled between Nadia Greenberg's brows, Lolly thought, *Hopefully that did it.*

Nadia Greenberg hurried out the door. Tick, Sophie, and Lolly stood in the trailer's doorway and watched until she had turned the corner of David Robinson Crocker's trailer and disappeared.

"Well," Sophie said. She sat down hard in her chair. "Ever shoot anyone, Lolly?" She lifted a bracelet of beads and added a bright blue stone to the string.

"You mean with a gun?" Lolly said.

"I mean with a bazooka! Shoot them so they're deader than a nit!"

"Hush, Mama," Tick said, and she crawled up on her mother's lap. "Remember what words can do."

"Oh, Lord, Tick. They *can't* take you away from me. I'd die, baby." Then Sophie scooted Tick off, jumped up, and went to the back of the trailer. She returned holding a *Reader's Digest.* "I have to know just how good you can read." She opened the magazine and plunked it down in front of Tick. "Read to me." Her frosted nail pointed to a paragraph.

Perfectly, Tick read the first paragraph of a story about a woman whose dog had rescued a kitten from a burning barn.

"See?" Sophie gloated. "What'd I tell you? Ain't she somethin'?"

"What does *incendiary* mean?" Lolly asked.

"What?" Tick looked at her perplexed.

"Incendiary. You just read it. In the first sentence."

Tick wound a curl around her finger. "Don't know."

"Oh, Lordy," Sophie said. "I ain't got the slightest idea what it means either. Oh, Tick, they can't take you away from me."

"Don't worry, Sophie," Lolly said. "I'll help you defeat that *incendiary* Nadia Greenberg. You've done a good job already. Tick just needs a little boning up. I read pretty well and I'm good with a dictionary and not too bad with numbers. She won't fail that test. I promise."

"Ain't Lolly the sweetest little ragged head girl you've ever met?" Sophie said as she nuzzled her face into Tick's serpentine curls. Then she drew Lolly close and hugged them both. "The sweetest." Sophie sighed. "Now get your ragged head home. It's gettin' on toward five."

"We buried Bo today," Lolly said.

"Oh, child, I'm so sorry you lost that little soul."

"Me too."

"You all right?" Sophie asked.

Lolly slouched out the trailer door but before leaving she called back, "I'll get her through that test!"

Chapter Sixteen

The next day at breakfast, Lolly watched her father sip his coffee, nibble dry toast, and read the paper. The placid look on his face reminded her of the way he looked the moment he tossed Bo over the levee.

He finally lowered the paper and looked at her. "What is it?"

"Nothing," Lolly said.

"Eat your breakfast, dear," her mother said. "We all have an early start today."

He went back to his paper, but her stare remained relentless and he looked up again. "What's bothering you?"

She took a breath. "Are you on a committee?"

He frowned at her, clearly puzzled. "I'm on several committees," he said.

"Are you on a committee that sends people over to the gypsy camp to test a kid there who doesn't go to town school?"

"Why do you want to know?" he demanded, throwing down the paper.

"Just do."

"The answer is: I'm on many committees, too numerous to go into this morning." He got up, kissed her mother on the forehead, and patted Lolly on the shoulder. "Be a good girl in school today. I don't want any more phone calls from Sister Superior."

Lolly looked up at him. "Are you on that committee?"

"Did you hear me, Lolly?" her father asked. "No calls from Sister."

"No calls."

"Good."

As her father hurried from the room, she realized he had answered her question.

Tick read well, pronouncing every word correctly, but when Lolly quizzed her on the meanings, Tick usually failed. As a consequence, they spent a lot of time looking up words in the dictionary.

"I can figure out what the story's about without knowing what every word means," Tick complained.

"Nadia Greenberg is going to test you on vocabulary," Lolly said.

"Are you sure?"

"She said she would. She'll want to know if you understand what you're reading."

Tick shrugged, stuffed a cracker into her mouth and continued reading the story out loud. As she spoke, crumbs flew onto the pages.

"That's enough of that," Sophie said. "That Greenberg woman thinks I neglect you. That ain't true, but maybe I do go a little light on manners. Startin' now, Miss Teresa, no talkin' with your mouth full, hear?"

"Yes ma'am," Tick said, burrowing her nose deeper into

The Sign of the Twisted Candles, the Nancy Drew book Lolly had assigned.

An hour later, Lolly used flash cards to grill Tick on addition, subtraction, and multiplication.

"Enough!" Tick cried. "Let's go back to Nancy and the twisted candle."

"Tick-a-roo!" Sam called from the doorway. "How's the studying going? You gonna pass that test?"

"Yep," Tick said, bounding into his arms. "'Cause of old Lolly here. She's my best friend, Sam. Outside of you and Bob Bob and Survie, of course."

Sam gently mussed Tick's curls. "Tell you what. You pass that test and I'll have a little reward for you."

"What?" Tick asked. "What is it?"

"Pass the test and you'll find out."

"Rectify," Lolly said.

"Rectify," Tick repeated. "To set right; to correct. To correct by calculation or adjustment."

"Good," Lolly said. "Now use the word."

"I'm damn tootin' gonna rectify what Nadia Greenberg thinks about me so I ain't gonna be sent to no foster home." Tick smiled and raised her chin defiantly.

"So I'm *not* going to go to *any* foster home," Lolly corrected.

"That's what I said!"

Lolly sighed and decided grammar lessons would come later.

On her way to the fifth tutoring session with Tick, Lolly had gotten about half way up the side of the levee, when a chorus of whinnies broke out behind her. She whirled around to see the grotto horses stomping the ground, their heads thrashing back and forth, their manes flying.

The Thoroughbred reared back and then galloped out of the knot of ponies. "Want to play horses with us?"

Lolly narrowed her eyes and looked from one horse to the next. That's when she realized that Christina, the Warmblood, was missing.

They don't want me, she thought. *They just need another body to round out the herd.* But this was her chance. In a short time they would discover what a fast and beautiful horse she could be. She chuffed her feet. "Yes," she said.

From the top of the levee, someone called her name. She looked up to see Tick standing in the back glow of the sun, her hair radiating spikes of light.

Lolly squinted up at Tick for a long moment, then a horse whinnied and she turned back to the Thoroughbred.

The Thoroughbred whinnied again and stomped at the dry, brittle grass. "Let's go," she said, snorting loudly. "Let's gallop." The Thoroughbred cantered back to the herd.

"Wait!" Lolly said. "Can I bring another horse with me?"

"What?" the Thoroughbred shouted. "You mean that one?" She pointed at Tick.

"Yes," Lolly said. "Can I bring her with me?"

"No," said the Thoroughbred. She tossed her mane.

The Thoroughbred, the Appaloosa, and the Brumby broke into a scuffle of trots that raised dust. They circled and pounded, whinnied, snorted, and chuffed.

"If you want to join us, you'd better come now," the Thoroughbred said as the horses continued trotting in a circle.

Lolly looked up and saw disappointment on Tick's face as she backed away over the dirt track and disappeared down the river side of the levee.

Lolly turned back to the herd. Every fiber of her body craved to join them. "Tick!" she called over her shoulder.

There was no answer. She took a couple of steps up the berm and, when she spoke, her voice broke. "If the other horse can't come..." She looked from one pony to the other. "If the other horse can't come, I won't play with you."

The Thoroughbred tossed her mane. "Your choice." She reared, then nudged gently against the other horses and, together, they cantered down the levee.

Lolly watched them until they galloped down the street, rounded a corner, and were out of sight, their whinnies and cries fading.

Trudging up the levee, she found Tick sitting just on the other side. "Let's go," she said. "We still have work to do."

The next morning, Lolly didn't get up when her mother called. Instead, she lay groaning in her bed.

"What's the matter, darling?" Her mother pressed her hand over Lolly's forehead. "You don't feel hot."

"It's my stomach. I have a head hammer in my stomach."

"I'll call Doc," her mother said.

Lolly sat straight up. "No, Mama. I just need to rest. Please call Sister and tell her I can't come to school."

"Lolly, I have huge commitments at the club today, and your grandfather's on one of his art trips."

"It's okay," Lolly said. "I'm almost eleven. I can stay alone."

"Almost eleven," her mother scoffed affectionately. "In eleven months and two weeks, you'll be eleven."

"I'm a big girl. I'll be fine."

"Well..." Her mother paced the room. "I suppose. You have my number at the club, and I'll call you every hour."

"Not every hour, Mama. I feel very, very tired. Too much work on my essay. Don't worry. I just need to stay home for one day."

As her mother tucked her in, Lolly added, "And if you call and I don't answer, I'm sleeping." She opened her mouth wide and yawned like a cat, which made her think of Bo. A throbbing sob lodged in her throat.

Listening to her mother's car drive away, she pulled clothes out of her closet, bundled them together, and stuffed them into her bed, arranged the covers carefully.

Not bad, she thought. *Lolly Candolin's sleeping in her bed like a good girl.*

Nadia Greenberg stood on the porch of the unicorn trailer. Her brown linen suit was fresh, the skirt creased across her lap from her drive to Cougarville. She had piled her black hair on top of her head, causing her face to look more severe.

Lolly, Tick, Sophie, and Sam gaped at her through the screen. Finally, Sophie opened the door and let Nadia Greenberg in.

"Good morning, Teresa, Mrs. Peckinpaw, Lolly." Nadia

Greenberg turned to Sam.

"Mornin' ma'am," he said, thrusting out his hand. "I'm Sam Maple and I'm a close friend of Tick's. How you doin'?"

"Fine," Nadia Greenberg said, straightening her back and tucking in her chin. "Well, let's get started."

Lolly joined Sophie and Sam, and they landed together on the couch as if they were school children who'd just been told to sit.

Nadia Greenberg smiled wanly. "You will all have to leave. Teresa must be alone to take the test."

"But, I'm her mother," Sophie protested. "I ought to be here."

"She'll be fine," Nadia Greenberg assured her.

Lolly took Sophie's hand and they moved toward the door, Sam following. Sophie blew Tick a kiss.

Lolly whispered, "*Haram infata cum.*"

Tick giggled and Sophie shot her a questioning glance.

There was a gathering of Cougarville residents outside. "Go on home," Sam ordered them. "All of you. Sophie knows you're concerned, but she'll let you know as soon as she knows anythin'."

The group dispersed.

"Lolly, you hold the fort here," Sam said. "I'm gonna take Sophie for a walk. Her nerves will leak right through the trailer and Tick won't be able to think."

Lolly nodded and perched on the top step while Sophie and Sam wandered in the direction of the cottonwoods.

Waiting was difficult. Now and then, Lolly heard Nadia Greenberg's voice murmuring. After a while, she paced in front of the trailer. With a stick of Madrone, she began to draw pictures in the dust. Then she practiced the weird twisting jumps she'd seen Tick do. She wondered how many times her mother had called her at home, and how she would be punished if her mother discovered she had lied. And would her mother tell her father? Lolly cringed when she thought about her next confession.

Finally, the door opened and Tick shot out. "That test near whipped me," she said in a whisper.

"How'd you do?"

"Goat Breath's correcting it now. Where's Mama and Sam?"

"Taking a walk. They went that way."

"Let's go," Tick said. "It'll take Goat Breath a little time to figure out if she's gonna put me in some gol-durn foster home or not. If she does, I won't go."

"What'll you do?" Lolly asked.

"Run," Tick said. "I'll run away and Mama will come with me. It's simple."

As they galloped toward the trees, Tick said, "I wish Mama'd get hitched to Sam."

"That means Sam would be your daddy."

"Bingo!" Tick crowed. "Give the genius a blue ribbon!"

"Do you think that would change anything with Nadia Greenberg?" Lolly asked as she raced to keep up with Tick.

"Maybe," Tick said.

"You think they *will* get married?"

"I don't know," Tick said. "My mama's damn stubborn. There they are! Don't let them see us."

Sophie and Sam sat at the base of an enormous tree, and the girls ducked behind another, close enough to hear what the adults were saying. Tick peered around one side, and Lolly peered around the other, careful not to be seen.

Sam reached over and took Sophie's hand in his.

"Sophie, when are you gonna come to your senses?" he

asked, turning her face gently toward his.

"Don't rush me, Sammy," Sophie said. "Besides, you need time, too. You need to heal before you run off and jump quick back into the fryin' pan. It's barely been a year."

Lolly pressed her hands against the tree. What were they talking about? What did Sophie mean about him having to heal?

"I ain't jumpin' to you 'cause of grief or loneliness," Sam said. "I want you to know that."

The girls craned to get closer.

"I love you, Sophie, with all my heart. And I love Tick too."

Tick reared back, her mouth open, and gave a silent cheer.

"But, wasting time apart is down right sinful," Sam continued. "We should be together."

"I don't know."

"Do you like me?"

"Of course, I like you, Sam. I like you a lot. You know that." Sophie's voice trembled.

Tick broke into wild, silent applause. Lolly grabbed Tick's hands, trying to restrain her.

Lolly wondered if, sometime, before she was born, her parents were tender like this. *Did I ruin things for them?*

"Do you think you could love me?" Sam asked.

Tick put her hands together in prayer.

"There's not a woman on earth who wouldn't love you, Sam," Sophie said.

"Well, then, shrug off that fear and love me, Sophie. I'll take good care of you and Tick."

"That's what that lazy and mean yahoo Darrell said before I married him."

"I ain't Darrel, damn it."

"It's just that that mistake has cost me dearly. Can you give me a little more time?" She leaned her head against his shoulder, and Tick beamed.

Lolly pointed to a pretend watch on her wrist and they headed back for the trailer. When they got there, Nadia Greenberg stood in the doorway, her pale face stern, her mouth a slash of red.

"Where's your mother?" she asked Tick.

"She's comin'."

Lolly looked back to see Sophie and Sam hand-in-hand, hurrying toward them. She also saw Hattie Berg and David Robinson Crocker huddled together in a shadow of a trailer; and Andrea and Charlie, arm-in-arm, slipping around the corner of another trailer. Matilda and Ducky, silent for a change, leaned against one another in a slice of shade by a sycamore tree. Bob Bob didn't seem to notice the heat as he stood in the sun, jingling what sounded like keys in his pockets.

"Well?" Sophie asked, breaking away from Sam. "Wasn't I right? My baby's smart." Sophie took the steps up to the trailer.

"Maybe we should do this inside," Nadia Greenberg said.

"Inside, outside it don't matter," Sophie said. "Just tell me. Are you takin' my girl away from me?"

Lolly clutched Tick's hand as Nadia Greenberg opened her folder and studied it.

"Teresa?" she called, looking up at last. "Where are you?"

"Here, ma'am," Tick said. "Right here."

"Your score," Nadia Greenberg cleared her throat. "Your score on each test was high."

Applause and whistles erupted from the little gathering.

"However..." She let the word hang. "I still have reservations about your home life."

"What can you say ain't right about her home life?" Sophie

asked. "The trailer's clean and I feed her good."

"I can't say anything negative about the home, Mrs. Peckinpaw. But the committee is concerned that your finances are questionable and..."

"And *what?*" Sophie said, stepping closer to Nadia Greenberg, who moved back. "And what?"

"For the time being, Teresa will continue to live with you."

A cheer rose in the gypsy camp.

"But the investigation is not closed."

"What do you mean by 'not closed'?" Sophie asked.

"Well, the committee is concerned about...stability."

"Miss Greenberg," Sam said, stepping forward. "What's not stable about a mother providing a loving home for her child? Can you answer me that?"

Nadia Greenberg ran her tongue over her lips. "The committee thinks that..."

Lolly looked from Sophie to Sam to Tick.

"The committee thinks what?" Sophie snapped. "Who is this committee? I want to meet them. I'd bet all my stones and beads that they can't find fault with my mothering! Please, Miss Greenberg, can you tell me one thing wrong I'm doin' with my baby?"

Lolly thought she saw a softening in Nadia Greenberg's face as the woman sighed and shook her head in a way that said, "What am I doing here harassing these people?"

Sam put his arm around Sophie's shoulder. "We're all doin' the best we can, Miss Greenberg. Yes, ma'am, we're doin' the best we can."

Sophie smiled. Tears shimmered in her eyes, and she reached out to both Lolly and Tick. She grabbed Tick and held her so tight, Tick had to pry free.

"I can't breathe, Mama!" she shouted, then got Lolly in a

strangle hold of her own. "Thank you!"

As the girls jumped up and down, the residents broke out in more cheers, hoots, and hand-clapping.

Out of the corner of her eye, Lolly saw Nadia Greenberg descend the steps of the trailer and pick her way through the small group.

"Miss Greenberg," she called, "are you going to tell my daddy you saw me here?"

Nadia Greenberg took a handkerchief from her purse and dabbed at her face.

"Because if you do," Lolly continued, "I'll tell him that you liked Tick and her mama so much you didn't have the heart to take Tick away, and you changed the answers so Tick wouldn't flunk. You'll lose your job."

"Do you think my job makes any difference to your father?" Nadia Greenberg said. "If Teresa hadn't passed the tests, it would have been just the ammunition your father's looking for."

Lolly hadn't thought of that. She scraped at a tuft of dry grass. "Are you going to tell him?"

"Just what on earth are you doing here with these people?" Nadia Greenberg asked, her voice sharp and accusing.

"They're my friends."

Nadia Greenberg frowned. "You don't belong here. You should go home."

"Are you going to tell him?"

Nadia Greenberg watched some crows bellyaching at two small brown birds. "No. I'm not," she said, then turned on her heel and walked away.

When Lolly went back to Tick, Sam encircled them both in his muscular arms and lifted them high. She breathed in sweat and detergent.

"Okay, Tickaroo," he said, depositing them on the ground. "Are you ready for the reward? If you are, go jump in the truck. Bob Bob and I are takin' you to town."

"Can Lolly go, too?" Tick asked.

Sam rubbed his hands together. "I'd sure like to take you, Lolly, but where we're going...well, I don't think it's a good idea."

Sophie put her hands on Lolly's shoulders. "Where you plan to go, Sam Maple?"

"It's a surprise," Sam said.

"I doubt you'd take Tick someplace you can't take Lolly. Plus, it just ain't fair."

"You don't understand, Sophie," Sam said. "Her bein' Regan Candolin's kid and all..."

"What her daddy does ain't got nothin' to do with Lolly. Sam, both girls worked so hard."

"It's nothin' I got against Lolly," Sam said. "It's just him being who he is. It wouldn't be a very good idea."

"Please," Tick said. "Please, Sam."

Sam looked around for somebody to take his side, but the others had gone back to their trailers, and Bob Bob just swayed back and forth.

"That's okay, Sam," Lolly said. "Maybe I should just go home." She turned to leave.

"Wait, Lolly. Maybe we can work this out." Sam paced in front of her. "The problem is, we have kind of a small...war goin' with them folks in town."

"I don't care one hoot about what those townies think," Lolly told him.

"I know," Sam said. "But *they* care. They think people over the levee are..."

"They think we're different," Sophie cut in. "And we durn

sure are, thank the Lord!"

"Good different," Lolly said.

"Yes," Sophie said. "Good different. But what Sam's tryin' to say is, sometimes folks are afraid of people who are different. So if you go to town with him and Tick, and people see you and tell your daddy, you may get into a heap of trouble. And Sam might, too."

"Would we be going to a place where people there would tell on me?" Lolly asked, determined to be included. The more they talked about it the more she wanted to go.

Sam thrust his hands into his pockets. "Okay. Here's what we do. You go with us. When we get there, I'll check out the place and, if I think it's okay, I'll take you in. If it ain't, I'll take you home. Deal?"

"Deal," Lolly said as Tick jumped up and down and clapped her hands.

"Where we goin', Sam?" Tick asked. "Where we goin'?"

Sam kissed Sophie on the cheek, then motioned for the girls to follow him. "Come on, Bob Bob," he called. "Let's give these girls a treat!"

Chapter Seventeen

Lolly thrilled at the way Sam's truck bounced and jolted over the gravel-studded track, rocks clanking up against the undercarriage. She cocked her head to steal a glance at the watch on Sam's wrist. It was almost noon. She knew that her mother had called her at least once by now. *I should go home,* she thought, but her yearning to find out what was at the end of this adventure tugged at her. To keep her mind from home, she turned to Bob Bob.

"Can I ask you a question, Bob Bob?"

"Sure, my friend Lolly."

"Why do people call you Bob Bob?"

"It's my name."

"But, why *two* Bobs?"

"There's a story about that," Sam said. "Should I tell it, Bob Bob?"

"Yeah, Sam," Bob Bob said. "You tell the story."

"Well, it goes like this. His mama, bless her soul in heaven, wanted to call him Robert."

"Yeah," Bob Bob said. "My mama wanted to call me Robert."

"But his daddy, bless his soul in heaven, wanted to call him Bob."

"Yeah, my daddy wanted to call me Bob."

"Not willing to give up, his mama compromised and started calling him Robert Bob."

"My mama started calling me Robert Bob," Bob Bob smiled proudly at Lolly.

"But after a while, Robert Bob was too much work so she just called him Bob Bob," Sam continued.

They were driving faster now than Lolly had ever gone before, causing her and Tick to come off the seat when they hit deep potholes. Sam turned the truck sharply and they took the levee road down into town where the road grew smooth.

"Ain't this the bee's knee?" Tick said, her eyes bright as beads. She seemed to feel no fear.

Sam took the truck around a corner, straightened for a second, then turned sharply again and drew to an abrupt stop.

"Wow!" Lolly exclaimed, exhaling. Clamoring out of the truck after Tick, she gazed around. Nothing looked familiar, but she knew her parents wouldn't approve of this part of town.

Many of the windows along the street were boarded, and the people wandering up and down were ragged and dirty. A man layered in dark capes lurched toward them. He looked confused and worn, smelled sour, and went straight toward Lolly, who ducked behind Sam.

"That's okay, cowboy," Sam said. "Here's a quarter, now push on."

"God bless," the man said, and continued down the street.

A gong suddenly vibrated the hot air. Lolly moved closer to Sam and Tick. When the gong rang again, she felt the reverberation in her chest.

"It's the *Bok Kai*," Sam said, nodding at a building across the street with an ornately carved entrance painted deep red. A large brass medallion connected the doors like a lock, and tasseled lanterns hung on either side next to long, narrow scrolls. The roof was red tile, the corners molded into hook shapes.

The third crash of the gong was followed by drums that rumbled like thunder.

"They're getting' ready for the festival," Sam told them. "It's somethin' to see. A hundred and fifty-foot dragon'll dance out of that there temple and do the two-step right down Main Street, with firecrackers poppin' to beat the band."

"Yeah, to beat the band," Bob Bob said.

"I've seen it!" Tick said, doing three leaps down the sidewalk. "Last year Sam brought me. It was neato. They say unless them Chinese folks do all that dancin' and drummin', the river would flood Cougarville and the town. Right Sam?"

Sam grinned the way he did when Tick had something to say. "Them dragon dancers help Cougarville. The levee helps the town."

"What Chinese?" Lolly asked. "I've never seen them. Where do they come from?"

"From that temple, dummy," Tick said, and she tossed her head.

"Okay, young ladies, now for your reward," Sam said. I'm taking you shootin'."

"You mean guns?" Tick asked.

"Yep, that's what I mean," Sam said.

"Oh, boy!" Tick crowed.

Lolly tried to smile, but concern grabbed her by the stomach. She wasn't used to guns. What if she accidentally shot somebody?

She clutched Tick's hand tightly as they followed Sam up the street. He turned toward a wooden building which had probably been white at one time. Over the front door, a sign hanging from rusted chains proclaimed the property to be the *Chiseler's Inn.*

"Wait here," Sam said. "I'm goin' to do a little scoutin'."

"How long?" Lolly asked. She was worried about getting home before her mother.

"Seconds," Sam said, and he disappeared into the worn building.

Lolly took a deep breath. If Sam hadn't come back by the time she counted five, she was going to have to walk home.

"Coast is clear," Sam said.

Thank you, God.

Sam motioned Lolly, Tick, and Bob Bob out of the hot spring day into the chill of the bar. Darkness sucked away Lolly's vision, and she put her hands out in front of her to feel her way. She found Tick's cottony hair, her arm, and finally her hand. In the blackness, the air was spiked with the smell of liquor and the musty smell of leftover cigarette smoke. As her eyes adjusted, she could see a dim light glowing in an adjoining room.

"You ever been in here before?" she whispered to Tick.

"No."

Sam's hand was on Lolly's shoulder, guiding her. "Every kid should know how to handle a gun and today you girls are gonna learn." His voice was gruff and all business.

A door opened directly ahead, murky light washing over them, and they entered a large room where a mahogany bar stretched along one wall. Behind it stood bottles of liquor, backlit so their amber and ruby contents glowed like jewels. Small round tables covered with grimy felt stood here and there and, at the back, a hanging lamp burned over the stained, dull green of a pool table. A man was bending over the table and banging balls against the sides with a long stick. Two other men sat at the bar.

"Don't have no concern," Sam said, nodding toward at the bar. "That's Lenny Torrey and Phil Dinglebrook. They practically have those bar stools growing out of their bee-hinds. And that's Gary Hendricks shootin' pool. Another fixture."

The men at the bar turned toward them, their faces cracked like old leather. Something about them seemed familiar to Lolly, but maybe it was only the sadness in their eyes.

Behind the bar, a tall thin man with yellow skin and baggy, bloodshot eyes saluted Sam.

"Howdy, Mo," Sam said. "How's the best barkeep in town?"

"Real good, Sam. Real good. Who're the kids?"

"Just a couple of little scrubs from the other side," Sam told him.

"You know, partner, no kids are allowed in here," Mo said. "Do me a favor and take 'em on into the gallery. I'll turn on the targets and bring 'em Cokes in there."

A loud crack came from the pool table. "Hey, Gary," Sam called to the man.

"How ya doin', Sam?"

"Can't complain, my friend," Sam replied. "Come on, girls. Time for your first shootin' lesson. What you're about to learn here is as important as any of those lessons Nadia Greenberg was so fired up about." He reached for Lolly's hand, but she wouldn't move.

"What's wrong?" Sam asked.

"You suppose my daddy comes in here?" she asked.

"No doubt," Sam said. "Just about every yahoo from these parts partakes of this waterin' hole from time to time. You can stop your worryin', Lolly. There's nobody here today that crosses paths with your daddy. And for sure they got no recognition of you, unless you've been hangin' out here after school."

Lolly laughed and nestled her hand in Sam's as he guided them through a door to another room even darker than the last. At one end against a black velvet wall, a spotlight shone on a line of chipped and yellow mechanical ducks paddling effortlessly in a line, going nowhere.

"Are we going to shoot them ducks?" Tick asked.

"Yes, ma'am," Sam said.

"I don't shoot things," Lolly said. "It's a sin."

"They're not real!" Tick said, letting out a little shriek. "Did you really think they were real?"

"I know they're not," Lolly said, feeling her face flush.

"Ducks aren't real," Bob Bob said. He picked up a rifle from a wall mount, butted it into his shoulder, and began firing. *Ping!* A duck fell over. Each time he fired, the same result. *Ping! Ping!*

"Bob Bob never misses," Sam said. "He wins every shootin' match he enters, don't you, Bob Bob?"

"Yep," Bob Bob said. "Win every match." He fired quickly, every mechanical duck taking a hit and laying on it side until making the turn and reappearing upright.

Sam let go of a long, slow whistle. "Bob Bob's got the eye of a hawk. Okay, Tick, you give it a try." He moved a chair into range and lifted her up onto it. Then he placed the rifle in her hands. "Rule number one. Check if your gun is loaded. Rule number two. Never point a gun at anything or anyone unless you intend to use it. Got that?"

The girls nodded.

"Rule number three. Use your eyes. Look real careful. Which way them ducks swim?"

"Left to right," Tick said.

"Left to right," Sam said. "Okay. Choose a duck, line it up in the two sights, hold your breath, and squeeze the trigger."

Tick tried to lift the rifle, but when its weight caused her arms to shake, Sam put a hand under the barrel and stabilized it. Lolly held an empathetic breath as she watched Tick close one eye, slip her finger around the trigger, and squeeze off six shots. At the end of the round, all of the ducks were still swimming.

"Shucks," Tick said, her lower lip turned down in a pout. "I ain't no good."

"Not true," Sam said. "That was a good try. Hittin' takes practice. Lots. Let's give Lolly a turn."

"No, thanks," Lolly said.

"Why not?" Tick asked. "It's fun. Go on, Lolly, give it a try."

Lolly stood on the chair and raised the rifle. It was too heavy for her also, so Sam supported it. "Same thing goes for you, Lolly," he said. "Sight, hold your breath, squeeze."

She felt her heart pounding. The dull rifle felt alien, but at the same time, comfortable in an odd way. Its long barrel and tight mechanisms had a strange beauty about them. A thrill thrummed inside of her.

She closed one eye and tucked the butt into her shoulder. The metal pressing against her cheek smelled oily. The ducks swam fast. She picked one, aimed, and squeezed. *Ping!*

"I hit it!" she said. "I hit a duck!"

"Son of a gun!" Sam said. "Try again."

She turned around to see if Bob Bob had seen her, but he had disappeared.

"Where's Bob Bob?" she asked. "I want him to see me knock over a duck."

"You done real good," Bob Bob said.

"Where are you?" Lolly asked. "I can hear you, but I can't see you."

"I'm here," Bob Bob said.

Sam nodded toward a dark area near the gallery entrance where an overhang of stairs cast a deep shadow. Though Lolly stared, she saw nothing there.

"You done good, my friend Lolly," Bob Bob said again as he stepped out of the darkness. "Real good."

"Wow!" she said. "You were invisible. I couldn't see you at all."

"Come on, Lolly, try again," Sam said.

Lolly chose another duck. Its little body glowed as it moved along the line. Just before it turned the corner, she squeezed. *Ping!*

"You're a natural," Sam said. She missed the next two, then hit the third. Tick tried again and managed to hit one. For the next half-hour, they guzzled Cokes, shot ducks, and laughed. Lolly felt almost giddy, like the day she had stepped into the cage with the cougar.

"Excuse me, ladies. I have to see a man about a dog," Sam said. "Don't touch those guns until I get back, you hear?"

"Yes, Sam," Tick said. "We hear."

Sam left the room and Bob Bob wandered into the bar, mumbling that he meant to play some pool.

"What man about what dog?" Lolly asked.

Tick's eyes grew big, then she threw her head back and laughed. "There ain't no man or no dog!" Tick said. "Sam's gone to take a pee!"

While waiting for Sam to return, Tick counted how many times she could jump on one foot. When she missed, she began the competition on the other. Finally, she crossed her feet and did a quick turn. "Ta-da!" she cried, her arms spread, and bowed.

"Too bad Sam doesn't have any kids," Lolly said, running

her hand down the rifle barrel.

"Don't touch the gun!" Tick ordered. "Sam said."

Lolly removed her hand. "I mean, he's so nice."

"He used to have a kid," Tick said.

"What do you mean?"

"He was married, too."

"Is that what your mama was talking about when she and Sam were out there by the river?"

"It's a real sad story," Tick said, rubbing her eyes. "Happened 'bout a year ago. Merilee was Sam's wife. She had a baby and it came early or fast or somethin', and Sam couldn't get them to the hospital. He tried to get help from the po-lice, but I guess that weren't no good. By the time the doctor got to Sam's trailer, Merilee'd gone dead. Along with the baby."

"Oh, no," Lolly said. "That's terrible."

"Sam says there weren't no good reason for them to die. Says it were the doctor's fault 'cause he took his sweet damn time gettin' to 'em. Sam says them town doctors don't give a crumb about folks in Cougarville. He says town folks'd be just as happy if folks in Cougarville would drown in the winter river. He says town folks think it'd be better if Cougarville washed away."

"That's not true," Lolly whispered, lowering her eyes because she knew what Tick said was true.

A loud laugh hacked from the other room. Lolly peered out of the shooting gallery into the dimness beyond. She could see that another man had joined the two at the bar. He tossed his head back and, in one gulp, emptied a squatty glass. Lolly narrowed her eyes. The man looked exactly like Doc, but it couldn't be. Certainly Doc didn't take medicine like her father did. And why was he here at this time of day? Didn't he have patients to take care of? She blinked and took a step closer.

The man *was* Doc. Lolly quickly ducked back into the shadows.

"Who you hiding from?" Tick asked her.

"That man at the bar. He's a friend of my daddy's."

"Uh, oh," Tick said. "I better go get Sam."

"No," Lolly said. "Don't attract attention. Sam'll be back in a minute."

Like cartoon characters, one head above the other, Lolly and Tick craned their necks past the doorjamb to see better. Doc ordered another drink and downed it in one swallow. He *was* taking medicine the same way her daddy did.

"That's Doc Pine," Tick said. "He knows your daddy?"

"Yeah," Lolly said. "And my mama."

"Wow," Tick said.

"Wow, what?" Lolly asked.

"It were him who didn't come to take care of Merilee and Sam's baby. He's no good. Mama says that when it come time for him to hang up his old clothes and get new ones, there won't be nobody there to help him."

Lolly was silent. She realized it must have been Sam's wife and baby Doc Pine had been talking about when he spoke to her father about the people over the levee. She picked up the rifle.

"Don't touch that!" Tick exclaimed. "Sam made the rule."

Lolly rested the butt into her shoulder, the weapon suddenly light in her hands.

"What are you doing?" Tick demanded. "Sam said don't touch the gun."

Lolly aimed through the door at Doc Pine just as he turned and saw her. He left his barstool and hurried over to her, the expression on his face stern.

His mouth smiled, but not his eyes. "Well, well, well," he

said. "What are you doing here, Miss Candolin?"

Lolly raised the gun so it was pointed directly at his belly.

"I wonder what your daddy would say if he knew you were hanging out in the shooting gallery?" Doc went on in a low tone.

"My daddy wouldn't care," she said. The next confession she made with Father O'Connor was going to be a doozie.

"I think you and me need to come to a little understanding," Doc said. "It wouldn't be good for me if your daddy knew I was here at this time of day, do you understand? So you and me are going to do some favors for each other. Right?"

Lolly knew there was only one answer that would be acceptable to him. With one finger, he moved the gun aside. "You're not going to mention you saw me here, and I'm not going to mention I saw you here. Or in Cougarville, for that matter. Agreed?"

Lolly nodded. *It's certainly been a day for secrets and deals!*

Suddenly Doc yanked the gun out of her hands. "And never point a gun unless you mean to use it," he said.

Sam came up from behind him and pulled Doc around by the shoulder. "And never be a doctor unless you mean to make people better," he said in a threatening voice that surprised Lolly. "That includes *all* people." He took the gun away from Doc. "This man bothering you, Lolly?"

Lolly wanted to say, "Yes," but she merely shook her head.

"You remember me, Doc?" Sam said. "Maybe you don't. I expect there's a lot you don't remember about what goes on in Cougarville."

"Okay, okay, easy goes it, boys," said Mo, who had worked his way out from behind the bar. "The past is the past, Sam. Let's all go on about our business."

Sam nodded and shoved past Doc, almost knocking him

down. "Good," Mo said. "Now let's settle down. Can I buy you boys a drink?"

Sam shook his head and stomped into the shooting gallery. Doc also declined, but before he left, he turned back to Lolly and glared directly into her eyes. He made a little *cluck* with his tongue, then walked out of the bar.

Lolly's hands shook, and it felt as if she'd stopped breathing.

Tick was looking at her with huge eyes. "Wow!"

"Yeah," Lolly said. "Wow."

Sam came up to her, the worried expression on his face deepening the lines around his eyes. "Ready for another round?"

"I—I've got to go!" Lolly said. She had to get out of the gallery. Seeing Doc had changed everything. It wasn't fun anymore. Now there was a sense of danger about the place and everyone in it. "If my mama comes home and finds me gone, she's going to kill me."

"Righto, young'un," Sam said. "I'll give you a lift."

At the corner of her block, Lolly said, "Better let me out here, Sam. I don't think it's a good idea for you to drive me up to the house."

"Nice houses around here," Tick observed.

"Real nice," Bob Bob said.

"Thanks, Sam, for the best day of my life," Lolly said and hopped out of the truck.

Sam rolled the window down and said, "Be good."

Lolly placed her hands on the door and whispered, "I'm

sorry about your wife and baby. Real, real, sorry."

Sam nodded, and she ran down the street. When she reached the Remington's, she stopped to look back. She saw Tick's face framed in the rear window of the old red truck as it rocked its way back to Cougarville.

As she made her way up the driveway, she wondered if Doc's daughter knew he took medicine. She felt sorry for her if she did know, and even sorrier if she had tried to get him to stop. Because, failing to get your daddy to understand hurts more than anything the grotto horses could do to you.

Maybe I'm not the only kid who can't make a deal with her father.

Footsteps rushed up the stairs, then Lolly felt her mother's cool hand pressing on her forehead. She turned onto her back and opened her eyes.

"I called you several times," her mother said. She was wearing a crisp backless white top and full black skirt. A black patent belt that accentuated her small waist matched the high heels. She would look perfect on the cover of *Vogue*.

"I guess I was sleeping."

"You feel hot as a pancake."

"That's just because I've been buried under the covers," Lolly said, hoping her voice sounded sleepy.

"You might have a flu. If you do, you need fluids. I'll get you some ice water." Her mother fussed over her, pulling away the covers, and felt her forehead again. "Take off that awful hat," she said and tugged the cap off.

"But Mama..."

"It's too hot and you have a fever!"

"But if Daddy comes home and finds me without it."

"I don't care!" her mother said, her voice tight. "He can shave my head if he wants, but I will not have you wearing it when you're sick. I shouldn't have left you. That damn art show isn't worth it. It's making us both sick."

The quaver in her voice was a sign that a head hammer wasn't far away.

Lolly watched her stride out of the room, massaging her temples and mumbling about the decorations for the luncheon being a disaster. Lolly knew it was only a matter of time before her mother went to bed.

Then Lolly remembered what Tick had told her about Sam and grief engulfed her completely. She felt sad for her mother, for poor dead Merilee, for the dead baby, for Bo. And sad because she was going to have to go to confession.

Barefoot as usual and wearing shorts and a halter, she pulled on the cap and went downstairs to sit on the top step of the porch and wait for her father to come home. A hot breeze ruffled around her, so she yanked off the cap, but pulled it back on again when she heard his car coming up the drive. It was precisely 5:30 p.m.

"Oh, oh, a reception committee," he said as he drew his long legs out of the Capri. "That means something's wrong. What's up, kiddo? I didn't get any calls from Sister Superior. You must not have busted any noses today."

When she looked at him, all Lolly could see were two paws clawing from the inside of the burlap bag.

"I didn't go to school today," she said. "Felt sick."

"You don't look sick," he said. "You okay now?"

"Sort of."

"Is your mother upstairs?"

"She's in bed with a head hammer." *How many times have I told you that?* she wondered. *How many times have you used her as an excuse to get out the vodka bottle?*

But he surprised her. "I know," he said. "When I called her from the office, she didn't sound well so I called Doc. He should be here any minute."

"Doc Pine is coming here? Now?"

"Yes. He said he'd be here in a jiffy."

"Just like that?"

"That's what a doctor does, Lolly." Her father mounted a step. "When somebody's sick, he leaves everything to go help."

"Would he do that for anybody?" she asked.

"He's supposed to," he said, taking the steps two at a time as if he couldn't wait to get to the kitchen. She wondered if Doc was making a bee-line for his kitchen at this same moment.

"How do you put somebody in jail when they commit murder?" she asked, seeing Bo's stiff body stretched out, his fur dull and dirty.

Her father stopped short. "What are you asking, exactly?"

"If somebody murders somebody, how do you go about putting them in jail?"

He put his briefcase down, came back down the steps, anchored his foot two steps up, and leaned his arm across his thigh. "That's a mighty big question, and it takes a mighty big answer. All kinds of things have to happen. What's brought this on?"

"I just want to know."

"In a nutshell, a person has be proven guilty in a court of law," he said. "After that, the judge sentences him or her, and then they either go to jail for a very long time or they're executed."

"Executed?" she said. "You mean killed?"

"That's right," he said as his eyes flicked over her. Lolly knew then that he was thinking there was something more behind her questions other than a sudden interest in the workings of the law. "Any more questions?"

She pictured Bo wrapped in a woolen blanket and lying in a deep hole. "But how do you get somebody proved?"

He took a deep breath. "I'm tired and I have a meeting tonight," he told her. "This is going to be a very long day. We'll talk another time." He reached out for her hand, but she pulled away.

"Please," she begged. "Tell me now."

"It sounds to me, Lolly Candolin, as if you have somebody in mind," he said frowning. "Quit beating around the bush."

She examined the white marks under her fingernails. The grotto horses had told her that every time she told a lie, a white mark appeared.

"The mother and baby that died in the gypsy camp. What if they died because Doc didn't get there in time? Not because he couldn't, but because he didn't care enough about them?"

"Where'd you get that kind of hogwash?" he asked, annoyed. "I don't have time for nonsense. Your daddy's tired and he needs a horn of corn. Let me know when Doc arrives. And not a word about this to him. Understand?"

"But what if..."

He whirled on her, arm straight, finger pointing. "I told you! I don't want to hear any more about babies and murder!"

"All right, all right," she said.

Lowering his arm, he stormed into the kitchen, leaving Lolly to wonder if crows and jays were flying over Bo's grave.

When Doc Pine knocked, Lolly opened the door. Doc had changed from what he'd worn in the bar to khaki trousers, a white as snow short-sleeved shirt, and an electric blue bow tie. She backed away, and he stepped in.

"How you be, Lolly girl?" he asked, indifferently.

They looked at each other for a moment. Should she say something about what had happened earlier? She stared directly into his eyes, something she never had done. Somehow, she felt it her right to confront him. After all, they were in cahoots, partners so to speak, and partners needed to communicate. She felt her lips draw into a tight line, an expression she had seen Sister Theodora take on when she was about to lower the boom.

"Cat got your tongue?" Doc said. He was acting as if they hadn't crossed paths today. "Well, okay," he said. "Guess I better get up there and see how your mama's doing." He nodded and trudged up stairs, Lolly following.

She heard her mother crying from behind the bedroom door. Doc knocked and her father said, "Come in."

Doc turned and looked back at her, not winking exactly, more like a narrowing of his eyes. "Best you stay out, Lolly," he said and closed the door behind him.

She sat at the top of the stairs and waited. A few minutes later, her father and Doc emerged.

"Your mama's going to be fine," Doc said, the lid of one eye falling to half-mast. "She's going to sleep for a while."

So what's new? Lolly thought. *You always put her to sleep. I wonder what she'd be like if she stopped taking the pills and shots?*

Her father's warm hand on her shoulder guided her downstairs. "Your grandfather's coming over to be with you. He'll make you dinner," he said. "Doc and I have a meeting at the Reclamation Board." He looked at his watch. "We have to get a move on or we'll be late."

He tapped her on the nose playfully and walked toward the front door.

Doc hesitated, then winked. *That must be the signal to say that our secret is safe*, she thought. She hated this alliance with Doc and wished it never existed.

"By the way, Lolly," he said. "Do you think I could borrow that twisted candle book for Pamela?"

Now what's he doing? Why not just leave?

"Sure," she said. "I'll have to look for it."

"We don't have time now," her father said from the doorway. "Have it for Doc when he brings me back. We won't be gone more than a couple of hours."

She watched her father and Doc hurry down the porch stairs.

"I understand Drake Halliday is planning to show up tonight," she heard her father say as he hurried around Doc's new Buick. "The bastard's dogging me."

"Don't worry, Regan," Doc replied. "Halliday's a weak sister and everybody knows it." He opened the door and slipped into the driver's seat. "Do you think we can get a consensus at this meeting?"

"Doubt it," her father said as he opened the door on the passenger side. "The gypsies are like the common cold. Nobody can figure out a cure for them."

As the car sped away, Lolly realized that she would have to cross over the levee tonight to get the book she had left at Tick's.

Chapter Eighteen

"**D**addy, the drug's taking over," her mother's eyes swam in their sockets. "I have to tell you what's in the fridge for dinner."

Lolly covered her mother with her favorite light silk throw. The sun washed the bedroom with deep magenta, and a warm breeze caused the gathered nylon curtains to flutter.

"Don't worry about dinner," Grandpa said and put down a large, flat package wrapped in brown paper. "My princess and I'll figure it out. You sleep. That's the best medicine for you right now, not these damn drugs. I don't think Regan should let that quack doctor give them to you."

"Daddy," her mother said. Her eyes closed momentarily but opened again.

"Before you go to the land of Blinken and Nod, Clarry, take a look at this." He tore the paper from the package to unveil a painting of a beautiful woman. She had short, white hair that capped a nut-brown oval face,

"Is this the lady you were telling us about?" her mother asked.

"The one and the same. What'd you think?"

Her mother gasped and leaned weakly toward the portrait. "Oh, Daddy. It's wonderful. I admit I'm surprised." Her mother's eyes flickered over the canvas. "I expected to see fur. I'm glad to see you're painting something other than wild animals for a change."

"This one has a wild soul," Grandpa said and turned the painting to get a better look at it. "Yes, a beautiful, wild soul." He looked back at her mother. "You like it?"

"Of the two of us, you're the real painter." Her mother fell back into the pillows and, smiling, closed her eyes.

Her grandfather motioned for Lolly to follow him, and they crept downstairs.

"Who's the lady in the painting?" Lolly asked.

"Willow," he said. "Her name is Willow." He wrapped up the painting and leaned it near the front door. Rubbing his hands together, he headed for the kitchen. "Let's see what we can rustle up for dinner."

"We don't have time," she said. "I have to go over the levee."

"What? You've been there again?"

"Yes."

"Princess, that's not a good idea. Those people are not so welcoming to us folks. They operate a little differently than we do."

"Yeah," she said. "They're nice and they like kids and they spend time with them and they don't drink and I buried Bo over there!"

"You found him?"

"Yep," she said. "And I need to go over there tonight to get my books. See, I loaned them to Tick so Nadia Greenberg wouldn't take her away from Sophie."

"Who's Tick?"

"My friend."

"And Sophie and Nadia Greenberg?"

"It's too complicated to explain right now, but if Daddy comes home and I don't have *The Sign of the Twisted Candles* to loan to Doc's daughter, I'm going to be in big trouble."

"The book's over there?"

"Yes," she said. "It and a few others. You don't have to come with me. I'm not afraid to go by myself. I'll go and be back before you even know I've been gone."

"Believe you me, princess, I'd know if you were gone. Besides, do you really think I'd let you go over there by yourself? Tell you what, tomorrow we'll go together."

"If I don't have that book when Daddy comes home tonight, I won't be alive tomorrow. He knows how careful I am with my books. I don't lose them. He'll force me to tell him where it is. I know him. Please, Grandpa, I'm begging you."

"No, princess. I just can't. Come on, now. Let's rustle us up some grub. You can tell your daddy you loaned the book to a friend and that you'll get it to Doc the next day or so."

If only he was right, she thought. But the fear that prickled up and down her spine told her he was wrong. If she lied to her father, he would browbeat her into the truth. And the truth would bring about consequences that she and her mother couldn't risk.

"That won't work, Grandpa. I *have* to get it tonight."

"I'm not letting you go over there. No way."

She threw him a kiss before bolting out the front door, galloping down the steps, and heading down the driveway.

"Lolly!" her grandfather called. "Lolly, please."

"Sorry, Grandpa," she called back. "I have to."

"All right, child. Hold on, I'm coming."

Lolly turned to see her grandfather stiffly maneuvering his way down the steps.

Grandpa, no. Please don't come with me.

But she waited for him to catch up.

"You're as stubborn as clotted milk is to pour," he said. "All right, we'll go. But no dilly-dallying. It'll be my hide tacked up on your garage door if we're not here when he comes back."

True, she thought, trying to ignore the image of her father punishing her grandfather.

She had to walk more slowly than she would have liked, but she knew that he was just as stubborn as she was and he was coming with her.

She held the flashlight in one hand and slipped her other arm around her grandfather's waist. Together they stumbled up the last couple of feet of the levee and onto the road. Grandpa's breath stuttered in short gasps and sweat shone on his face.

"Whew!" he said, his chest wheezing. "That was quite a climb. What're you trying to do to this old man?"

"You stay here," Lolly told him. "I'll run down to Tick's place, get the books, and be back in a snap."

"What? You think your grandfather's a wimp?" He pulled his handkerchief out and dabbed at his face. "Give me a minute." The cover of night lowered itself over the valley and gold light burned in the windows of the trailers. "It's been a long time since I've star gazed. My God, it's beautiful. It's like looking at a jeweler's cloth with all the diamonds laid out for you to admire."

Lolly slipped her hand into her grandfather's. "Come on, Grandpa, we better hurry."

"Okay, show me the way."

She switched on the flashlight, and they started down the

road in the direction of the camp.

She led the way down the easiest berm path, cautioning her grandfather as they went and keeping a hand on her cap: she didn't have time to make the trip twice tonight.

Once at the bottom, they cut through the warren of vans. When they came to Tick's, Lolly jogged up the steps and peered through the screen door. Tick was sitting at the table reading *The Sign of the Twisted Candles*.

"Pssst," Lolly hissed.

"Lolly!" She dashed to the door. "Come on in. I ain't never been so glad to see anyone. I love this book. I'm almost at the end."

"I have to make this fast," Lolly interrupted. "I need my books. Sorry, but my father wants me to loan the one you're reading to Doc's daughter and I have to give it to him tonight."

"Golly," Tick said, her face falling. "A creep like Doc has a kid?" Her eyes flicked past Lolly. "Who's that?"

"My grandfather."

Tick's hands flew up to her mouth. "A real grandfather?"

"Yes," Lolly said, grinning. "He's real."

"You lucky bum," Tick said, glancing over at the newspaper clippings she had framed. "To tell you the truth, Lolly, I don't got no grandfathers. Not a real one. Can I meet yours?"

"Sure," Lolly said. She and Tick went outside. Grandpa extended his hand. When Tick took it, her eyes shone as if she were meeting a king.

"Good evening, Tick," he said. "My, my, that hair. I doubt I've seen a prettier halo on any angel."

Tick giggled. "Want some lemonade or crackers?"

"No, thank you," he said. "I 'spect we better keep on going."

"A real grandfather!" Tick exclaimed. "I never seen one in

the flesh. How about some Jello or milk? My mama buys special milk. We mix the cream into it ourselves."

Lolly found herself wondering why she had never realized how special her grandfather made her feel.

"That's mighty kind of you," he said, "but we have to get home before Lolly's daddy returns."

"Can you get the books?" Lolly said. "Don't worry. I'll bring them back. I just need them for a little while."

"Okay," Tick bounced into the trailer that flickered with candlelight, and returned with the cloth bag sagging with books. "Do you really have to go?" Tick asked. "It ain't every day I get to talk to a real grandfather. Maybe I could give him one of my mama's bracelets."

"Where is your mama?" Lolly asked.

"Over at Andrea's. Mama says Andrea's 'bout to hang up her old dress." Tick whirled around to Grandpa. "Want to see our secret?"

"Your secret?"

"We don't have time," Lolly said.

"Want to see a cougar?" Tick asked.

"A *cougar?*" he repeated. His eyes crinkled. "You don't mean a real cougar."

"Sure do. It'll only take a couple of minutes. Hurry!"

"Come on, Lolly," Grandpa said, as Tick tugged at his arm. "I've never seen a cougar up close. We've haven't been gone all *that* long."

They hurried through the maze of trailers, the pungent scent of the cougar growing as they got closer. When they reached the cage and Lolly shined her light on him, the cougar raised his head. He sniffed and a deep, breathy growl rolled from his throat.

"That don't mean he's mad," Tick said. "He makes lots of

different kinds of noises."

Grandpa moved closer. "He's flat out magnificent," he said, and curled his gnarled fingers through the metal fencing. "Look at that wonderful creature. All that beautiful wildness. What I wouldn't give to paint him."

Tick came up and leaned against him, both hands on his arm. "He's really friendly," she said eagerly. "He loves to be petted and it's real good for him to be touched. Want to see me go into the cage and pet him? I'll go get Bob Bob and the key."

"No, Tick," Lolly said. "We don't have time."

"I'll be right back."

"Wait," Lolly said, but Tick was gone. When she and Grandpa followed her, they found her standing on the porch of Bob Bob's trailer pounding on his door.

"Bob Bob! It's Tick and Lolly and…" She looked back at them. "What do I call a real grandfather?"

"You can call me Jeb, or, if Lolly doesn't mind, you can call me Grandpa, too," he said.

A smile broke across Tick's face as she turned to Lolly for permission. "What do you think?"

Lolly had never thought about sharing her grandfather with anyone. *But, Tick would be a good one to start with!* She smiled and nodded.

"Grandpa," Tick whispered. Then she yelled, "Tick, Lolly, and Grandpa are out here. We want to pet Survie!"

Still no answer. Tick's face fell. "I guess Bob Bob ain't home."

"Nope," Lolly said. "Another time, Tick." The minutes were speeding by and even Grandpa didn't seem to realize it. In fact, he seemed as fascinated by this place as she had been the first time.

"Wait," Tick said. She turned the handle and Bob Bob's

door opened.

"Tick, what're you doing?" Lolly asked.

"Nothing," Tick said. She disappeared inside. Seconds later, she stood on the porch with a key dangling from her hand. "I'm borrowing it. I know Bob Bob won't mind." She jumped the steps and headed back to the cage.

Lolly ran after Tick and caught her by the arm. "Sam will have your hide. You know the rule."

"Rules are rules, Tick," Grandpa said.

"Look, Sam says we must take very good care of Survie. And Survie's lonely. So, to take *really* good care of him, we need to go into the cage and give him a good scratch." Tick ran toward the cage and slipped the key into the lock. It wouldn't turn.

Bob Bob emerged from a stand of cottonwood trees opposite the cage. "What are you doin', my friend Tick?"

"Bob Bob!" Tick exclaimed. "This is Grandpa and he wants to see me go into the cage and pet Survie."

"Now, Tick," Grandpa said. "That's not exactly true, you know."

"Please, Bob Bob," Tick pleaded.

"Sam says it ain't right for you to go into the cage, my friend Tick," Bob Bob said as he continued toward them.

"Please," Tick begged. "It ain't a good idea to let Survie get lonely."

"Sam says nobody but me goes into the cage when he ain't here," Bob Bob said.

"I know," Tick said, "but Grandpa's here. He's a *real* grandpa, so that makes a difference."

"We don't have time," Lolly insisted. "We have to go."

"She's got that right," Grandpa said. "We've got to be getting back."

"Please, not yet," Tick said, slipping her hand into Grandpa's. "We have to do something special for you." Tick jumped up and down. "Please, Bob Bob, please. Let me go into the cage. I want to show Grandpa how brave I am, and see if I can make Survie purr like Lolly does."

"Another time," Grandpa said.

"No!" Tick said. "Now! Bob Bob, *please*. I mighten never get another chance to show a real Grandpa how brave I can be. And he'll go away thinkin' I ain't nothin' special. I bet if you could show *your* grandpa how brave you are, you'd do it!"

"Sam says nobody but me goes in the cage unless he's here," Bob Bob said.

"Grandpa's older than Sam," Tick said. "Don't that count?"

"My dear child, I'll come again," Grandpa said. "We really do have to go."

Lollie watched Tick clinging to her grandfather's arm like a koala bear hugging a eucalyptus tree, and she knew there was only one way to satisfy her.

"For cripe's sake, Bob Bob," Lolly said. "Let her give the cougar a scratch so she'll be still. It'll take about five seconds and then we can go."

"Yes!" Tick said, breaking into a jig. "Five seconds! Now watch, Grandpa. Watch real good."

"I'm watching," Grandpa said, giving Lolly a reassuring look that told her they'd be leaving soon.

Bob Bob took the key from Tick, slipped it into the lock, turned it, and yanked the padlock open.

"Are you watchin'?" Tick asked Grandpa as Bob Bob pushed open the door of the cage.

"Yes, Tick," he said. "I'm watching."

Tick stepped into the cage, and the cougar's eyes closed to slits.

"Hey, there boy," Tick said, her voice low and soothing, trying to imitate Sam. "Hey, you beautiful boy. It's Tick, Survie. I've brought someone special. I've brought a real grandpa to see you."

She extended her hand, and the cougar craned his neck to smell her palm.

"See?" Tick said. "He's real friendly. Lolly, come in and make him purr."

"No!" Grandpa said quickly. "She's not to go in there. I'll go in. I've lived a lot of years and painted a lot of wild animals, but never have I touched one."

"Maybe you shouldn't," Lolly said. "Survie doesn't know you."

"I'd like to touch something wild before I move on from this world," Grandpa said. "Run my hand over a true natural being."

Before Lolly could try to stop him, he had pushed his way into the cage. Pressing her face against the mesh of the cage, her flashlight casting a pool of light in front of her, she watched Tick step aside and make room for Grandpa. Beside her, Bob Bob squatted on his haunches, one hand on the lock.

"Put your hand out and let him get a sniff," Tick instructed. "And don't make any fast moves."

As Grandpa slowly stepped forward, the cougar gave a throaty hiss and pounced. In an instant, the cage became a maelstrom of fur, claws, and teeth. Tick screamed and clawed blindly at the wire, trying to find the door. Lolly rushed forward, but Bob Bob grabbed her arm and threw her to the ground behind him. As she got to her feet, she saw the giant reach into the cage and snatch Tick. Grandpa was on the ground, curled into a ball, his cries for help drowned out by the cougar's shrieks.

"Grandpa," Lolly cried. "Get out of there!"

But the cougar was on top of him, massive claws tearing his clothes, raking his skin, raising streams of blood.

Lolly pounded on the cage and screamed as Tick stood frozen, watching. Bob Bob swayed back and forth.

"Help him, Bob Bob!" Lolly cried.

He continued rocking. "Sam said no go in the cage...Sam said no go in the cage."

Lolly dashed to a nearby pile of old hubcaps and broken tools, rummaging desperately for something—anything—she could use to help Grandpa. Finally, her fingers closed on a rusted tire-iron and she turned back to the cage.

The cougar had clamped his jaws around Grandpa's throat and was shaking him like Bo used to shake mice. She knew there wasn't much time. She thrust the tire iron into Bob Bob's hand.

"Help him! Please, help him!"

Bob Bob's eyes seemed to catch fire and he charged into the cage brandishing the tire-iron, a deep bellow issuing from his chest. He grabbed Grandpa's blood-covered arm, the torn flesh hanging like frayed curtains, and pulled. The snarling cougar would not relinquish his hold.

"Let him go!" Bob Bob waved the tire iron.

The cougar hissed loudly, the whites of his eyes shining in the dim light. Bob Bob moved in swinging the iron club fiercely, and the cat backed off, slinking to the far side of the cage. Bob Bob slipped his hands under Grandpa's arms and pulled him out, slamming the cage door behind him and snapping the lock.

"Lolly...Lolly," Grandpa moaned.

"I'm here, Grandpa. We need to call an ambulance," Lolly wailed. "Where's a phone?"

"Sam said no go in cage...Sam said no go in cage."

She whirled on Tick. "Where's a telephone?"

Tick blinked as if just awakened. "Over the levee," she said in a hoarse voice. "At Tony's Grocery."

"Go!" Lolly ordered. "Go call. Hurry, Tick, unless you want him to die!"

Chapter Nineteen

In the hospital, Lolly laid her head on her mother's lap while her father paced the waiting room.

"What in the hell were you doing in the goddamn gypsy camp?" he demanded. "Especially after I told you never to go over there? And what in God's name were you doing?"

"She's exhausted," her mother said. "You can interrogate her when we get home, Regan."

"No," he said. "She's going to answer some questions now. Lolly, I want to know how many times you've gone over the levee."

She sat up, her face striped with levee dirt, her hands ingrained with grime and grease.

"I don't know."

"Twice, three times?"

"More."

"Ten, twenty?"

"Something like that."

"You defied my rule?"

"Yes," she said. "I'm sorry."

"You're sorry now that your grandfather's in there fighting for his life."

Lolly continued to cry silently. Her mother stroked her

head. "I have a feeling he's going to make it. He's a strong man. He's going to be all right."

Lolly stood. "*Haram infata cum…*"

Her father turned to look at her, his eyes opaque with fury.

"*Lo epoodo sonesta tum. Ray deponda slatin fey—*"

"What in the hell is that?" he demanded.

"Nothing," Lolly sniffled. "A nonsense rhyme. It only works if you believe in it."

"It's gypsy talk. That's what it is," he said, flatly. "Goddamn gypsy talk. So help me God, Lolly Candolin, if you ever…"

"Not now!" her mother said with startling authority.

Her father became silent. Tears continued to roll down Lolly's face. She felt as though she was the levee and the winter river had broken through her banks.

"Baby, don't," her mother said, trying to soothe her. "Let's pray for your grandfather. Praying will help him. And us."

"If Grandpa dies will he still be able to see me?" Lolly asked through her sobs.

"Well…" her mother began, "it's difficult to say…"

"It's *easy* to say," her father cut in. "You die, you're dead. That's it. No hocus pocus can change that."

"That'll do, Regan," her mother said, her back straightening as Lolly nestled closer to her. "She's had enough for one night."

"Don't you tell me what to say to my own daughter!"

The waiting room door swung open and Tick, Sophie, and Sam came in.

"Tick!" Lolly pulled out of her mother's arms. "What are you doing here?" Lolly was confused. She wanted to run to Tick and hug her, but wasn't it Tick's fault that her grandfather had gotten hurt? Wasn't it Tick who had insisted Grandpa see the cougar? Wasn't it Tick who had to show how brave she was?

Yes! And it was Tick who had convinced Bob Bob to let her go into the cage, Tick who had invited Grandpa to go in with the cougar.

Without a leap or a skip, Tick said, "I'm sorry." Tears shimmered in her eyes as she pressed close to Sophie, who was painted into a white Spandex skirt and a print halter that exposed the mounds of her breasts.

"Mr. Candolin," Sam said. He wore his dirty red shirt and snakeskin belt, but his boots were clean. He rubbed his hand against his jeans, before thrusting it out. "Sam Maple. I'm real sorry about your father-in-law. I have to tell you that the cougar's mine."

Lolly's father looked from Sam to Sophie and finally to Tick. "Get out," he said. "My family's going through a difficult time. Get out."

"Daddy," Lolly said, "these are my friends. And none of this is their fault. You can't blame them. If I hadn't been so stupid and disobeyed you, none of this would have happened."

"Get out!" her father roared.

Sam nodded and opened the door for them to leave.

"Come on, baby," Sophie said, gathering up Tick. "These folks need to be alone."

"But I have to know if Grandpa's gonna be all right," Tick said.

"I don't think he's ready to hang up his old dress," Lolly told her. "Something tells me he's going to wear it a bit longer."

Tick, her mother, and Sam backed out of the room.

"You'll be hearing from me, Sam Maple!" Lolly's father spat out the words. "You haven't heard the end of this!"

Lolly buried her face in her mother's lap.

"White trash," her father went on. "They think they're untouchable. Well, I'll show them."

The door swung open again. This time it was Doc. Lolly stood with her mother, who asked, "How is he?"

"The cat was close to making dinner out of that old man," Doc replied wearily. "But he's much too tough, even for a cougar. He's going to make it, but I'm keeping him here for several days. I want to monitor him. Need to be sure none of those wounds get infected."

"Can we see him?" Lolly asked.

"For a few minutes," Doc said. No winks or secret communication. This time he looked genuinely worried. "He's had a hard fight and he's tired."

She and her parents followed Doc down the long hall. "Remember, only a couple of minutes. And Regan," Doc put his hand on her father's arm. "Go easy, my friend."

In the room, Grandpa lay on his back, attached by tubes to upside-down bottles hanging from stainless steel staffs. Bandages covered his throat, arms, and legs, with a huge one around his chest.

"Hey there, princess," he said in a raspy voice. "Before you say one word, I want you to get it out of your head that this was anybody's fault but my own." He raised his hand and motioned for her father to come closer. "Regan, listen to me. Don't be hard on Lolly. This wasn't her doing."

"I understand," her father said. He patted Grandpa's hand, but he glared at Lolly.

"How many people get to touch nature in its prime?" Grandpa winked at her mother. "This old man did. Boy, do I have a story to tell. I wouldn't trade that rumble for a million bucks."

"Okay, Lolly, your lion tamer needs to rest," Doc said and, spreading his arms, swept the three of them out of the room.

Her father's hand on her shoulder seared through her

blouse, and he didn't say a word until they were out of the hospital and back into the warm night.

"Consequences," he whispered as he opened the car for her.

Lolly wanted to tell him that there would be consequences for everyone. She knew that now. He could punish her if he wanted to, but that wouldn't be the end of it. Not for him, not for any of them.

Chapter Twenty

The scene in the cougar's cage played over and over again in Lolly's head, the fear and shame of having let Grandpa get near the big cat clogging her throat.

Soon as they got home, her father walked directly to the kitchen, and she heard the clink of the vodka bottle against the jelly glass.

It took all of her energy to haul herself upstairs. She slipped on her baby doll pajamas, but she was too tired to brush her teeth. When her mother came in to hear her prayers and sat on the bed brushing the stubble of her hair with cool fingers, the weight of her guilt seemed too enormous to bear.

"In the name of the Father, and of the Son and of..." Her voice trailed off. *Listen to me, God!*

"Go on," her mother said.

"Dear God, thank you for letting Grandpa not have to hang up his old dress yet, and thank you for making him my grandpa," she whispered into her closed hands. "God bless Mama and Daddy, Sam, Sophie, and especially Tick, even though I'm so mad at her I could spit. And don't forget Bob Bob, God. He needs your help, too. Amen." She made the sign of the cross.

"Who's Bob Bob?" her mother asked.

"My friend," Lolly said. She turned over and closed her eyes. "One of my best friends."

For a moment, Lolly had lost what day it was or even what had occurred the day before. It was as though she had awakened empty. She felt sweaty and her pajamas stuck to the sides of her body. She lay quietly, her arm shielding her eyes from the light as she tried to figure what it was that hovered just outside her head.

Then she saw the dust-covered bag of books. She had managed to keep it near her, through all that had happened, like some kind of talisman that would make everyone safe if the Nancy Drew book was presented to Doc Pine.

Men's voices threaded up the stairway from downstairs. One voice belonged to her father, but she didn't recognize the other.

She scooted to the door, opened it a crack, and listened.

"When can we go, Moose?" her father was speaking. "I want this done as soon as possible."

"Moose" had to be Moose Perry, the sheriff.

"In about an hour," the sheriff said. "Maybe longer. Have to get the paper work in order. Call me around ten, and I'll let you know the status of everything. We need a warrant and all, but it'll be done today, Regan. You can count on that." Their voices trailed off as they went toward the front door.

What was the sheriff doing here so early in the morning? What was a warrant? And why was her father home? It was Friday. He was always at the office no later than seven on weekdays.

Her mother came to the door. "Oh, you're up," she said. Dressed in blue pedal pushers and a paler blue sleeveless blouse, she looked like she'd stepped out of a magazine ad for deodorant.

"I'm late for school," Lolly said.

"You don't have to go," her mother told her. "I talked to Sister. We decided your time today would be better spent with your grandfather. Good news. He's feeling better. Maybe you can read your essay to him. I'll get your breakfast while you get dressed. Then I'll drop you by the hospital on my way to the art club."

"Why was the sheriff here?" Lolly asked.

"On business, I suppose," her mother said, and headed for the door.

"What business?"

"You know your father doesn't talk to me about office things. Hurry up. Grandpa needs you."

"But why would they do their business here?" Lolly insisted. "What is it that they're going to get done today?"

"I don't know."

"You do know. Tell me!"

"Please, Lolly. Everyone's a little on edge. Last night was hard on us all. Get dressed."

Her mother hurried downstairs and, from the landing, Lolly saw her father pass into his study. Dressing quickly into jeans, a green and white-checkered t-shirt, and tennis shoes, she went downstairs to stand outside the door to her father's study.

"Well," he said, looking up from the pile of papers he was flipping through. "How are you this morning?"

"All right, I guess."

"Lolly," he said quietly. "I've always taught you to do what you think is right. Do you think it was right to disobey me and go over the levee?"

"No—well, in a way," she said.

"Yes or no? Do you think it was right to disobey me?"

"No."

"But you went ahead and did it anyway."

"I helped fix it so Nadia Greenberg wouldn't take Tick away from Sophie. That was right. Do you know Nadia Greenberg?"

He ignored her question. "I've told you many times *not* to go over there. Correct?"

"Correct," she said, and chewed on her cuticle while he patiently tapped his fingers on the desk. "What's a warrant?"

"Why do you ask?" He sat back deep in his leather chair and smoothed his mustache.

"What's a warrant?" she repeated.

"The law says you can't enter on to somebody's property without one." He clapped the book shut, anger pouring from his eyes.

She ventured a few inches deeper into the room where he barricaded himself nightly and played his saxophone. "Whose property are you going to enter?"

He left the chair, went to the window, and yanked a cord that sent the Venetian blinds clattering up and caused her to jump. Then he raised the window. The warmth of the outdoors invaded the coolness of the room.

"Why does Moose Perry need to get a warrant today?"

"Go find your mother, Lolly." He sat down again and opened a file. "I have work to do."

"But I want to know whose property you are..."

"Go!" he barked, and she backed out of the room.

Her mother drove up the hospital's circular drive and stopped in the passenger zone. "I'll be back about one," she said, kissing Lolly's cheek. "Can you find your way to Grandpa's room?"

"Yes."

"If you can't, just ask at the reception desk."

"I can find it."

"Watch that tone of voice, young lady."

Lolly climbed out of the car, hauling the bag of books with her, and watched her mother drive off. It was unusual for her mother to scold her. But, since last night everything had changed.

Grandpa's room smelled stale. He was sleeping as she put down the books and kissed his hand because she couldn't reach his face. Checking out a covered tray, she found two eggs over easy sitting like stained linen beside a piece of white toast curled at its edges. From the large window, she could see the levee that surrounded the town looming on the horizon, and imagined Cougarville on the other side.

The law says you can't enter somebody's property without a warrant.

The connection snapped inside her head: her father and Moose Perry were going to Cougarville. That's why they needed a warrant!

"I love you, Grandpa," she whispered in his ear, then left the hospital for the levee—the one place she wasn't supposed to go.

Sweat dripped from under Lolly's woolen cap as she charged up the steps of Tick's trailer and banged on the door.

"Hey, Lolly," Tick said, holding open the screen. "I'm glad you're here. I need to..."

"Have you seen my daddy or the sheriff?" Lolly asked.

"I ain't seen nobody," Tick said gloomily. "Mama's in town, and she told me not go out for nothin' or nobody."

"This is all your fault, you know," Lolly said, turning.

"Wait!" Tick said.

"I've got to go," Lolly said, jumping off the stairs and hitting the ground hard.

"But, Lolly!"

"Not now!" Lolly turned and zigzagged through the trailers until she reached Bob Bob's. His door was standing open.

"Bob Bob?" she called. No answer. She stepped inside. One wall was covered with cheaply framed black and white pictures of what appeared to be the same man in different stages of life: young, middle-aged, and old. She wondered if they were photographs of Bob Bob's father who'd died when Bob Bob was in jail. Rifles resting in wooden gun racks hung on the wall.

Clattering out of Bob Bob's trailer, she dashed toward Sam's. Just as she rounded the corner, she saw them.

Her father stood, legs apart, in an unfamiliar pose. He was dressed in a linen suit, his white shirt opened at the neck in a way that made him appear like a stranger to her. Beside him, Moose Perry loomed, a pillar of khaki in his starched uniform, a red rash on his pocked face blooming in the hot sun. His silver sheriff's star was pinned to his shirt and he carried a rifle. Next to him stood Sam, his face hard, his mouth closed in a tight line as though something terrible trembled inside of him. Behind Sam, Bob Bob stood silently.

Moose walked up to the cougar's cage.

"No!" Lolly screamed, running into the circle of men.

"What the hell are you doing here?" her father demanded as she threw herself against him, pounding at his chest with her fists.

"Please don't hurt Survie! Please!" Tears spurted from Lolly's eyes. "He didn't know what he was doing. It's a rule. Nobody goes into the cage without Sam, and Grandpa went in and made a quick move. The cougar just followed his nature!"

Her father pushed her aside and walked slowly over to Sam. He stopped when he was only inches away and looked him straight in the eye. About the same height, they appeared to be two pieces of wooden sculpture, one finely honed, the other rough and splintery.

"Consequences," her father said.

Sam said something back, but Lolly couldn't make out the words.

"Want to say that so everyone can hear?" her father asked him. His voice was mean.

Sam's jaw worked so hard it looked as if it might grind his teeth to powder. Then he turned his back on her father.

"You hear that, Moose?" her father said. "The gypsy here said he'd like to shoot you and me in the head."

Sam whirled around. "That's not what I said, Candolin, and you know it."

"The sheriff's my witness. He heard you threaten both of us. Threaten our lives."

Sam's hands curled into fists.

Lolly ran to her father. "Please, Daddy. Don't hurt the cougar."

Her father yanked her roughly behind him. "You heard that, didn't you Moose? You heard what he said?"

Moose Perry nodded.

Lolly wiggled out of his grasp. "Daddy, he's a good cat. It was instinct that made him attack Grandpa. He couldn't help it. He's never hurt Sam, and when Bob Bob feeds him, he doesn't hurt him." She looked around wildly until she found Bob Bob. "Has Survie ever hurt you, Bob Bob?"

"The cougar never hurt Bob Bob," Bob Bob said.

"He practically smiles when Tick pets him, and when I scratch his jowls, he purrs. He's just like any cat only he's..."

"You were in the cage with that animal?"

"Not exactly."

"Don't lie to me."

He was talking to her but he was watching Sam.

"Yes, I went in the cage. But Sam was with me, and the cougar was quiet and calm and sweet. It was just that Grandpa surprised him."

"You took my daughter into that cage?" her father said, his mouth shaping into a snarl. "I'll get you, Sam Maple." Then he whipped around to Moose Perry. "Let me get her out of here, then you go ahead and get this thing over with."

"You gonna kill our cougar?" Bob Bob said, stepping forward.

"Yeah, Bob Bob," Moose said. "I'm going to kill your cougar." The sheriff raised the rifle to his shoulder.

"No!" Lolly screamed. "Please, no!"

"Lolly, I will not have this!" her father said. "Go!"

"He's not bad, Daddy. I promise you, he's not. He's just a cat!"

"Enough!" her father bellowed. "This is a dangerous animal and he has be destroyed."

"Lolly," Sam said, his voice quiet as he squatted down beside her. "You're makin' it harder for Survie. He did somethin' bad and there ain't nothin' you or I can say that'll change that."

The flat voice of Bob Bob caused everyone to turn toward him. "Moose Perry kill my daddy." Bob Bob swayed from side to side, his voice expressionless. "Moose Perry kill my daddy and now he wants to kill Survie."

Moose looked at Bob Bob. "If I'd a known this simpleton was going to be here, I'd a brought a deputy. Simmer down, Bob Bob. You got me once, but you can count on it that you won't get me again."

"Moose Perry kill my daddy."

"Go on, Bob Bob," Sam said. "Go on home."

"Moose Perry kill my daddy."

"Go back to your trailer!" Sam said again, this time with an edge of real authority.

Bob Bob looked at Sam and blinked, then switched his gaze to Regan Candolin. "Go back to trailer," he said. Raising his hand, palm out in a kind of salute to the cougar, he turned and shuffled away.

"You go, too," Sam said to Lolly. "Say good-bye to Survie and let him hang up his old dress without no fuss."

A sob hiccuped from Lolly's throat. "Can I say good-bye to him from inside the cage?" she asked. "Can I make him purr one more time?"

"Absolutely not!" her father told her.

"You tell him goodbye from here," Sam said and, as he rose, he muttered something to her father.

"What was that, Maple?" her father demanded. "You threatening us again?"

"Say your good-bye and go," Sam told Lolly, his voice thin and tight, as if he were holding everything inside of him.

She turned toward the cage. "Good-by, Survie," she said. "If you need me, come to me in my dreams. I'll be there."

Scratching her cheeks as if they were the cougar's, she then flung her hands forward as if sending Survie her affection. In response, he stretched out his legs toward her, his paws kneading the ground. To everyone's astonishment, he purred.

"Wait for me up on top of the levee, Lolly," her father told her, pushing her away. "When we finish, I'll take you home."

She began running as fast as she could, the echo of her father's voice scraping at her heart. When she reached the levee, she climbed to the top.

"I hate him!" she shrieked, picking up rocks from the road and throwing them wildly.

Bang!

She froze.

Bang!

Lolly snatched the black woolen cap off her head and raised it to the screaming crows flying in confused circles overhead.

"Good-bye, Survie," she said, tears running down her face. "When you get where you're going, try and find Bo!"

Chapter Twenty-One

She climbed the levee, but the surface dirt gave way and she slid back. She heard the crack of the gun and saw the cougar's skull exploding, a spray of blood forming a stylized halo like those around the heads of holy children in her Catechism. It happened over and over: the climbing, the slipping, the gunshot, the exploding skull....

Then she slid back, *thunk*, into her bedroom. A breeze played with the window curtains as the unseasonable heat gave way to a cool front. In the corner of her room, the cougar lay under cottonwood trees next to a slow summer river. Bo was curled beneath the bigger cat's tawny blaze, and both of them purred in unison.

"Lolly." Her mother stood over her. "Lolly, you were talking in your sleep."

Lolly rubbed her eyes and looked at her mother, who looked different, older somehow. Sadness had collected under her skin and her eyes were in caves of shadows. A slight tremble seemed to have inhabited her hands.

"How do you feel?" her mother asked her.

"All right," she murmured. The heat had returned and the air in her room burned.

"You've been sleeping on and off for three days, Lolly," her mother told her. "Doc's been here twice to check on you, and I've called him again. I want him to take a look at you now that you're awake." Her mother kissed her cheek and hurried out of the room.

Lolly wanted to call out that she didn't want that man near her, but the dream had stolen her voice and her strength.

The only person she wanted to see was her grandfather. Just the thought of him brought all the sad things rushing back to her: *Bo is dead. The cougar is dead. Grandpa's in the hospital.*

Her mother returned and sat on the bed. "Doc'll be here in a few minutes," she said. "I'm worried about you, baby."

Lolly tossed restlessly. She wasn't sure what day it was, and she didn't want to ask because that would show her confusion.

"Grandpa," she said. "How's Grandpa?"

"He's home, sweetheart, and he seems to be no worse for wear. He'll be over to see you this afternoon. Can you eat something now?"

"Grandpa," Lolly said again. There was no other person on earth that could help her now.

"He's coming to see you today. I promise."

Lolly turned her head away. She'd had her fill of their empty words.

She heard the voices of her father and Doc Pine outside the door. "Thanks for coming over, Doc," her father said. "She's a bit under the weather."

"I'll take a look at her in a minute," Doc said. "I suppose that since you got the case, you're spending every waking moment at the shooting gallery?"

"Not much, Doc. After umty-ump years of making it my weekend watering hole, like you, I pretty much know the place like the back of my hand."

Case? What case are they talking about? And what does it have to do with the shooting gallery?

The door to her room opened.

"Well, young lady!" Doc stood in the doorway, clean and pressed, his skin scrubbed pink. "I hear you're a little off your oats."

Lolly pulled the sheet over her head. "I don't want to see him," she said so low that only her mother heard.

"Don't be silly, baby. Doc's here to help you. Come on." Her mother tugged at the sheet. "Let him take a look."

"That's all right. Clarissa, why don't you go downstairs and get a dish of ice cream for our girl."

Lolly heard the sound of the door closing and the creak of the white wicker chair beside her bed.

"Ah, me," Doc said. "Sometimes it's difficult being an intelligent kid. You're a bright girl, but going over the levee, or to the shooting gallery, for that matter, wasn't so smart."

Lolly yanked the sheet off her face and glared at him. He looked thin and more papery than usual. *You hypocrite*, she thought. *Is it smart for you to go the bar in the middle of the day?*

Getting out of bed, her head reeled and she lurched toward the book bag, pulled out *The Sign of the Twisted Candles*, and thrust the book into Doc's hands.

"There," she said as she crawled back into bed. "You got what you came for."

Doc opened his black bag, stashed the book, and pulled out his stethoscope. He put the rubber ends into his ears.

"Raise your jammies and let me take a listen."

With both hands, she held the sheet against her chest. Doc tried to loosen it, but she wouldn't let go. He leaned back in the chair. "Remember what you asked me? About medicine for your daddy? The answer is: there isn't any. You see, Lolly, often people can't help the things they do."

"I don't want a drunk and a murderer to be my doctor," Lolly said, her voice flat and quiet.

Doc's face hardened. Taking the stethoscope out of his ears, he coiled it, and put it back into his bag before clamping his fingers over her wrist to take her pulse. He was close enough for her to count the freckles and moles on his beak-like nose.

"Normal," he said. "You've been through quite an experience, miss. Seeing your grandfather mauled by a wild animal and not being able to do anything about it. That in itself is enough to put any child into a state of shock." He cocked his head. "I'm going to give your mama some pills for you to take. They'll calm the willie-waws in your stomach."

"I don't have willie-waws and I won't take the pills!"

"Lots of things have happened to you since you took to going over the levee," Doc said. "Lots of things. Certainly, it hasn't enhanced your manners."

"If you'd gone over when Sam called you, Merilee and the baby would be alive today," Lolly told him. "You didn't go to help them because they're gypsies. You didn't go because you want the people across the levee to go away. You didn't go because you and my daddy think you're better than they are. You killed that woman and you killed that baby and that's why you go to Chiseler's to drink. I think you'd better go to confession or you'll go to hell when it's time to hang up your old dress."

Doc's flaky skin paled and he fell back in his chair. Lolly was shocked at the power of her punch. His eyes wandered the ceiling and, for a few seconds, she thought that he'd stopped breathing. Then he pulled out of the chair, did an old-fashioned bow, and opened her bedroom door.

Lolly saw her mother, standing just outside the door, pull back as though she were startled and Lolly wondered how much she had heard.

"What's wrong with her?" her mother asked.

"Nothing but a good dose of the truth," Doc said.

"What truth?" her mother asked, her face contorting in worry.

Doc's back stiffened as though he had just enough military discipline to get him out of the room and down the stairs.

"Lolly, what was Doc talking about?"

Lolly turned her face to the wall.

"All right, we'll let it go for now," her mother said, straining to paste a smile on her face. "How about something to eat? I have some cold roast chicken and grandpa's homegrown tomatoes, his beefsteak specials, and a slice of watermelon."

"You knew, didn't you?" Lolly got out of bed and went into the bathroom, splashed water on her face, and dressed in shorts and a sleeveless shirt.

"Knew what?" Her mother busied herself with straightening the bed covers.

"You knew what they were going to do to the cougar. You knew what the warrant was for. You and Daddy always tell me to do the right thing. Do you think it was right to kill the big cat?"

"Lolly, please. That *thing* almost killed your grandfather."

"I *know!* I saw the claws and the blood and heard the—the sounds!" Gulps of tears rushed up, scalding her eyes. "If it hadn't been for Bob Bob, Grandpa would be dead! But the cougar was an animal like Bo. What did you do when Daddy threw Bo off the levee? Nothing! You never do anything but go along with him. You're just like him!"

"Those are pretty rough words, princess." Her grandfather had stepped into the room.

At the sound of his voice, the sobs broke through, big

wracking hiccups, and she ran over and hugged him for a long time. His rough hands petted her nubby hair and rubbed her shoulder.

"Are you all right, Grandpa?" she asked through her tears.

"I'm fine," he said. "But I don't think I can say the same for you."

She stepped back to take a better look at him. Stains of blood had seeped through the large square of gauze taped around his throat. Another bandage covered his lower arm.

She shuddered. "I'm so mad at that Tick. If it hadn't been for her, you'd never gone into the cage."

"Come on over and sit down," Grandpa said. He patted the bed, and motioned for Clarissa to leave them alone. "You know, princess," he said softly, "sometimes it's like playing a game of pool. You hit the eight ball and it hits another ball and it hits another. All because you connected with the first one. When I went into the cage with the cougar, I hit the eight ball. I have to take full responsibility for what I did."

"I know, b-but she..."

"No, Lolly," he said. "Tick didn't take a gun to my head and make me go in. I went in all by myself. Just like you made the decision to go over the levee all by yourself."

"I guess." Her stuttering sobs lessened.

"If you unwind all the strands, they lead back to you going over there. But you know, because you crossed over, not everything that's happened has been bad."

The more Grandpa talked, the less empty that place in her stomach felt. She looked up at him. His face shone and his ice blue eyes smiled.

"I love you, Grandpa," she said.

He put his arm around her shoulder. "As you know, princess, I don't give a gnat's elbow for you." He chuckled and hugged her more tightly.

Lolly's mother knocked and entered. "Lolly, your father wants to see you downstairs."

"Okay," Lolly said. "Don't leave, Grandpa."

"I won't go anywhere. In fact, I want to spend a little time with your mama. I'd like to take a gander at her new paintings."

Lolly left her room and then stood for a long time outside her father's study. *I wish I would never have to lay eyes on him again.* Finally, she raised her hand and rapped.

"Come in," he said, his tone lower than usual. She opened the door but didn't go in. The light slicing through the blinds made it difficult to see, but she knew from his silhouette that he was sitting at his desk and appeared to be leaning toward her slightly.

"Yes?"

"Lolly," he said gravely. "I have something to tell you."

She didn't know why, but her stomach lurched and she gripped the edge of the door in preparation for what he was about to say.

Chapter Twenty-Two

H
e got up, came around the desk, and sat down in a wing-backed chair beside his saxophone, which was lodged in its stand. He picked it up and, drawing it close, touched the mouthpiece to his lips. He ran his fingers over the keys, but the room remained silent.

"Why are you standing there? Come in."

Lolly inched into the room and sat in a chair that was the twin to his. Her mother had bought them at the antique auction in Sacramento. Her father put the mouthpiece between his lips and blew. Notes spun through the air, loopy, lonely sounds and, even though anger was tying slipknots in the pit of her stomach, the music made her want to put her arms around him and take his sadness away.

A full jelly glass of vodka sat on his desk. It might be the first horn of corn for the evening, or the second, or the third. For once, she didn't care.

He shifted in his chair and the music changed to a haunting melody that reminded her of the harmony she had heard from one of the trailers over the levee. His eyes were closed and his cheeks were puffed. She visualized them popping and him flying around the room like a released birthday balloon, hitting walls, bumping into corners.

What's this all about? she wondered. *What is it he wants to tell me?*

When the music stopped, he opened his eyes and placed the saxophone back into its stand. "I got a call today," he said. "From the sheriff's office." He rubbed his hands over his face as if trying to massage away everything that pricked and needled him.

"Moose Perry's dead," he said.

"The sheriff?" she asked. Relief rushed through her. She had been afraid he was going to tell her something bad had happened to Sam.

He nodded.

"What happened?"

"He was shot." He stared at her intensely. "In the shooting gallery at Chiseler's Inn."

She curled her lips into her mouth and looked down at her feet swinging back and forth. This must have been what her father and Doc had been talking about. She was afraid to ask the next question, because she knew they wouldn't be having this conversation if the answer didn't have something to do with her.

"Sit still!" her father said.

She froze. The question had to be asked. "Who killed him?"

"Sam Maple."

"Sam!" Her voice cracked. "Impossible! Sam wouldn't hurt a flea!"

Her father stood and paced the room. "How would you know that? You'd have to know somebody pretty damn well to know they wouldn't hurt a flea."

Here they were, talking—exactly the thing she had longed for. Never before had he been so direct. But, the strangest part of all was that he was completely sober, and that frightened her.

"I know him well enough," Lolly said. "Some people you don't have to know long."

"Well, I want you to be aware of a couple of things," he said and shoved his hands in his pockets like he was about to launch into a lecture about her behavior at school. "I'm going to prosecute him."

Lolly stared at her father, who stood tall and powerful, his eyes clear. He hadn't yet had a horn of corn. "I'm going to put that son of a bitch away."

Now she understood why her father had abstained from drinking tonight. Not because he had wanted to talk to her about something he knew would concern and upset her, but because he was preparing to use Sam Maple for his own purposes.

"It's very important that I win this case," he said as Lolly focused on her shoes. "Are you listening to me? Because you may not know it, but your old daddy here has had a string of bad luck. I've lost a couple of big cases, and there's another fellow after my job."

"Maybe you both could do the job," she said.

He snorted. "If it were only that easy. No, Lolly, I'm going to try this case and I'm going to have to win it. I just wanted you to understand. Do you have any questions?"

"How do you know Sam did it?" she asked.

"Oh, he did it," her father assured her, holding up a stack of papers. "We've got witnesses, fingerprints, and motive. He even threatened Moose and me the other day at the cougar's cage. You heard him."

She shook her head.

"You heard him."

She shook her head again.

"I'm going to see he goes down," her father said angrily. "Whether you like it or not."

"What does that mean?"

"I'm going to ask for the death penalty. Sam Maple killed an officer of the law, and for that he's going to pay with his life."

Lolly's hands turned into fists and she shot him the darkest glance she could muster.

"Where're you going?" he demanded when she got to her feet.

"Nowhere."

"Have you been excused?"

"No."

"Sit down, then."

Lolly sat down.

He came over to her and gently removed the cap. "Your hair's growing back," he said, his voice soft. "It won't be long before you'll have something to comb."

He touched her chin, but she stiffened. She grabbed the cap back and tugged it down over her head.

"Lolly, I have to try this case. It's the right thing to do. It's my job to see that justice is served. Do you know what that means?"

I wish you would die. "It means it doesn't matter who did it. It means the most convenient person is punished."

"No, ma'am," he said. "It means that..."

"Where's Sam now?" she interrupted.

"Down at the jail. He'll be there through the grand jury hearing and then the trial."

"Can I go see him?"

"Absolutely not! I don't think you understand. He's a murderer. You think they're going to let you into the jail so you can talk to a murderer?"

"Can I be excused now?" Lolly asked.

"I just wanted to try and explain to you about—"

"Can I go now?"

He backed away as she got up and headed for the door.

"I know Sam didn't do it," she said. "I know it!"

Lolly strode through the kitchen and plunged through the back door into the heat of the backyard. Everything spun downward. Yanking off the cap, she hurled it against the trunk of the weeping willow.

Her feet pawed at the ground as she reared her head back, snorts fumed from her nose. She galloped around the tree, under the long tendrils dangling to the ground, and as they brushed over her, she ripped at the leaves.

She had a strong inclination to race over the levee, pull Tick out of her trailer, and squeeze her until her eyes popped out of her head.

Then the truth hit her: they were going to kill Sam!

She charged into the house. "Grandpa!"

She found him with her mother in the dining room. They were appraising several paintings that rested here and there on chairs.

"Grandpa, I have to talk to you!" She tugged at his arm, trying to pull him out of the room.

"You're being rude, dear," her mother protested.

"But it's really, really important," Lolly told her.

"Give me a minute, princess," her grandfather said. "Have you seen these paintings your mama's done? Some of them are down right extraordinary."

"They're great," she said. "Grandpa, this is a matter of life and death!"

"Lolly, please," her mother said. "What do you think of

that one, Daddy?" She turned a chair. "This angle is better because it doesn't get the glare from the window."

"Good," he said. "Very good."

"Grandpa!"

Her grandfather turned to her. "All right, Lolly. We're about finished here. Your work has crossed a line, Clarry. Your control and the emotional context are really fine. You should have these photographed and present them to a gallery in San Francisco."

"You think so?" her mother said.

"I do," he said. "I definitely do. I'll come over next week and we'll choose which ones. You've taken huge leaps. Your mother would have been proud." He leaned toward Lolly. "You proud of your mama?"

"Yes," she said, "but I need to talk to you."

"Okay, princess, what's on your mind?"

She signaled with her eyes that she wanted to talk alone.

His eyebrows raised. "These old legs aren't what they used to be. Let's go out on the porch and sit a spell." He chuckled. "Especially since my lion taming exploits."

The swing squeaked as he rocked it. "Okay, what's so all powerful important?"

"I want to go down to Chiseler's Inn," she said.

His eyes widened and a flicker of amusement played in them. "Is that right? You want to down a couple of beers and shoot a round of pool?"

Despite herself, she smiled. "I need to see the shooting gallery. Daddy told me Sam killed Moose Perry there. I've got to see it."

"Yes, sir, I heard about that. Terrible." He shook his head. "What human beings do to each other. Why do you want to go down there?"

"I'm not sure," she said. "Sam took me once and I guess I just need to see the place again."

"Sam Maple took you to Chiseler's? That's no place for a little girl."

"Please, Grandpa."

"Your daddy know about you going to Chiseler's?"

She shook her head.

"Why in the world would that man take you to a place like that?"

"It was a treat. Besides, all kids should know how to shoot a gun. It's as important as stuff we learn in school."

"Going to Chiseler's is not exactly like learning the three R's. Besides, your daddy'll have me thrown in the clink if he catches me taking you down there."

"Sam's my friend. I have to help him."

"Tell me something, princess. When you went to Chiseler's with Sam, did you ever see him shoot?"

"No, he only showed us how. I saw Bob Bob, though. Wow, Grandpa. He never missed. Bam, bam, bam, bam. One after the other, those ducks *fell*."

"Well, that's fine, but it's not Bob Bob who's in trouble."

"We have to go down there. That's how they do it on TV. On *Dragnet*, Joe Friday always goes back to the scene of the crime."

"I didn't think you liked TV."

"*Dragnet*. Sometimes. Please, Grandpa. I'm begging you. Sam's my friend. Maybe if I see the place again I'll think of some way to help him."

Her grandfather shook his head. "Lolly, going to Chiseler's isn't going to do anybody any good. In fact, it might do a lot of damage."

"If you had a friend in as much trouble as Sam, wouldn't

you try and think of ways to help him?"

"I would," he agreed. "I would do what I could. But I surely wouldn't try and make things worse."

"This won't. I just need to see the place. Please, Grandpa. I'm begging you."

"The things you get me into, princess. I have a hard time saying no to that pretty face of yours. So, all right, but you hear me good. We're in and out, understand?"

"I understand," Lolly said. Her stomach turned with excitement. She felt just like Nancy Drew on the trail of solving a mystery.

"Go tell your daddy and mama we're going out for ice cream. Which, by the way, is exactly what we're going to do. Get some ice cream. And maybe, just maybe we'll stop by Chiseler's."

She kissed her grandfather's cheek and dashed into the house looking for her father. She didn't have to go far as she ran into him in the hallway.

"Why in such a hurry?" he said.

"Can I go with Grandfather to get some ice cream?"

"*May* I go with Grandfather to get some ice cream," her father corrected her.

"Yes, Sir. *May* I go?"

"Put on the cap. You're still wretched-looking and Lolly..."

"Yes, Sir. Thank you." She ran to the backyard and retrieved her cap.

"Let's go," she said and sprinted toward her grandfather's car.

"Whoa! Slow down. Don't you think it looks a might suspicious you running like crazy legs? Your daddy and mama may wonder what all the excitement's about. After all, you're just going for ice cream with your old grandpa. Calm down, princess, and grab a hold."

The police had closed the street facing the Chiseler's Inn, as well as three more blocks.

"I think it's the Bok Kai parade," Grandpa said. "I'd almost forgot about it."

Throngs of people lined the streets and braved the noon-time sun that bleached the sidewalks. Chinese drums throbbed in the distance.

Grandpa parked his car and they made their way through the buzzing crowd toward Chiseler's.

"You know, Lolly, this town was quite the place during the gold rush. I've heard tell that Chiseler's was the number one watering hole between here and the gold fields."

Firecrackers bit the air. They clustered in loud cracking bouquets, and the smell of sulfur was heavy.

"Would you look at that!" he said, guiding her through a fence of people.

Men in bright red and gold outfits beat on gongs while another group pounded on drums. Out of the drifting fire-cracker smoke plunged a glittery gold dragon more than thirty feet long. It undulated over the street, winding back and forth, an enormous centipede with fierce bulging eyes and a mouth filled with fangs that Lolly thought capable of tearing apart the devil himself.

As the dragon came closer, she leaned against her grandfa-ther. When it danced opposite them, its head wagged and nod-ded, and then it suddenly turned its penetrating gaze directly on her. She peered back into its face.

For a brief moment, everything drifted in graceful slow movements. In that strange ellipse of time, a voice that seemed to be the dragon's spoke to her: *Do what you know is right.*

She blinked and buried her head into her grandfather's side. It wasn't until she felt his gentle hand on her head that she turned back and things felt normal again.

The firecrackers continued their dazzling stutter, the drums pounded, the gongs crashed, and the dragon danced away, winding its long beautiful body past the crowd.

Lolly slipped her hand into her grandfather's and they made their way across the street and into the Chiseler's Inn.

The bar was as empty and dim as it had been on her first visit. The bartender, polishing the glasses at the front end of the bar, didn't seem to notice them. Lolly went straight into the shooting gallery, where duck after duck swam in their endless line. She looked at the rifles hanging on the wall and tried to imagine Sam taking one down, cocking it like he had done for Tick and her, raising it, then turning the gun on Moose Perry.

Site, hold your breath, squeeze.

She tried to imagine him pulling the trigger. The image refused to live. She'd never seen Sam raise a gun, but she knew he'd never kill anything.

The ducks swam and she watched. To her left, a voice spoke, "Think you better get her out of here, Jeb."

She turned, but saw only velvety blackness that swallowed whoever had spoken.

The bartender stepped out of the shadows. "Ain't no place for a kid, especially after what happened last week."

"Okay, Mo," said her grandfather. "Let's go, princess."

She nodded. The way Mo had been hidden in the darkness was exactly the same way Bob Bob was hidden the day she fired the gun.

"Ready for a double dip?" Grandpa asked.

"Ready," she said.

Back on the street the smell of sulfur hung in the air. It reminded her of incense at High Mass. She still heard the drums, but the dragon was gone.

Chapter Twenty-Three

For a long time Lolly's mother sat on the bed, tapping her cigarette into the ashtray she had brought with her.

"A dragon talked to me today," Lolly said, slowly running her hand over her mother's pale arm.

"A dragon?"

"He had a long body and big scary eyes and he made everything slow down."

"We all have our demons," her mother said. "Be careful, darling, that yours don't get so big you can't control them."

"Mama, I have to talk to Sam."

"The man who came to the hospital?"

"Yes, I have to talk to him."

"From what I understand, he's in jail."

"I know," Lolly said. "But you could take me there."

"To the jail? Don't even think about it. It's impossible."

"I know," Lolly said. "But I have to talk to him."

"About what?"

"Killing Moose Perry. I have to hear the story from Sam."

"You'll hear it, my darling. Since your father's taking on that case, mark my words, you're going to hear more than you should. Batten down the hatches. It's going to be a stormy summer."

"I need to talk to Sam," Lolly said. "If you won't help me, I'll find a way. I'll—"

"Lolly, don't we have enough trouble around here? Don't push this, please." She took a drag on the cigarette. "Besides, even if I did take you down to the jail, they wouldn't let you in. The man's a murderer, for God's sakes! You think they're going to let a ten-year-old in to talk to a murderer?"

"He's not a murderer!" Lolly said. "He's not." She bit her lip and turned away from her mother. How could people think Sam's bad if they don't know him?

"If he's innocent, he'll be freed," her mother said, more hope in her voice than certainty. She stubbed out her cigarette.

"Daddy wants to get him."

"Who is it your daddy wants to get?" Her father asked, suddenly appearing in the doorway. He leaned against the doorjamb, his eyes blazing and his jaws clenched. "Tell me. Who?"

Lolly pushed herself up on her elbows, but her mother pressed a hand on her shoulder.

"Regan, dear, Lolly's about to go to sleep. I think it's best we keep things calm at bedtime. Tomorrow you can ask your questions."

"Goddamn it," he bellowed. The way he slurred his words indicated he was drunker than usual. "I want to know what you were saying about me!"

"We were talking about that man who shot Moose," her mother said.

"Sam Maple," he said, and his lips curled into a snarl. "I'm going to see that that son of a bitch *fries*! Those goddamn gypsies'll cut and run when I'm finished with him because they'll know if I can do it to Sam Maple, I can do it to any of them!" He slammed his hand down on the dresser and two glass figurines, a cat and a unicorn, wobbled.

"Daddy, what if Sam didn't do it?"

"Don't Daddy me! I'm prosecuting that white trash. He and his kind won't hurt my family ever again."

"But Sam didn't hurt anyone."

"Don't tell me what he did or didn't do!" He balanced himself with the back of the white wicker chair, his eyes wild like those of a wounded animal.

"Regan, please. Let her alone," her mother said and stepped toward him. He wheeled around, his open hand clipping her jaw. She reeled backwards, stumbled, and fell hard on her backside.

Lolly jumped out of bed and knelt beside her. Already her jaw was speckled with strawberries under the skin.

Her father staggered toward them and yanked Lolly away from her mother, tossing her across the room and against the wall where her legs buckled and she collapsed.

"Don't you touch her!" her mother screamed as she scrambled to stand, but her father knocked her down again.

When he came toward her, Lolly curled into a frightened bundle.

"Look at you," her father sneered. "Both of you sniveling messes." He made his way back to the door. "Forget it," he said, his breath coming in convulsive heaves. "Just forget it."

But Lolly knew she would never forget what had just happened.

Chapter Twenty-Four

She opened her eyes to see her father kneeling at the side of her bed.

"I'm sorry for last night." His breath smelled of toothpaste, but underneath was the stench of liquor. The lines gouged under his eyes ran deeper than usual, as though his fierceness had dug trenches in his face. His mustache, though perfectly trimmed, accentuated the downward turn of his mouth.

"What can I do, Lolly? What can I say to get you to forgive me? Tell me." He buried his face in the bedding. "I don't want to be like my father." He raised his face. Tears stained his cheeks. "I'll do anything."

Lolly's insides turned to stone. She opened her mouth to speak, but then changed her mind.

"Say it," he said. "Please! Say it!"

She wanted to ask him not to prosecute Sam, but to defend him. But she knew now that that was too much to ask, so she went for the next best thing: "I want to talk to Sam."

He blinked. "Lolly, dear, the man's in jail on a murder charge. Only his lawyer has access to him right now. I don't know if even *I* can get in to see him. Certainly not if his attorney wants to get sticky about it."

She slid back down to lie flat in her bed and stared at the

ceiling.

"Lolly, please," he pleaded.

She knew that he wanted forgiveness, but she would not relent. Not this time. "I want to see Sam," she replied stubbornly.

He exhaled a long, deep breath. Tenting his fingers, he tapped them against his mouth. "All right. I'll try and arrange it, but I can't give you guarantees." He cocked his head, waiting for her reaction, but she offered nothing. He stood and backed toward the door. "I'll see what I can do."

Lolly pulled the sheet up to her chin and closed her eyes. She didn't open them again until she heard the door to her room close.

She sat in the front seat of the Capri as her father steered the car down the long driveway. The sour scent of his aftershave lotion filled the car. The hunch of his shoulders showed the degree of his fatigue. She wanted to show him how grateful she was, but when she moved closer to him, his withering glare pressed her back against the door.

"How did they get Sam?" she asked to end their latest silence.

"Do you mean how did they arrest him?" he asked, his voice strained.

"Yes. How'd they arrest him?" Lolly repeated.

"I wasn't there."

They drove past the sprawling houses of the Remingtons and the Berkeleys.

"What would it have been like?" she asked.

"Most likely a couple of deputies brought an arrest warrant to his trailer and cuffed him on the spot."

"And then what?"

"Then they took him to the jail."

"And then?"

"Why do you want to know all these details?" he snapped, glancing at her as though he didn't really want to see her.

"Because Sam is my friend and I want to know what they did to him."

He shrugged. "At the jail they probably took away his personal possessions like his wallet, watch, any cash he had on him, and put them in a manila envelope. He would have to sign for them."

"Would they take his snakeskin belt?" she asked.

"Yes," he said. "They'd take away his belt for sure and they'd probably gave him a TB skin test."

"Why?"

"To be sure he doesn't have the disease. It's standard procedure. Probably an officer took his medical history and then he had his picture taken."

"What for?"

She knew her questions were annoying him but she didn't care. Suddenly this ability to bite him like a mosquito gave her satisfaction.

Thou shalt honor thy father and thy mother.

"It's called a mug shot," her father said warily. "If he gets away, they post it around so people will recognize him and turn him in."

"Sam looks like you," she said.

Her father's knuckles whitened and she felt his glance shift between her and the road.

Buzz, buzz goes the mosquito.

"And then what?" she said.

He didn't speak for a long time and Lolly knew he'd had enough, but finally he said, "And then they probably got his fingerprints."

"I've seen them do that on *Dragnet*."

"Only the facts, ma'am," he said, his voice as low as Jack Webb's.

"Yeah," she said, but she didn't smile. "Did Sam tell you he's innocent?"

"All defendants say they're innocent."

She turned and looked out the window. They rode the rest of the way in silence.

When they reached the jail, he pulled into a parking lot and stopped the car but didn't get out. She watched as his hands traced a circle around the steering wheel.

"Dredge Craylor's going to be here," he said. He turned and looked at her. "He's Maple's lawyer. He okayed this meeting, I think out of curiosity. My bet is he wants to see how his client reacts to you. It might help him with the case."

She didn't look away. "So?" she said.

"Don't be defiant with me, missy," her father said. "Watch your tone."

"Sorry," Lolly said and looked away.

Within the jail it was cool and gray with grime. Lolly's insides felt wobbly and she wished she hadn't concocted this plan. What did she think she was doing? Maybe Grandpa was right. She might be making the situation worse. Maybe she was complicating things for Sam.

"Hey, Mr. Candolin," said an officer at the front desk. "How ya been?" His nametag read *Fred Lockley, Deputy*. His shoulders sat like an off-kilter board, nailed across his frame, straw hair frizzing around a bald dome. "It says here you have clearance to visit the gypsy," he said.

"His name is Sam Maple," Lolly said.

Her father leaned down and whispered, "Any more comments and I'll take you out of here so fast it'll make your head spin."

"Yes, sir," she said.

Her father signed in. "Is Craylor here yet?"

Deputy Lockley checked the log and nodded. "He's in the building, although I'm not sure he's with his client at the moment." He cleared his throat and then motioned to another officer, a paunchy man, to lead them down a dim hall.

When they entered an eight by ten, windowless room a stocky man wearing a gray suit and tie, who her father addressed as Drudge, greeted them. Lolly saw Sam sitting at a table wearing a khaki jumpsuit. The second he set eyes on her, his face lit up.

"What in tarnation are *you* doin' here?" Sam said.

"Hi, Sam," she said.

"I'm Dredge Craylor, Lolly, Sam's lawyer. Nice to meet you." Dredge Craylor extended his hand. She looked at her father for his approval, then shook Dredge Craylor's hand. It felt warm and soft.

"Are you all right, Sam?" she asked.

"Well, I've been better, but I'm okay," Sam told her and bowed his head.

"Cut the mincing, Lolly," her father said. "We only have a couple of minutes."

When her father and Dredge Craylor moved to the opposite end of the room, she lowered her voice. "I needed to see you, Sam," she said. "I have to know. Did you kill Moose Perry? I know you didn't, but I have to hear it from you."

Sam's eyes flicked toward the two lawyers, then he took a deep breath. "No," he said, looking directly into her eyes. "I did not kill Moose Perry."

"Did you hear that?" she called to her father. "Sam didn't do it. I told you." Dredge Craylor smiled indulgently and her father simply shrugged.

"Lolly, you ain't got no understanding how these things work," Sam said. "There ain't nobody that's gonna believe what I say."

"We'll see about that, Sam," Dredge Craylor said as he and Lolly's father came back to join them.

"*I* believe you," she said.

"I thank you for that," Sam said. "But there's a whole host of other things that ain't lookin' so good for me. Your daddy'll explain."

Her father resumed his position beside her. His hand on her back created an urgency in her. Something was going on that she didn't understand.

"What *did* happened?" she asked Sam.

"Don't say anything, Sam," Dredge Craylor said.

"I ain't got nothin' to hide," Sam said.

"As your lawyer I insist you don't say anything more," Dredge Craylor said.

"Everybody knows I was there at Chiseler's," Sam said. "That part's true. I heard the gun go off."

"Save the rest for the trial," Dredge Craylor snapped, no longer smiling.

Sam ignored him. "I saw Moose the moment he were shot," he told Lolly. "But I ain't the killer."

"Sam!" Craylor said.

"If you were there, then you saw who did it," she said.

Sam nodded. "Yep, I know who did it."

"I'm advising you not to say any more," Craylor said. "Do I have to remind you that this child's father is..."

"Who did it?" Lolly asked. "Tell me! Tell my daddy!"

Sam shook his head. "Can't."

"Why not?" Lolly persisted, her voice beginning to tremble. "Tell me. Why not?"

"This interview is over," Craylor said. He knocked on the door, and Deputy Lockley opened it from the outside.

"'Cause if I do," Sam said forcefully, "that person'll be in my seat and I ain't gonna do that to another human being."

Lolly's father had her hand and was tugging her toward the door.

"But Sam," she insisted. "If you don't, they'll say you're guilty. You have to tell. You have to!"

"Enough of this," her father said. "You've had your chance, Lolly. We're leaving."

"Not yet. Please!" She tried to pull away from her father's grip. "He's not guilty. Can't you see?" She clamped one of her hands around the doorjamb. "You need to hear what Sam has to say, Daddy!"

"Come on, Lolly. Time to go." Her father peeled her hand free and held both her wrists in his, nodding his thanks to Craylor. They were heading down the hall when she wrenched herself free and rushed back to the room, where the deputy had just clapped handcuffs around Sam's wrists.

"Bye, Sam." Lolly pretended to scratch fury jowls, then she threw the affectionate rub to Sam. A hint of a smile crossed Sam's face.

Suddenly she was jerked away as her father grabbed her

again. "I'll see you two in court," he said, pointing at Sam, then at Craylor. He turned and dragged her out of the jail into the blistering day.

When school let out for the summer in June, Lolly was more tired than she ever remembered. Her dreams, filled with gunshots and cougar howls, would awaken her, leaving her to lie in her bed, her mind turning with dread over Sam's trial. She finished the fifth grade without saying good-bye to a single grotto horse and offered barely a nod to Sister Theodora.

Every evening that summer, when her father dragged himself up the porch stairs precisely at 5:30, she was waiting to interrogate him.

"What happened to Sam today?" she asked one night.

Her father dropped his briefcase in the foyer, shifted out of his jacket, and loosened his tie before heading for the kitchen.

"Well, today your friend was indicted by the grand jury."

"What's indicted?"

"It's part of the process. A group of people called the grand jury listen to the prosecutor—that's me—lay out the case against the defendant," he said.

"The case?"

"If the grand jury decides there's enough evidence to hold a man and the evidence indicates the defendant *probably* committed the crime, they'll return a true bill, or indictment. If they don't think there's enough evidence, there'll be no indictment and the accused walks."

"Walks?" she asked.

"Goes free."

Lolly crossed her fingers behind her back. "What'd they do?"

"Indicted him."

"Can Sam go home now?"

"No," he said. His face pinched into small folds of satisfaction. "The judge denied bail."

"What does that mean?"

"That means Sam Maple's in jail until the trial."

"Why do they make him stay in jail and not let him go home?"

"They're afraid he might run away or go out and hurt somebody again," her father said righteously.

Lolly could tell that simply talking about the case made him feel as self-satisfied as though he had already won it.

Lolly licked the beaters after her mother had whipped a batch of brownies. "What's the date today?" Lolly asked.

"Let's see," her mother said. "I think it's the first."

"Five more days," Lolly said.

"Yes, five more days."

"I want to go to the trial."

"I don't think that would be a good idea," her mother said, and dipped her own finger into the batter and licked it. "And your father wouldn't think so either."

"It's a learning experience. How else can I find out if I want to be a lawyer?"

Her mother smiled. "You're too smart for your own good, Lolly Candolin."

That night, between horns of corns, Lolly posed her argument for attending the trial to her father.

"I thought you wanted to be a reader," he said. "Isn't that what you said last year? When I grow up, I want to be a reader."

"I've thought about it. Nobody will pay me to read. Maybe I should be a lawyer."

"Maybe you should. Not so easy for a female though."

"That's okay," she said, chewing on her cuticle. "So, can I go to court?"

"It's not going to be easy. I'm going to rake your friend over the coals. You may not have the stomach for that."

"I've got the stomach for what's right."

He looked at her thoughtfully for a long time. "All right," he said finally. "You can sit in. But I warn you, Missy. One wrong move and you're out on your ear."

On the sixth of August, the heat in the valley rallied with such exuberance that Lolly wondered if the devil himself was breathing down their necks. Pulling her cap further down on her head, she followed her mother into the courtroom, which was filled to standing room only. She and her mother sat in the front row. She saw Tick, Sophie, and Bob Bob sitting behind them. Grandpa sat far in the back.

On the other side of the railing, her father sat at a table to the left, his assistant seated beside him. Birch Stolheim was a shy, young man who had been with him for only a year. At the table to their right sat Dredge Craylor, Sam sitting next to him.

"All rise. Court is now in session," called out Ned Smithy, the bailiff. His already ruddy skin flared scarlet under the pressure of this public display. "All stand for The Honorable Thaddeus Edmunds presiding."

Lolly craned to see as Judge Edmunds entered from a side door. The judge's skin was oily and his eyes, nose, and mouth were so small that it almost seemed they weren't there. He reminded Lolly of an egg.

"Please be seated," Judge Edmunds said.

The clerk, a sour-looking woman with flat hair, held up a document and squinted at it. "Case number 55-949043, the People of the State of California v. Sam Maple," she announced and sat down.

After Lolly's father and Dredge Craylor told Judge Edmunds they were ready, the judge instructed her father to begin his opening statement.

Shrugging his shoulders to reposition his off-white linen suit, he walked up to the jury box. The way the sun was shining on his back, he looked to Lolly like a bad angel. She couldn't take her eyes off him. She heard him address the jury as if he were talking to one of his long time friends. He spoke in a close, easy way, promising that he would arm them with all the evidence they would need to convict Sam of murder.

Then Dredge Craylor rose and put his hand on Sam's shoulder. Sam wore a bright white shirt so carefully pressed that Lolly guessed Sophie had ironed it for him. His boots were shined and his snakeskin belt was buckled around his waist.

As Craylor approached the jury box, his speech came in starts and stops. He appeared to be practically trembling with his own belief that his client, Sam Maple, had not killed Moose Perry. He assured the jury that at the end of the trial they could come to only one conclusion: Sam Maple was innocent.

Lolly felt a tap on her shoulder and she turned to see Tick's face close enough for a kiss.

"Please, Lolly, you gotta listen," she whispered. "I'm sorry about Grandpa."

"He's not your grandpa!"

When her mother shushed her, Lolly looked straight ahead.

"Please," Tick said as red curls filled Lolly's peripheral vision. "I feel real bad. I'd do anythin' to make it right."

Tick's hand on Lolly's shoulder was scalding, reminding her of Tick's handprint on the windshield of her mother's new car. It seemed magic then and it seemed magic now.

Lolly shrugged out from under Tick's hand. She knew Tick hadn't meant harm to her grandfather, but she was not yet ready to forgive. Lolly glared at Tick and gestured for her to sit back.

For the next week, Lolly's father called a string of witnesses to the stand, men who were in Chiseler's the night of the shooting: Mo Townsend, the bartender; Phil Dinglebrook and Lenny Torrey, who had been drinking at the bar; and Gary Hendricks, who had been shooting pool.

Her father even called Bob Bob, who'd been seen drifting in and out of the shooting gallery that night. When his name was called to testify, Bob Bob had trouble figuring out which hand to raise and which hand to put on the Bible. Once, in the middle of his incoherent testimony, he looked out into the gallery and called out, "Hello, my friend, Tick!" Lolly's father finally gave up and asked the judge to excuse him.

That afternoon during the recess, Lolly and her mother were standing in the hallway when Bob Bob came toward them.

Lolly's mother put a protective arm around her shoulders, but Lolly stepped away.

"My friend, Lolly. Your daddy was real nice to me, Lolly. I

guess I don't hate him so much no more."

"You did really well up there, Bob Bob," Lolly said. "I could hear every word you said."

"I didn't do nothin' wrong? You're still my friend?"

Lolly smiled. "For sure I'm still you're friend," she said.

Bob Bob beamed. "Thanks, Lolly. Thanks a lot." The giant tipped an imaginary hat to Lolly's mother before shuffling away.

"See you," Lolly called after him. Bob Bob raised a finger but he didn't look back.

During the afternoon session, Lolly's father submitted the rifle into evidence. He was careful to point out that Sam's fingerprints were found on the gun.

Craylor countered with the fact that other prints were found on both the stock and the barrel. "Bob Bob Jones' prints were found on the murder weapon as well as a partial set of my own," he told the jury. "And, oh yes, another print was found, one belonging to a highly admired person in this community who also likes to hone his skills as a marksman and was in the shooting gallery with me the night before the murder. Our own Regan Candolin."

The onlookers buzzed and Judge Edmunds gaveled the courtroom to order. Lolly wondered what this revelation would do for Sam.

Craylor then called several of the townsfolk, including William Hall, the owner of the stationery store; Dino Lucca, a truck driver; and Juan Garcia who worked in the fields. He interrogated them about their visits to the Chiseler's Inn. It soon became apparent that there were few men in town who didn't stop at Chiseler's at least once a week for a beer, a game of pool, or maybe a quick round of target shooting.

Lolly's father cleared his throat as he approached the jury. "I want to thank Mr. Dredge Craylor for this colorful parade of town folk and the insights to their Chiseler routines." He paused as a wave of titters rolled across the courtroom, then straightened his back, appearing to grow inches taller.

"Permit me to refocus us on something much more important," he continued. "Let's look at the motivation for the killing. It's clear and simple. Sam Maple shot Moose Perry not only because the sheriff put down his cougar, but because a year ago Sam Maple's wife was giving birth at the gypsy camp and he called the sheriff to request a police escort for the doctor. But, when the doctor didn't reach his wife in time, she and the baby died. Sam Maple blamed Moose Perry for their deaths."

"Objection, your Honor," Craylor said, leaping to his feet.

"Objection overruled," Judge Edmunds said.

By the second Friday afternoon of the trial, the heat had taken its toll on everyone. At three o'clock, Judge Edmunds called for a recess. "We'll have closing arguments on Monday," he decided, slamming down the gavel as the courtroom broke into a loud hum.

Sam stood, his face haggard, his eyes framed by dark circles.

"Sam!" Tick called out to him and hugged her mother as Sam sternly shook his head and was led away.

Lolly felt sad and wanted to console them all. She was afraid that Sam was doomed and there was nothing she could do.

On Saturday, Lolly awakened to the growl of her father's car driving away. He was probably heading to the office to prepare his closing statement. Since her mother was still asleep, she dressed quickly and high-tailed it over the levee. She realized Tick and Sophie knew things were serious for Sam, but she wasn't sure they understood the depths of her father's desire to convict him and that they needed to be prepared for the worst.

"Tick!" she called as she rapped on the trailer's door. "Tick!"

Tick appeared looking sleepy. "What are you doin' here, Lolly?"

"You need to know. My daddy's going to do whatever it takes to put Sam away."

"Away where?"

"In jail, or worse," Lolly said. "I just want you to be ready for what might happen."

"I'll tell Mama," Tick said.

"Another thing," Lolly said. "I want you to know that I'm still mad you coaxed my grandpa into Survie's cage, but I'm trying not to be."

"How hard you tryin'?" Tick asked.

"It's a sin to be mad and I hate going to confession."

"Uh," Tick grunted. "Well, I guess that's good enough reason. When you gonna get all the way unmad?"

"I don't know yet," Lolly told her. "I better get back home. My mama's sleeping. She'll go nuts if she wakes up and I'm gone."

Sophie wandered into the trailer's main room wearing a baby blue sateen robe. "Lolly, what a surprise! You ever drink champagne for breakfast?"

Lolly smiled. "No, ma'am. Never have, but I don't think this is a good time for it. Maybe when Sam's free."

"Your daddy's doin' his best to see that ain't gonna to happen," Sophie said sadly.

"That's why I'm here," Lolly said. "I wanted to tell you

what he intends."

"It's pretty clear what he intends," Sophie said and pulled the robe tighter. "Lord knows, this is an awful time. The Lord also knows that what your daddy does ain't your fault, you pretty little ragged head. Come on in, for Heaven's sake, and have something cold. The sun ain't up but I can tell it's gonna ravage us."

"Thanks," Lolly said. "I've got to go. Maybe after this is over we can...well, we'll see."

"When you gonna take off that cap?" Sophie asked.

"That's another thing we'll see about when this is over." Lolly took the first step down from the trailer. "I miss you, Tick," she said and jumped over the rest of the stairs.

Bang!

It was exactly the same sound she'd heard when Moose shot the cougar.

Sophie and Tick came out onto the porch. "Dear, God," Sophie said. "What now?"

Tick and Sophie threaded their way through the trailers. Lolly followed them, dreading what the sound could mean.

Chapter Twenty-Five

No other resident of Cougarville had turned out to investigate the sharp crack.

"How come no one else heard that shot?" Lolly asked Tick and Sophie.

"It ain't such an unusual sound in Cougarville," Sophie said. "Now and then a couple of hot heads might settle a personal dispute."

"You mean shoot at each other?"

"Naw, more like posturing," Sophie said. "It's a little early in the day for them kind of shenanigans, though."

"Maybe somebody getting' himself a duck breakfast," Tick said.

When they arrived at Bob Bob's van, Lolly and Tick scrambled up the steps.

"Bob Bob," Tick yelled, and pushed the door open. "Are you in there?"

The strange faces in the photographs were still on the wall, the guns in the rack on the other.

"He's not here," Lolly said. "Where would he be?"

"Most likely over at Sam's," Tick said. "He hangs out there a lot, whether Sam's home or not."

"The sound definitely came from this part of the camp,"

Sophie said.

"Probably just a hunter," Tick said.

"Ain't huntin' season," Sophie said.

"That don't much matter around here," Tick said.

"Let's go back," Sophie said, and it was clear from the way she took Tick's and Lolly's hand that something was worrying her.

"Wait," Lolly said. She pulled away from Sophie and started toward Sam's trailer. Something was wrong.

"I feel it, too," Sophie said. "I ain't sure we should risk going one inch closer."

Lolly nodded and squeezed her eyes shut. Then she took three big steps that brought her around the trailer and positioned her directly in front of the cougar's cage.

Help me, dear Jesus.

She took a deep breath before she opened her eyes and gasped. Someone had dumped a large rumpled pile of old clothing inside the cage. And then she realized that the pile was Bob Bob, lying up against the fence, his enormous legs stretched out in front of him. He wore jeans and he was barefoot. A rifle lay on the ground between his legs, the barrel facing him.

Lolly stepped closer. Bob Bob's head hung down like he was saying prayers, but the top of his head was gone. What looked like dark red curd seemed to have boiled out of his skull and the sun glinted off smears of moist blood on his shirt. Lolly began to shiver so hard that, even when she wrapped her arms around herself, she couldn't stop.

Behind her Tick was whimpering. She turned to see Tick clinging to Sophie, her face pressed into Sophie's stomach.

Sophie unwound Tick's arms and grabbed for Lolly, trying to pull her away from the scene. "Come on, sweet thing."

Lolly resisted with all her might, so Sophie gave up and

held Tick.

"In the name of the Father, and of the Son, and of the Holy Ghost." Lolly blessed herself. "If you're here, God," she began and then her voice gave out. Maybe this wasn't the proper time to ask God for anything. And if it was, what should she ask for?

"Come on, Lolly," Sophie said. "Let's go call the police."

"He killed himself," Lolly said to Sophie, her voice hoarse. "He took that gun and turned it on himself and pulled the trigger."

"Lolly, come on," Sophie said, this time more urgently. "You've seen enough."

Lolly laced her hands through the cage's wire fencing and leaned her forehead against the metal. The sharp struts pressed into her skin as she took in every detail: Bob Bob's dirty feet, the broken toenails, his swollen ankles, the worn denim straining from the pressure of the huge legs, the tire of stomach bulging over his waistband. He wore a plaid shirt, but so much of the pattern's white squares had been stained by blood that it appeared to be solid red. His right hand lay over the gun and under his left was a piece of paper.

She stiffened. She had to know what was on that paper.

"Please, darlin'," Sophie said. "We have to report this. I don't want you to look at him no more."

"In a minute," Lolly said.

Inching to the entrance of the cage, she stepped inside.

"Come with me, child," Sophie demanded.

Lolly took a deep breath. Wiping away her tears, she stepped toward Bob Bob. As she got closer, his smell burned her nostrils. She held her breath as she bent down and reached for the paper.

"Lolly!" Sophie called.

With one quick tug, not touching Bob Bob, Lolly snatched the paper from under his hand and stumbled out of the cage. She lost control as her stomach jackknifed and she vomited. Tears ran from her eyes and she didn't stop retching until she got back to Sophie and Tick's trailer, where she slid into a chair, the paper crumpled in her fist.

"You'd better go, Lolly," Sophie said. "The police will be coming after I call, though God knows they won't be hurryin'. A dead man in Cougarville don't give them much to worry about."

"Yeah, you're right," Lolly said.

"I've ain't n-never s-seen a..." Tick's voice trailed off.

"Got to go," Lolly said.

"What's that you took from Bob Bob's hand?" Sophie asked.

"Nothing," Lolly said and took off for the levee. When she reached the top of the berm, she stopped and read the note in Bob Bob's messy pencil scrawl:

Dear Who Ever,
I kilt Mose Peray. He a Bad man. Bad for the world.
He kilt my daddy and my frend the cooger. Sam ain't bad.
I hid in the blin spot and shot over Sam. Sam need to go free.

Yours trulie,
Bob Bob Jones

Lolly raised her tear-stained face to the sky. "God bless, you, Bob Bob," she said. "You're going to save Sam!"

At home, Lolly crept into her father's study. From a legal pad on his desk, she tore two pages and placed Bob Bob's note between them. She folded the three pieces into a neat package and stuck it in her back pocket. Then she hopped on her bicycle and rode hard and fast to her father's office. It was still early and there was little traffic.

His Capri was in the parking lot. She dropped her bike on the sidewalk and dashed up to his office. It was locked, so she pounded on the door.

"Daddy! Daddy!" she called. "It's Lolly!"

Knowing that he was probably too involved in his work to hear her, she picked up pebbles in the garden beside the entrance and tossed them at his window.

The door opened. "Lolly," he said, stepping back as she pushed past him. "What're you doing here?"

"I have proof," she said, her breath coming in quick pants. "I have all the proof Sam needs."

"Go home, Lolly," he told her impatiently. "I've got a lot of work to do."

She followed him into his office where he sat down heavily at his desk. "I'm in the midst of a murder trial, Lolly," he said. "If I don't win this one...well, it won't be good. I'm in a bind and I'm working hard to get out of it. This isn't just for me, you know. It's for you and your mother, too. I want you to know that. My father never worked. My mother had to...but that's not important now. Go home and let me do what I have to do!"

"How's it going?" Lolly said.

"How's what going?"

"The trial." *He's so strange,* she thought. *It's like his mind flies off to another planet.*

"I think I'm going to put Sam Maple away for a very long

time," he told her.

She slipped the ragged piece of paper out from between the two yellow-lined sheets. "I think I have something that can save him," she said.

His face pinched. "What in the hell are you talking about? Go home, Lolly."

She hesitated.

"Well? What are you waiting for?"

"A little while ago," she said, keeping her voice quiet and calm, "I went over the levee to..."

"Goddamn it! Do I have to lock you up? Hasn't your defiance caused enough trouble?"

"I went over to tell Tick I was trying to forgive her."

"Stop going over there!" He said angrily. "It's a beehive of liars, cheaters, and murderers."

"Sam is not a murderer!"

"Sam Maple shot the sheriff in cold blood."

"No, he didn't! Sam respects everyone, and he respects what guns can do."

"And how would you know that?"

She lifted her chin and folded her arms across her chest. "Because he taught me never to point a gun at anyone unless I intend to use it."

"A man like that wouldn't think in those terms."

"Well, Sam does!"

"How do you know?"

"Because he said never to point a gun. He said that."

"I don't believe you."

"He did!"

"Why did he say that to you?"

"We were at the shooting gallery. He took Tick and me there to teach us to shoot."

The silence that followed pounded in Lolly's ears. When had she begun enjoying making her father angry? Why did it give her such a sense of satisfaction, make her feel powerful? When she said just the right words, she could make his eyes water and the veins in his neck thicken. But now, she was sorry she'd said what she said. She hadn't done Sam any favors.

"That man took you to the shooting gallery?" The words were slow, deliberate, and ominous.

"It wasn't any big deal. It was just to celebrate Tick's passing the tests."

"He took you to the Chiseler's Inn?"

Lolly looked out the window.

"Sam Maple took my daughter to the Chiseler's Inn. That son-of-a-bitch."

"He didn't mean to do anything wrong," Lolly said, thinking it probably wasn't the best idea Sam had ever had, but he did it for the right reasons.

"That son-of-a-bitch." He paced. She heard fury whistle through his nose, and his eyes became small. "I'll get him. Mark my words, I'll get that white trash gypsy. Now you go home and stay home!" He slumped back into his chair and slammed a book down on the desk.

Lolly stood frozen, the note pressed against her chest.

"What've you got there?" he demanded.

Suddenly she didn't trust that he wouldn't destroy the note. She folded the paper quickly and stuffed it into her back pocket. "Nothing," she said. "Bob Bob killed himself today." The image of Bob Bob's bloody shirt flickered in her head, and though she sucked hard at the tide of sobs, she couldn't hold them back.

"The simpleton?" he asked.

She nodded.

"How do you know?"

"I saw him."

"Where?"

"I heard the shot. This morning when I was in the camp." She trembled. All she could see was Bob Bob slumped in the cougar cage. She pulled the back of her hand across her face, smearing the tears.

"Goddamn it, Lolly. Goddamn it."

"I-I'm s-sorry." Now she felt no sense of satisfaction.

"You went over there and saw a dead man?"

She nodded. "The top of his head...the top of his head was gone."

"My God," he exclaimed as he pulled himself out of the deep leather chair, came around his desk, and tried to put his arms around her. She snaked out of his embrace. "This is too much," he said. "Too much! Those people over there are dangerous and crazy. You are never to set foot over there again. Never!"

Hatred burned in her throat. "I'll never forgive you," she said, the words ironed and flat. She stomped out of his office.

"Come back!" he called, sounding plaintive and regretful.

It was the same singsong voice she'd heard so many times, the one that had always kept them connected. As she rode her bicycle away from the office, Lolly felt the connection snap, and a breeze of relief fluttered over her like the flapping of a hundred river crows.

Chapter Twenty-Six

The *Appeal Democrat* lay open on the table. The secondary headline in the lower right side of the front page declared "Gypsy Found Dead in Cougar Cage." Lolly picked up the paper and read the story, which indicated that residents in the trailer camp had found Bob Bob and called the police.

"Those poor people," her mother said. "It must be hard for them."

Lolly closed the paper. "I'm not hungry," she said, nudging her bowl of cereal away.

She wandered outside, cap in hand, and stood on the porch waiting for her mother to finish dressing. It was too hot to put the cap on now. She would wait until just before she walked into the courtroom. Across the levee, she heard the relentless summer sound of irrigation pumps pushing water into the fields surrounding the town. Her grandfather always said water was like blood to the valley.

Finally her mother appeared dressed in a tailored beige linen dress, ready to drive them to the courthouse, but never going over twenty-five miles per hour. "You feel all right, Lolly?" she asked.

"Yes," Lolly said. She watched the houses with manicured lawns slip by. "Mama, do you believe in justice?"

"What do you mean?"

"I know Sam is innocent. I *know* he is. But Daddy keeps saying things that make it look like he isn't. How can there be justice if they can make a man who is innocent look guilty?"

Her mother pulled the car over and stopped next to the lake in the park across from the courthouse. "Sometimes things don't go the way they should," she said. "Remember when Mrs. Stevenson down the block got cancer and died and left three little children without a mother?"

Lolly nodded.

"It wasn't fair to those children or to that family, but it happened."

"That was God's fault," Lolly said.

Her mother ignored the comment. "Then there was the time when that teacher, Mr. Bolton, was accused of hurting one of the girls at school? Do you remember?"

"I remember and I knew he wouldn't hurt anyone. That was God's fault, too."

"It's not a matter of fault. It's just that sometimes things happen. In Mr. Bolton's case, it turned out you were right. He hadn't done anything wrong, but he still lost his job, the truth didn't help him."

Lolly rolled the hem of her cotton pinafore. "What you're saying is that sometimes there's justice and sometimes there isn't?"

Her mother took the keys out of the ignition then jammed them back in. "Things happen," she said. "When my mother died, I was younger than you and..." Her mother's voice trailed off and she looked away. Her chest caved in as if the weight of the memory deflated her. "It's just that I want you to be prepared for what might happen in this case. You've been hearing two stories. One from Mr. Craylor and one from your father.

After they make their final arguments, the jury will have to decide which one to believe. And what ever happens, Lolly, you must accept their decision."

Lolly turned away from her mother and watched a line of ducks paddling across the lake.

"Lolly?" Her mother touched her hand. "Will you accept the outcome?"

Lolly traced a big S over the window glass.

"Lolly?"

"No!" she said sharply. "If they say Sam is a murderer, I won't accept that because I know he's not!"

"Please, Lolly. I'm just trying to prepare you."

"Yeah," Lolly sighed. "I'm prepared."

The courtroom was packed, the air stuffy. A fan whirred overhead. Sophie and Tick sat behind Lolly and her mother, with Andrea and Charlie behind them. Charlie wore a bright orange Hawaiian shirt and Andrea was vibrant in heavy make-up. Andrea winked at Lolly, then motioned with her head toward Sophie and mouthed, "She done it. She made me well." David Robinson Crocker was slumped next to Andrea, his hands stacked on the head of his cane, and next to him was Hattie, gently dabbing at her face with a lace handkerchief. Behind Hattie, Matilda and Ducky whispered like a couple of kids in school. As he had done every day of the trial, her grandfather sat in the last row.

"All rise. Court is now in session," Bailiff Smithy sang out as Judge Edmunds entered the courtroom, imposing in his long, black robe and gaveled the third week of the trial into session.

Lolly's father stood to begin his closing argument. The light coming through the east windows shimmered over his white linen suit, white shirt, and pale blue tie.

He presented a figure of authority, righteousness, and truth, staring at the jury for a long moment before beginning. His voice sliced like a silver knife, every jury member sitting up straighter, some leaning forward.

"Consequences ladies and gentlemen," he said in a deep, resonating voice. "Thomas Huxley said, 'Logical consequences are the scarecrows of fools and the beacon of wise men.' When Sam Maple raised the gun against Moose Perry, was he not a fool?

Murder is the crime," he said, walking the length of the jury box. "By definition murder is the unlawful killing of one human being by another, especially with premeditated malice. Malice is the intent without just cause or reason to commit a wrongful act that will result in harm to another." Her father turned and looked at Sam. "Murder is precisely what Sam Maple committed. Without just cause or reason, he took the life of Robert Pearson Perry, whom we all knew as Moose. Without just cause, Sam Maple murdered Moose, stealing his life from him. When Sam Maple chose to aim that gun and pull the trigger, he made a conscious decision to steal Martha Perry's husband from her. He also made the decision to take ten-year-old Jennie Perry and three-year-old Robert Perry's father from them. And, as if that weren't enough," he went on turning to the gallery, "when he pulled the trigger, he stole from this town one of the most responsible and important figures in its history. Moose gave his life for us. I say to you, Sam Maple, in the words of William Shakespeare, 'If you prick us do we not bleed? If you poison us do we not die? And if you wrong us shall we not revenge?'"

The silence that followed her father's summing up was absolute. Lolly scooted forward in her chair. She had never heard her father argue a case before and now she felt a combination of awe at his eloquence and fear of his power.

"Let's turn our clocks back in time," her father went on. "Five months and three days to be exact. Come with me, folks, into the Chiseler's Inn." He extended his hand to the jury and then to the people in the gallery, offering them all an opportunity to follow him.

"Chiseler's was relatively empty on the afternoon in question. You heard Mo Townsend, the bartender, testify that he had just pulled a couple of beers for two patrons sitting at the bar, Lenny Torrey and Phil Dinglebrook. Now, it's true they were in the bar and not the shooting gallery, but you've heard all three of them say—while under oath—that Sam Maple and Moose Perry were in the shooting gallery. We know that Gary Hendricks was playing pool at the back of the bar, and that Bob Bob Jones, who tagged after Sam Maple like a puppy dog, was drifting in and out of the gallery."

Her father turned away from Lolly as if avoiding her glare.

"Since a particularly brutal brawl at the bar about three months ago, the one we all read about for days on the front page of our esteemed newspaper, the sheriff made a stop at Chiseler's Inn part of his afternoon routine. On the day of the murder he arrived about four o'clock.

"It was a perfect setup for a murder, ladies and gentleman. Only a few days before, Moose Perry had been required by law to shoot and kill Sam Maple's pet cougar, an animal that had mauled and almost killed Jeb Hitchcock. Maple had imbibed a fair amount of alcohol at the bar: two beers. Maybe not enough to inspire a killing spree in most men, but in Sam Maple, who was consumed with anger for the killing of his cougar, it was the right amount to ignite his rage."

Lolly chewed on her cuticle as she listened. The longer her father spoke, the more frightened she became. It was as though everyone in the courtroom was clay in his hands. It didn't matter if what he said was actually true. It was the way he said it that made it true.

"Imagine that you're Sam Maple and you have witnessed the execution of an animal you've raised from a cub. Now, add to the mix the fact that the executioner was the sheriff, someone you and others in the gypsy camp have had numerous clashes with over the years. A man you *hate* because you blame him for the death of your wife and your newborn child."

Her father walked over and paused next to Sam. Every eye in the court followed. He returned to the jury box, placed his hands on the railing.

"Remember, please, that you are now Sam Maple. You come to the shooting gallery today around three-thirty p.m. knowing the sheriff will be here. You enter the bar hoping for one thing and one thing only: that Moose Perry will not break his routine, because you want to kill him and make it look like an accident."

He's so clever, Lolly thought. *He's making the jury imagine that they had been there. But they're not seeing what really happened. They're only seeing what Daddy wants them to see.*

"You have a couple of beers," her father continued. "The sheriff arrives. He greets Mo Townsend, Lenny Torrey, Phil Dinglebrook and Gary Hendricks. Then, as he does on every visit, he moves through the bar and into the shooting gallery. That's where you're waiting. You've been shooting at the mechanical ducks for maybe eight or nine minutes. Shooting and waiting, shooting and waiting. You think to yourself: I can fire a couple of times at the ducks as they swim by and, when I get to the last one, I'll go just a little farther. Just a couple of degrees, maybe less than a foot, and fire one more time. Ah, but this time it won't be a duck that falls."

Ed Reginald, sitting in the front row of the jury box, exhaled, "I'll be damned." The judge glared at him.

Ignoring the comment, her father went on. "You have a rifle in your hand. A twenty-two. Not a high-powered gun, but lethal at short range. And there, within spitting distance, only a few feet away, stands the man you despise. You raise the rifle to your shoulder, your bitterness and anger rising with it, and take a bead on the yellow metal ducks passing by."

Lolly straightened and moved to the edge of her chair. Her mother put a hand on her shoulder, forcing her to sit back.

"We're going to pretend that Birch Stolheim, my assistant here, is Moose Perry." Birch's face and bald head reddened at the sound of his name. "With the Judge's approval, Birch, I'm going to ask you to stand in for our late esteemed sheriff and take a position over here."

The judged nodded his assent.

What's he doing now? Lolly wondered.

"Good," her father said. "I'm going to ask the members of the jury to once again use your imaginations. We're going to switch roles. I am now Sam Maple."

He looked into the eyes of each member of the jury before continuing.

"The police report tells us that Moose was standing to the right of Sam, about four feet away. Just about the way Birch and I are positioned now."

Birch shifted from one foot to the other. Her father backed up and mimed picking up a rifle. Then he stepped up, raised the imaginary gun, and drew it menacingly across the jury box, tracking imaginary duck targets from left to right. His finger tightened around and pulled the imaginary trigger. He imitated a slight kick and in a loud, sharp voice barked, "*Bang!*"

Mildred Pringle, sitting in the front row of the jury box, jumped.

"The first duck falls. *Bang!* The second duck falls. *Bang!* The third duck falls. *Bang!* The fourth duck falls. *Bang!* Moose Perry's temple is pierced by a twenty-two caliber bullet. The stunned sheriff takes one step forward, and then collapses. With the murder weapon in his hand, Sam Maples looks at the sheriff dead at his feet."

The jury's gaze moved to the floor where her father pointed. If Lolly had been asked, she would have sworn that she saw Moose Perry lying dead on the courtroom floor.

"No!" she leaped from her seat.

Startled, her father wheeled around, his hands still holding the imaginary gun.

"Sam didn't kill Moose!" Lolly said. "Somebody else did!"

Chapter Twenty-Seven

The judge pounded his gavel and the clamor subsided. Lolly felt lightheaded. Everything swam around her and before she allowed herself to think about the consequences of her actions, she said, "Bob Bob Jones was standing in the dark spot under the stairs just beyond Sam and Bob Bob shot past Sam and killed Moose Perry!"

Her mother grasped her hand.

People in the gallery came out of their seats shouting, "What did she say?" and "I can't believe what she said!"

Judge Edmonds rapped his gavel. Confusion roiled through the room like hot molasses. Lolly didn't glance up for fear she would have to look into her father's eyes. Surely his hands would be shaking, and his face pale with fury.

Her mother stood and took Lolly's chin in her hand and forced her to look up. "Do you have any idea of what you've just done?"

"It's the truth," she whispered.

"The bailiff will expel anyone who doesn't come to order," Judge Edmonds crowed. The chatter quieted and the people sat down. Lolly saw an unutterable sadness in her father's eyes and she knew a big part of it was her fault. She felt small and very frightened. But it was too late to turn back. She pulled Bob

Bob's note out of her pocket.

"What's that?" her mother asked.

"Bob Bob's confession. It proves that Sam didn't kill Sheriff Perry."

Her mother read the note.

The judge pounded his gavel. "Mrs. Candolin, please take the child out of the courtroom."

To Lolly's amazement, her mother stood up. "Judge, I think you'd better read this." She pulled Lolly by the hand and led her out of the row. "Take this to the judge, Lolly. Go on. Take it up to him."

Lolly pushed through the swinging gates, walked up to the judge's bench, and rose on her tiptoes to hand him the slip of paper.

"Thank you, Lolly," he said. "Now you go sit down." The courtroom erupted and the judge banged his gavel. "This court will come to order!" he said, his eyes scanning to the note Lolly had handed him.

"I want to see counsel in my chambers." His voice was very grave. "Court will resume at one-thirty."

When the court reconvened, her father looked like a doll that had lost its stuffing. Judge Edmunds announced that both parties had agreed to allow the note Lolly had presented to be entered into evidence. Dredge Craylor recalled Mo Townsend, Gary Hendricks, and Phil Dinglebrook to the stand. One after the other they confirmed that they had seen Bob Bob Jones in and about the bar on that afternoon, though they couldn't be sure they had seen him in the shooting gallery.

Then Dredge Craylor called Lenny Torrey to the stand. "Now you understand, Lenny, the same goes for you as for the other fellows. You swore on the Bible the other day to tell the truth and you are still under that oath. Do you understand?"

Lenny Torrey was a roughened man, his skin sunburned, his hands swollen. "Oh, yes, sir, I understand. I swore on the Bible just like Phil and Gary and Mo. Just like them'ums did."

"You saw Bob Bob Jones in the shooting gallery?"

"Yes, sir, I did."

"Where exactly did you see him?"

"I saw him back around the pool table, yeah, and in the bar, and I said, 'Hey, Bob Bob,' but he didn't say one word. Not one. Youda thunk he was walkin' in his sleep. I thought it were strange so I followed him. Saw him take a rifle down, but he didn't shoot. Just stood in that dark place under the stairs we call the blind spot. The light don't reach back there and when you're standin' in it you can't be seen even if somebody knows you're there. I watched for Bob Bob for a while, but he just stayed there in the blind spot. Finally I went back and finished my beer but I member thinkin' it funny at the time."

"What did you think was funny, Lenny?" Craylor asked.

"That he weren't shootin'. I ain't never see him come in that he don't shoot a round or two. Even though he's simple, he's a crack shot. I ain't never see him miss. No, siree. Not never."

Craylor turned to Lolly's father. "Your witness."

Her father thrust his hands in his pockets and approached the witness box. "Lenny," he said, "how do you know nobody can be seen in the blind spot?"

Lenny grinned a jack-o-lantern smile. "Well, see, I was standin' in it one night and heard some things said about me that made me gol-durn mad, but that's another story. Alls I can say is I knows from experience, when you're in that spot, people ain't got a clue you're there."

Her father nodded. "And why haven't you told us about the blind spot before now?"

"I suppose 'cause nobody asked."

One of her father's hands snaked out of his pocket and combed through his hair. "This is a murder trial, Lenny. Did it not occur to you that a man who might be standing in the blind spot would be important information?"

"Look, Mr. Candolin, my toothbrush knows more than Bob Bob. He's so simple, there's no way I could've fathomed him thinkin' about poppin' someone, let alone plannin' a pop."

Her father paused as if considering Lenny's words, then said, "No more questions." He returned to his seat, but not before catching sight of Lolly. She looked down and examined her nails. There were no white spots.

What have I done? she thought. Her actions were producing, as her father would call then, huge, enormous consequences.

Dredge Craylor called Deputy Lockley to the stand. Lolly remembered him from her visit to the jail. Her father objected to him testifying on the grounds that he had not been listed as a witness during the discovery phase of the trial but the judge overruled his objection.

Dredge Craylor asked the deputy to describe the incident in the sheriff's office three years ago, when Bob Bob had shot and wounded Moose Perry.

"Bob Bob came in unexpected like," the deputy told him, speaking in a cracking voice. "And he was a huffing and puffing about it being Moose's fault his daddy died. Then he pulled a gun and started shooting like a crazy man. Everybody ducked, but Moose caught a bullet."

Then Craylor introduced Bob Bob's suicide note as evidence. "Permission to read the note?" he asked.

The judge turned to her father, who nodded.

"Go ahead," the judge said.

Once Craylor read the note, Lolly knew the battle was over.

The jury was ushered out. It was time for them to deliberate.

As the courtroom emptied, Lolly asked her mother, "Can I go out and walk around the hall?"

"I've been through these big cases before, darling. There's a pack of reporters out there. After that bombshell you dropped, they'll eat you alive." The trial had taken on some notoriety—*Gypsy Accused of Killing Sheriff*—and the halls were swarming with newspaper reporters from as far away as Sacramento.

"Where's Daddy now, Mama?"

"I don't know," her mother said. "Somewhere pacing the floor, I expect."

"Do you think he's all right?"

"No, I don't think so."

"What I did. Was it bad?"

"You must be so uncomfortable," her mother said.

The cap is the least important thing, she thought. *What's going to happen to Sam? And what have I done to my father?*

"Do I need to go to confession?" Lolly asked.

"Oh, Lolly, that's a big question. You probably saved Sam, but what the consequences will be is hard to tell. No, I don't think you need to go to confession, but I do think praying for your Daddy would be a real good idea."

Lolly slumped low in her seat and chewed on her cuticle. She looked around for her grandfather, but she and her mother were alone in the courtroom.

When the jury filed in that afternoon, the crowd became silent.

"That didn't take long," her mother said, checking her watch.

"Is that good?" Lolly asked.

"Darling, this thing isn't good no matter how it ends."

"Has the jury come to a verdict?" Judge Edmunds asked.

Ed Reginald stood. "We have, your Honor." Bailiff Smithy took a folded paper from Ed and presented it to the judge.

"Sam Maple, please stand," the judge said.

Sam glanced to both sides as if he were looking for someone to okay the judge's order. Then he stood with Dredge Craylor beside him.

Her father leaned forward, his elbows on the table, his fingers tapping his mouth.

Lolly scooted forward in her seat. She felt the weight of her mother's hand on her back.

"Mr. Maple," the judge said solemnly, "the jury has found you not guilty."

Lolly leaped out of her seat, but her mother jerked her back down.

Thank you, God!

Cheering and clapping broke out behind them and Lolly

turned to see Tick standing, her arms above her head, practically crowing while Sophie pressed her hands together as if praying. Hattie Berg waved her lace handkerchief, Matilda and Ducky bounced up and down and hooted, Charlie clapped, Andrea stood on her chair and yelled, "Sam! Sam! Sam!" and David Robinson Crocker thumped his walking stick hard on the floor.

Lolly laughed at their demonstrations and clapped her hands loudly until her mother wrenched her around in her seat.

Judge Edmunds pounded his gavel. "Order!" he said in a loud voice. "I will have order!"

Then Lolly saw her father. She could see only his back, but the hunch of his shoulders told her defeat had landed heavily. That wild skip of jubilation that had fluttered in her chest now twisted into a painful knot and she heard a gasp. It was her mother, her fist jammed against her lips.

The judge pounded again. "The court will come to order." He was shouting now, but the residents of Cougarville continued to demonstrate.

Lolly looked over at Sam. He had sat down, his hands stretched out in front of him on the table, his fingers splayed, his head bowed. Then he stood and turned to the gallery.

"Please," he said in a voice louder than the judge's. "Respect this place."

The courtroom fell quiet. The only sound was a soft keening from Moose Perry's wife, her face pressed into the neck of a friend, who petted her by smoothing her hair.

"I want to thank the members of the jury for their service," the judge announced. "You are now dismissed. And you, Sam Maple, you are free to go."

Sam shook Dredge Craylor's hand and crossed the room to her father, where he paused. When her father didn't stand, Sam said softly, "I'm sorry," then he made his way through the well of the court and pushed open the swinging doors. He stopped at Lolly's row. A smile shone in his eyes as he unbuckled his snakeskin belt, pulled it through the keepers, and passed it to her.

In minutes the room was empty, except for her father, who remained in his seat, and Lolly and her mother. Lolly felt cold and confused. She wanted to curl up on her grandfather's couch and look at photographs of her dead grandmother, or sit in the school's sunlit chapel.

Finally her father got up. Unsteady, he picked up the papers strewn on the table and slipped them into his briefcase. He snapped it shut and pushed through the swinging gate. He stopped to look at Lolly. Without warning, he snatched Sam's snakeskin belt out of her hands. The leather stung when it ripped over her palms and tears welled in her eyes as she watched him stride down the aisle and through the double wooden doors, which slammed closed behind him.

Chapter Twenty-Eight

olly had been sitting under the weeping willow tree reading, but it was too hot and she was thirsty. She decided to go into the kitchen and get a drink. It wasn't until she heard the vodka bottle against the glass that she noticed her father sitting at the breakfast table. It had been a week since the trial and he hadn't gone to the office. Instead, he stayed home drinking and playing his saxophone.

"I didn't see you," she said, pouring a glass of water.

He knocked back his drink.

She walked quickly out of the kitchen and headed for the stairs.

"Are you proud of yourself?" he called.

She stopped.

He stood in the kitchen doorway, his hands pressing against the doorjambs. "Uh? Feeling like you're sitting in the catbird seat, are you?" She moved away. "Look at me, Lolly."

"You told me to do what I thought was right," she said.

"True," he said.

She said nothing.

"Don't give me that holier-than-thou look." He lurched to the sink and grabbed hold of the counter to balance himself and Lolly realized just how much medicine he had taken. "Do you think what you did was right? You kept that note from me. And if that wasn't enough, you walked up that aisle and gave it to the goddamn defense attorney."

"I gave it to the judge."

"Same as giving it to goddamn Craylor!"

But didn't I save Sam?

He took an unsteady step toward her. "Don't you see? It's not so much I lost the case. It's the fact that you didn't trust me. My own daughter didn't trust me with the goddamn note. How could you side with that Maple man...that...poor excuse for a human being? You chose him over your own father. You betrayed me."

"No, Daddy. I just knew that Sam didn't kill anyone!"

"Haven't I done enough for you?" he demanded, his teeth coming together in an angry grind. "Haven't I been a good enough father? You have everything. Every goddamn thing a girl could want."

Now he stood over her, his face reddening. The veins on both sides of his neck bulged, purple chords tunneling under flushed skin. Lolly took a step backward. How well she knew his anger, but this was different. She had never seen him show this much intensity. The thought flashed through her mind that she and her mother should get out of the house.

"I work my ass off for you and your mother," he told her. "To give you two the life you want. This house, the cars, clothes, the private school. I never left you. Never walked out so you had to go to a foul little room and identify my body by the scar on my cheek. I never did that, did I?"

Lolly stumbled up against the first riser and landed hard on her backside as he came closer.

"The nerve of you to speak out in that sacred place!" he said. "Who the hell do you think you are? I taught you to do what's right and you *betray* me. In court! I should beat you." He leaned down, his face inches from hers. "I should beat you until you're raw."

"You were going to have him executed!"

Backing off, he began to walk in smaller and smaller circles. "Don't you understand? He killed a man. He broke the law and he must be punished!"

"But he didn't kill anybody!" Lolly wailed. "Bob Bob killed Moose Perry! The note said he did! I took it out of his hand," she protested as her sobs piled up in her chest. "And he was dead!"

Her father's eyes had an oily glisten to them. She was afraid and she buried her face in her lap. He reached down, grabbed her arms, and shook her so hard her head thrashed back and forth. "I wanted to win!" he shouted. "I *had* to win!"

Her mother appeared at the top of the stairs. "Leave her alone, Regan! It's done. Can't you accept that?"

He kept his grip and looked down at Lolly for a long moment. Her mother rushed down the stairs. "For God's sake, let her go!"

He did and the skin beneath his eyes darkened. "You both betrayed me. Both of you. The only people in the world I thought I could count on."

Suddenly his eyes bulged and drool ran down the side of his chin. A rough hack barked from his lips and his body went limp, folding in on itself as he fell to the floor. He didn't move.

"Regan!" Her mother knelt next to him. "Oh, dear God, Regan! Lolly, call Doc! Tell him to come over! Now!"

When Lolly didn't move, her mother rushed to the telephone and called for Doc.

Lolly remained on the bottom stair and watched. *Let him go. Let him go.*

Chapter Twenty-Nine

"Grandpa," Lolly called. Her body ached as if she had the flu. "Grandpa?"

"Princess!" His eyes brightened as he rushed to his front door. "Oh, princess," his voice softened as he looked at her bruised arms. "What happened to you?"

"I killed my daddy," she said.

"What are you saying?" He guided her to the couch by the big bay window overlooking the rose garden and covered her with a light blanket. "I'll be right back. Just going to call your mama."

"She's not home," she whispered. "She's at the hospital with Daddy. He might be dead by now. If he is, it's my fault. I killed him."

"Nonsense. Tell me what happened."

"I said things. Bad things. And he fell down and Doc came and then the ambulance and Mama told me to come here."

She looked up at her grandfather, her mouth dry, her eyes stinging. "The men who took him away said something about a stroke."

"Oh, dear," her grandfather murmured. His knees popped as he lowered himself beside her. "I guess you don't have to give me the details. When you stood up in court with the note from

Bob Bob—well. Look at me, princess."

She turned her head toward him listlessly.

"It isn't your fault. The fact that your daddy's body is rebelling has nothing to do with you. Let's get out of here and get some fresh air. You up to it?"

She shook her head.

"Come on. I promise it'll do you good. We've got some cobweb cleaning to do."

"What do you mean?"

"A little lady spider has been hard at work spinning webs of confusion in that pretty noggin of yours. We need to clean them out. Come with me."

She got up and they headed for the door.

"Off with the hat," he said and tried to removed the cap.

She grabbed it and held on tightly. "Daddy's the only person who can tell me to take it off."

He shook his head. "Have it your way."

They climbed into his old Ford and drove toward the levee. The car chugged up the dirt ramp and rumbled onto the crown of the berm, driving in the opposite direction from Cougarville. After a while, they rattled down another ramp to a road leading away from town, passing fields of dry grasses and overgrown weeds. In the distance, the blue-purple Sutter Buttes loomed. Her father had told her once that they were at least two million years old. Today they looked like dragon teeth and she turned her eyes away.

Soon, they turned onto a narrow dirt road which took them to two large stone columns where they stopped and got out of the car. The columns were decorated with writing similar to what she had seen across from the Chiseler's Inn. Rusty gates, partially open, creaked as she and her grandfather pushed through. Beyond the gates lay a vast field pitted with deep holes and small gullies.

Lolly saw gravestones, each cocked off-kilter as though the souls underneath were pushing up. All the stones were engraved with the same strange writing. "What is this place?" she asked.

"It's a Chinese cemetery," her grandfather said. "I come here when I want to clear out the cobwebs. It's quiet. These folks don't make a whole lot of noise."

Lolly wandered a bit. "Look, Grandpa," she said. "That grave has dishes on it. Somebody left food."

"Yep," he said. "Some days you'll see ten or twelve families out here piling food on the graves. The Chinese believe that the spirit needs sustenance for the journey to the other world. And who knows? That trip might be a long one."

"To Heaven?" she asked.

"To the other world," he repeated.

She ran her hand over a fairly new marker. Blue and white dishes and several little wooden boxes wrapped with delicate white ribbons were piled at the base. On top of the dishes lay a small teddy bear. The dates on the marker indicated that a baby had died.

"That's not right," Lolly said. "Babies shouldn't die."

"Who says so?"

"But this one lived only fifteen days." She picked up the teddy bear and held it against her chest for a brief moment. "What could this baby have done that it deserved to die? It didn't even get started."

"Maybe it's not a case of doing something wrong," her grandfather suggested. "Maybe the baby had done what it came to do in the few days it was here."

Lolly looked at him for a long moment, then ran her hands over the baby's stone. "Do you think I've done what I came here to do?" she asked.

He cocked his head. "I think you've done a couple of the things you were meant to do. My bet is there's still more. What do you think?"

"Is one of those things speaking out in court?"

"Yes, ma'am."

Lolly pressed her palms together. "I don't know. Sam's free, but my daddy's dying and it's my fault. How can that be right?"

"Lolly, your daddy's smarter than a whip, but he makes mistakes just like the rest of us. By the way, princess, mistakes don't always come from making wrong choices. They also come from making incorrect assumptions."

"It would have been wrong for Sam to be executed," she said.

"You got that right," he said. "Righter than rain. And it took a lot of courage for you to do what you did. Granted, you might have found a less public place to do it in, but you did what you had to do."

She scuffed at the dirt next to the baby's grave. "My daddy turned red and I thought his eyes were going to pop out and land on the floor."

"I'm sorry you had to go through that, but maybe it'll help you understand how wrong your father's assumptions are. He assumes that because he's your daddy, you have to go along with him. That you only have to do what he thinks is right. He assumes what you did was easy."

Lolly's finger traced the Chinese characters on the small headstone. "He'll never forgive me."

"That may be true, but what if you got up one morning to read the headline in the paper that said *Sam Maple Executed?* How would you forgive yourself?"

She stared at her grandfather. "I don't think I'd be able to."

"That's the right answer. And that's how to know if you've done the right thing: ask if you can live with yourself. My sweet child, what you did allows you to answer yes to that question. None of this means that you aren't going to feel bad for your daddy. But as you get older, you'll understand more and more clearly that his broken heart isn't your doing. Matter of fact, it's your daddy who's going to have to figure out if *he* can live with himself. Knowing him, that question might kill him."

She put her arms around her grandfather's waist. "Never leave me, Grandpa."

"On that score, bet your last dollar that I never will. This rat trap of a body might kick off, but you can be sure that my heart's lodged so deep in yours, you'll hear me whispering to you if you listen hard enough."

"Come in, Lolly," her mother said from the doorway of her parent's bedroom. There was another voice from within, raspy and primitive like that of an animal, and her mother repeated, "Come in, Lolly. Come and see your daddy."

Lolly ducked into her own room, slipped into her closet, and huddled beneath the hanging dresses. She heard her mother come in. "I know you're in here, Lolly," she said. "I don't have time to play games."

Lolly crawled out into the room, the cap in her hand.

"Daddy's home, darling. Please come in and welcome him."

"Later, Mama. I promise I'll come in later."

"Now, Lolly."

Since the moment her father had collapsed, Lolly's mother had been a different person. She didn't go to bed at five o'clock in the afternoon, her eyes were brighter, she stood straighter, and when she spoke she meant business.

"Yes, Mama," Lolly said and tugged on her cap.

"You can take that thing off," her mother said.

"When Daddy tells me to," Lolly said, repositioning it.

Her mother took her hand and led her across the hall and into the bedroom. An acrid smell lay heavy in the air.

"Go over and give your daddy a kiss," her mother said.

On a hospital bed lay an ugly creature that reminded Lolly of the papier-mâché figure she'd made in art class, the flesh stretched thin and transparent, the hair white, the fingernails blue.

Backing away, Lolly bumped into her mother, who kept her moving closer to the bed. "Regan," her mother said. "Regan, Lolly's here."

"Don't wake him, Mama. Let him sleep."

"The nurse told me it's good to stimulate him. It's important to keep his brain working."

Her father's eyes opened. The rims were red, the whites dull yellow. His pupils darted back and forth over her mother's face, then settled on Lolly. He gagged.

Lolly fled the room, dashed down the stairs, and ran out into the backyard where she slumped under the weeping willow.

Soon her mother came out and sat next to her. "Lolly?" she said in a low voice.

"He hated me before he had the stroke and he hates me more now. He blames me for making him sick. Well, Grandpa says it's not my fault!" She laid her face on the cool grass and smelled its green ripeness.

"Of course it's not your fault. Is that what you've been

thinking? No, darling, Grandpa is right. It's not your fault. Let's go in."

Lolly hung back.

"Maybe this will help you." Her mother held out the bracelet that Sophie had made. "I'm almost embarrassed to admit it, but I think it has helped me. Now it's time for you to wear it."

"But I gave it to you," Lolly said.

"And I thank you for it. Now I want you to put it on."

Lolly extended her arm and her mother fastened the bracelet to her wrist. As the small stones glistened in the sunlight she thought that maybe, just maybe it did have magical powers.

Chapter Thirty

"Your mama called," Doc said. He looked rumpled, the skin under his eyes dark, his mouth grimly turned down.

Lolly opened the screen door for him and he stepped aside. "My daddy's dying," she said.

Doc started up the stairs, but stopped. "You know, Lolly, you were right."

"About what?"

"About the gypsy woman and her baby. I have some fixing to do in that regard."

She wondered how he could fix the dead Marilee and her baby, and she hoped there might be ways she didn't know about.

He continued up the stairs. She followed. Together they entered the bedroom, and her mother rushed over.

"I'm begging you Doc, do something. Give him a shot. Put him out of his misery. He can't breathe."

Doc gently patted her mother's hand, then sat down on the bed. He opened his bag, pulled out his stethoscope, and listened.

"Can you hear me, Regan?" Doc asked. Lolly's father's eyelids fluttered and Doc took his hand in his. "It's Doc. Squeeze my hand if you can understand me." Lolly saw her father squeeze Doc's hand.

"Regan, you're lungs are filling up. I'm going to give you two shots. An antibiotic to fight the infection and a second to help you rest."

Again her father squeezed.

"Regan, I want you to listen to me carefully," Doc said. "I can't promise this treatment is going to work. You've had a stroke. A bad one. You're slipping, old friend, so it's time to make your peace. Get my drift, partner?"

Squeeze.

Doc opened his bag and pulled out two hypodermics and administered the medications. Again, he took Regan's hand.

"You've been a mighty good man," Doc said, a hitch in his voice. "I'm proud to say that you counted me as your friend. If you make it, I expect to whip your behind on the golf course in the very near future. If you don't, I'll miss you, and that's the damn truth."

She expected her mother to ask Doc for a prescription of smoothies, but her mother simply watched the two old friends hold on to each other.

"I'll be back as soon as I can," Lolly said and ran to her room. In seconds she'd pulled on a pair of jeans and a tee shirt and slipped into tennis shoes. She charged out the back door and made a bee-line for Cougarville.

Sophie appeared at the back of the trailer. She wore lemon yellow Spandex pants that reached just below her knees and a strapless, matching teddy. Her hair was down, held back by a yellow and white striped headband. Apparently awakened from a late summer's day nap, she ambled toward the door.

"Lookie who's here," she said. "Our beauty queen. Dish me the dirt on Bert Parks. Does he really sing 'Here she comes, Miss America' or does he lip-sync?"

"Sophie," Lolly said plaintively, "I have to talk to you!"

Tick peeked out of her room. "Lolly, girl! I'm so happy to see you." She flew toward Lolly.

"Come in, baby," Sophie said and swung open the screen. "You don't ever need to knock at our door. We've missed you." She clucked her tongue. "Why on earth are you still wearin' that cap?"

Lolly stepped into the trailer. "Sophie," she said. "My daddy's dying. He had a stroke about three weeks ago."

"Yeah, baby, I heard. I'm real sorry. No matter what daddy's are in life, we sure don't like to see 'em enter that closet to hang up their duds."

"My daddy's dead, ain't he, Mama?" Tick said. She turned out her toes, bent her knees, and dipped into second position. "But he's waitin' for me on the other side. When I die, he'll be there, right, Mama?"

Sophie ran her hand over Tick's curls. "Everybody'll be waitin' for you, my love."

Lolly took hold of Sophie's hand. "Please, come," she said. "Please come see my daddy and make him well. I know you can do it. You made Andrea well. You can do the same for him."

"Whoa, there, Miss America," Sophie said. "That's a tall order. Healin's tricky stuff." Taking a cigarette from behind her ear, she struck a match with her fingernail, lit it up, and took a long drag. "What color's your daddy?"

Lolly's eyebrows raised in puzzlement. "White," she said.

"I don't mean what race, darlin'. What color is he? When

people get to certain stages in illness, they take on a color. Some turn a greenish tinge, others blue. Some sink into yellow, gray, dark brown. I've seen combinations you'll never find on no color chart. What color's your daddy?"

"White," she said. "Like old sheets, one laying on top of the other."

Sophie drew her close and pressed her against her body. Sophie was warm and soft and smelled of mint and cigarettes. "That white color ain't so good," she said. "I don't think there's much I can do for him."

"Mama says in order to get well you gotta want to," Tick said. "Isn't that right, Mama?"

"Righto, darlin'. Right you are. Besides, Lolly, I can't say your daddy's one of my most favorite people on earth. He almost took Sam away from us."

"I understand," Lolly said. "He's not exactly one of mine either. But he's my father."

"That's true, darlin'. But Lolly, if your daddy gets a load of me in his house, he might bust a gut on the spot. That alone could make him step off this ever lovin' planet days earlier than scheduled."

Lolly pulled away from Sophie. "I know all these things, but please try. I don't want him to die."

"I'm gonna make my daddy wait forever, 'cause I ain't never gonna die," Tick said. "Too dern much stuff to do."

Sophie cocked her head to the left, as if she were listening to something. Then she cocked her head to the right and listened more. Finally, she said, "I don't think it's a good idea that I visit your daddy. I suggest you go home, Lolly darlin', and love him. And if you can't love him, forgive him. Forgiveness is powerful medicine."

"I will, Sophie, I'll do it, but we have to do it all. Please,

please come with me. I won't ever ask you for anything again."

"This ain't easy, Lolly. Anyway, it can be..."

"What?" Lolly asked. "It can be what?"

Sophie stubbed out her cigarette. "Dangerous," she said.

Dangerous for who? Lolly wondered. *Dangerous for who?*

Chapter Thirty-One

L olly, Sophie, and Tick trudged over the levee. Sophie had a cloth bag over her shoulder, and she had wrapped herself in a large swatch of blue silk that kept getting snagged by thistles and brush.

"Drat it," Sophie said, struggling to untangle herself. They stopped while Lolly and Tick carefully unhooked the silk before skipping ahead.

"Come on! Hurry!" Lolly said. Tick jogged next to her, but Sophie dragged behind. "What's the matter, Sophie?" Lolly asked.

"I'm just hopin' this ain't the wrong thing to do."

"It's the right thing," Lolly said. "I tested it."

Finally they came to the entrance of Lolly's driveway.

"That your house?" Tick asked.

"Yep," Lolly said. "Come on." Tick let out a low whistle and Sophie caught her arm. "Darlin', I want to help, but people like us don't belong here."

"Please, Sophie. You've got to at least see him." She started up the driveway, but stopped. The four grotto horses sat Indian style on Lolly's front porch. *Why are they here?* she wondered. She wasn't up to their insults, and if they gave her lip, she didn't have time to flatten any of them. She braced her chin to her chest, lengthened her spine, and walked toward them.

When she reached the bottom step, Vicky Clare said, "We heard your daddy's sick." The other girls gathered behind her.

"We're sorry," Christina said from the back of the group.

"Real sorry," Sabrina added.

"Yeah," Sonja said.

"We came by to see if you want to gallop with us," Vicky Clare said, apparently unable to keep her eyes off Tick, who was looking particularly artful today in cut-off overalls, a lime-green, gathered shirt worn off the shoulders, and a straw hat complete with a large orange flower attached to the band.

"Can't," Lolly said.

"Maybe later?" Vicky Clare said. She nodded toward Tick. "I suppose she can come, too."

Lolly allowed herself a slight smile. "Maybe later," she said. She stepped aside and the four ponies descended the stairs at a trot, eyeing Tick and Sophie curiously. They shambled their way down the driveway, knocking against each other, their horse energy straining at the bit.

Lolly dashed up the steps, stopping only once to turn back to the herd. "Hey," she shouted. "Thanks."

The four horses turned and waved. Vicky Clare reared, the others scraped at the ground, and the Thoroughbred led them in a gallop down the driveway.

Lolly watched until they disappeared before pushing through the screen door. Tick and Sophie followed. Once inside, Tick's eyes grew large, and she ran her hands over the cool mahogany entry table.

"Don't touch," Sophie said.

"Wow," Tick breathed. "You live in a castle."

Lolly grabbed Sophie's hand and pulled her up the stairs.

Tick, hat in hand, followed close behind. As they paused on the landing, Lolly heard Father O'Connor's voice. Motioning for Sophie and Tick to stay where they were, she ran up the stairs and peered into the room.

Father O'Connor stood on one side of her father's bed, her mother on the other. Her grandfather sat in a corner on an upholstered stool.

"In nomine Patris, et Filii, et Spiritus Sancti. Amen."

"Lolly," her mother said. "Come in." Lolly hesitated. "Please," her mother said. "You should be here." Her mother looked pale but calm. The startled glaze that had shaded her eyes for so long had disappeared.

Lolly glanced back at Sophie and Tick. "We'll be downstairs," Sophie whispered.

"Don't leave." Lolly mouthed the words.

"Don't worry, baby," Sophie told her. "We ain't goin' nowhere."

Lolly stepped inside her parent's bedroom. The room was chilly, as if summer existed only on the outside. With the curtains closed, most of the light came from a standing lamp in the corner. A table draped in white linen stood next to the bed and on it was a lighted candle, a small crucifix, a glass of water, a spoon, and a hand towel. It looked like somebody's failed attempt to crate an altar.

Father O'Connor leaned toward her father, dipped his thumb into a small shallow vial of oil, and rubbed it between his thumb and forefinger before tracing the shape of a cross on her father's forehead. Lolly sucked in her breath. Sister

Theodora had told her about the Last Rites. It meant you were going to die and the ritual would keep you out of Hell.

Father O'Connor continued to murmur Latin over her father, whose eyes suddenly opened and sounds came from somewhere deep inside his throat. His red-rimmed eyes flicked from her mother to Father O'Connor and back to her mother. Finally they came to Lolly and stopped.

The gurgling noises ceased. He looked at her for a long time without blinking. Then he said, "Lolly."

Lolly reached out, but he jerked his hand away.

He hates me. He hates me right down to his toes.

Grandpa tried to stop her, but she stomped out of the room and hurried down the stairs.

Sophie hovered at the bottom of the wood-turned balustrade, and Tick turned in rapturous twirls in the cool hallway.

"*Pssst*," Sophie hissed at Tick, but she was lost in her dance. "Tick," Sophie said sternly.

Tick froze. "Sorry, Lolly. This don't mean I ain't sad for you. I were dancin' a prayer."

"Thank you," Lolly said and rubbed her hands hard over her thighs. "Sophie, I tried to touch my daddy, but he wouldn't let me. He pulled away."

Sophie put her arms around her. "Darlin', your daddy's busy doin' somethin' that ain't easy."

Lolly breathed in Sophie's perfume. "What's that?"

"Dyin', ragged head. Livin' is a habit ingrained deep as the seed in a peach, and it's durn hard to give up. Cut him some slack, my sweet girl."

Lolly nodded. "We'll wait for Father O'Connor to finish, and then we'll go up." She sat down on the first stair. Tick sat next to her.

Sophie leaned against the wall and sighed. "You let us know when the time is right."

There was a rustle at the top of the stairs. They all turned and looked up. It was her grandpa. He winked at Lolly and then went back into the room. Minutes later, Father O'Connor came down the stairs. He nodded to Sophie and Tick and said, "May I have a word with you alone, Lolly?"

"I have to go upstairs," she told the priest, as he guided her into the living room. Suddenly it seemed very important to her that she be close to her father.

"A wee moment," Father O'Connor said. He turned away and blessed himself, then he turned back. "Listen to me, child. I'm going to talk straight. You're old enough to understand that this is no time to mince words."

Lolly's throat tightened. Why was everybody so sure her father was going to die?

"Your da's on his way out," Father O'Connor said. "What he needs most of all is for you to tell him you love him."

"Yes, Father, I will." *But I want to tell him while he's alive,* she thought, *so I need to get Sophie up there to fix him.*

"No settling scores," he said authoritatively. "Do you understand me, Lolly? Your mama's filled me in on a few things about you and your da. The most important thing now is that he knows you love him."

"Yes, Father. Thank you. Good-bye, Father."

Lolly headed toward the foyer, anxious to get Father O'Connor on his way. There wasn't much time left for Sophie to work her magic.

"One more thing." Father caught her by the arm. "What in God's name are you doing with those two?" He cocked his head in the direction of Sophie and Tick. "Gypsies? This is not the time for you to be bringing people like that into this house. It's vital that you be a good girl now."

She nodded. "I understand, Father. I'll be good."

Lolly watched him hobble off the porch and waited until his car disappeared down the driveway. Then she clambered up the stairs and motioned for Sophie and Tick to follow her into the bedroom where her grandfather and her mother stood at the foot of the bed.

"Mama," she whispered. "Mama, I have something I want to do."

Her mother looked around. A wan smile flickered across her face. "What is it, darling?" And then she saw Sophie in her blue drape and the ragged girl, and she twitched as though she'd received a minor jolt of electricity.

"I'm sorry," her mother murmured to Sophie, her voice low, "but you'll have to go. You see, my husband is dying."

"I understand," Sophie said.

"No, wait!" Lolly cried. "Mama, we have to try this. Sophie made Andrea well, and maybe she can make Daddy well too!"

"Lolly, this isn't the time," her mother said. "These people must go."

"We have to try, Mama. I did the test. I asked myself if it was right, like Grandpa told me to do."

Clarissa turned to her father. "Daddy, what do you have to do with this?"

Grandpa's eyes, narrow and inquisitive, were trained on Lolly.

"Tell her," her mother said, insistently. "Tell her this isn't right."

"Hi, Tick," Grandpa said, running his hand gently over Tick's curls.

"Hi, Grandpa," Tick said.

Lolly's mother's mouth opened in astonishment.

"Relax, Clarissa," Grandpa said. "So, Sophie, you've healed somebody else?" he asked.

"She fixes people all the time," Tick said. "Everybody in Cougarville comes to Mama even if they just have a toothache. Ain't that so, Mama?"

"He looks real bad," Sophie whispered. "Sometimes, there ain't nothin' nobody can do. We all have an appointed time to leave. This may be his."

Grandpa nodded. "True." Then he turned to Clarissa. "It can't hurt," he said. "And it may make Lolly feel better. She thinks she's responsible for this, you know."

"Daddy," Clarissa breathed, "it's a sin. I mean, the Church wouldn't sanction this."

"How can trying to help Daddy when he's sick be a sin?" Lolly asked.

"Clarissa, you're not the only one suffering," Grandpa said. "The girl is, too. Let her help the only way she knows how."

"But the Church..."

"What the Church doesn't know won't hurt it. Besides, O'Connor did his mumbo jumbo and I don't see that Regan's improved one hair."

"I won't fight you both," her mother said. "I'm too tired." She went to the door. Turning to Grandpa she said, "Whatever happens, it'll be on your head."

Grandpa drew Lolly close to him.

The room came alive with the flickering candles Sophie placed around the room. Lolly was about to move the table draped in white linen that her mother had prepared for Father O'Connor when Sophie said, "Leave it. There ain't nothin' there that's bad. We're gonna need it all."

At Sophie's instruction, Lolly and Tick held hands. Then Sophie took hold of each girl. Lolly glanced over her shoulder. "Grandpa?"

Grandpa joined the circle. They raised their clasped hands and Sophie began her chant: *"Haram infata cum, Lo epoodo sonesta tum.* Now, darlin', you lean close to your daddy and talk to him."

"What do I say?"

"There ain't but one rule. Tell the truth."

Grandpa motioned for Sophie and Tick to follow him, and the three of them quietly left the room. Without looking at her father, Lolly slowly approached the hospital bed and leaned against it. Her hands ran over the soft sheets. Her eyes traced a crack in the ceiling, focused on the folds in the curtains, then finally landed on the small bronze crucifix on the table.

Why do you just hang there? Do something!

But there was no voice, no shining light, no holy clouds drifting in through the window. Lolly was going to have to do this on her own.

She took several huge gulps of air as her eyes fell on her father. He was dry and used up, a piece of old cardboard bleached by the sun and he smelled of dead flowers. More than anything she wanted to run over the levee and sit under the cottonwoods.

She leaned close. Bile sprang into her throat and she knew how forgiveness tasted. "Daddy," she whispered. He lay silent. Maybe he was already dead.

Her next confession loomed.

"And how did you kill your father, Lolly?" Father

O'Connor would ask.

"By bringing gypsies around to his death bed."

She gripped the sheets in her hands and said, "Daddy, it's Lolly."

He didn't move, so she leaned closer, close enough to see the hair growing in his ear.

"Daddy, I don't want you to go," she said in a low voice, speaking very slowly so that he wouldn't miss a word. "I prayed for you to die, so maybe your getting sick is my fault. But you were mean and ugly. What you did to Bo, and the things you did to..."

She waved her hand as if fanning away a bad smell.

"No, that's not how I want to do this. What I really want to tell you is..."

Only tell the truth.

"...that I forgive you. I do. Actually, I think maybe forgiveness takes a lot of work, and I don't know that we have enough time for me to get it right." She touched her father's cheek. "So don't die now."

There was no response from this mummy person that resembled her father. She remembered how they did it in the movies when they wanted to know if somebody was alive. She reached over to raise an eyelid—and a hand free from the sheets grabbed her wrist.

"Do the right thing."

Chapter Thirty-Two

It's amazing!" Her mother's eyes were clearer than she had ever seen them. Everything about her was more vivid and, somehow, more defined. "Your father is so much better. Come in and see."

"You mean he's not going to die?" Lolly scrambled out of bed. Before leaning around the corner of the doorway to peer into her parents' bedroom, she pulled on the cap. Her father was sitting up in bed. He was still pale and meager, but a delicate rose color had risen in his cheeks.

"Good morning, Lolly," he said. Now his voice was more like a whisper.

Lolly stood with one bare foot planted on the other. She bunched seersucker pajamas in her fists and she felt queasy. Her mother slashed at the curtains and light bled into the room. Lolly turned from it and faced her father. His once-handsome face now wore triangles of shadow, making him appear fatigued and worn.

The bracelet Sophie had made felt warm on her wrist. She brought it up close to her face and she felt its heat on her cheek.

"Lolly." His voice was faint. His manner now was soft and almost kind.

If he gets well, she wondered, *will he go back to being a mad bear raging through our lives?* Maybe she shouldn't have pushed things and just let events take their natural course. Had it been the right decision to drag Sophie and Tick across the levee to his deathbed?

"What's the matter, Lolly?" her mother asked.

"It's all right, Clarissa," her father said. "All this must be difficult for her." He tried to laugh, but the attempt turned into a cough.

"Did you die?" Lolly asked.

"I think I came pretty close," he said.

"It's a miracle," her mother said. "Regan, Father O'Connor gave you the Last Rites."

"I remember everything," he said. "Doc was here and Jeb. And Lolly. And Father O'Connor."

Her mother took a step toward her father. "Do you think that Father's prayers helped you?"

"No," Lolly interrupted. "It definitely wasn't the oil."

"What do you know, missy?" her mother said sharply. "You don't think it was that woman you brought here, do you?" Her hand clapped over her mouth.

"What woman?" Her father tried to sit up.

A soft rap came at the door. Her mother opened it and Grandpa stepped in.

"Would you lookie there," Grandpa said.

Lolly grabbed his wrinkled hand and kissed his palm. "Daddy's better, Grandpa," she said.

"I can see that, princess. Mighty glad to see you, Regan."

"Not as glad as I am to see you, Jeb. Rate I was going, I was going to beat you to the promised land."

Her grandfather chuckled. "You're tougher than that, Regan."

"Jeb, I want to say something to you," Lolly's father began.

"No need, Regan." Her grandfather repositioned the hat on Lolly's head. "All you have to do now is get back on your feet."

"Daddy," Lolly said. "Do you remember a woman wrapped in blue material?"

"That'll do," her mother said.

"The blue sarong?" he said and his eyes glittered as if they were two highly polished stones.

"Enough," her mother said.

Lolly smoothed the top of her pajamas. "Did you feel afraid when you thought you were going to die?" she asked. If she wasn't going to be able to explain what Sophie had done, at least she wanted to know what the experience had been like for him.

"Lolly Candolin," her mother scolded. "I don't think that's an appropriate question."

"It's fine, Clarissa," he said. He folded his pasty hands and looked for a long moment out the window. When he turned back his face was sad. "Yes, I felt fear," he said. "But you know, Lolly, I *am* going to die sometime. I don't think I ever believed that before."

"We've all been give that assignment," her grandfather said.

"But not soon," Lolly's mother said, as if it were a rule, one that had been written down somewhere and couldn't be revoked.

"Delusion is a thief," her father said almost shyly before breaking into a spasm of coughs.

Her mother held a glass of water to his lips. He rested his head against the pillow.

"At the trial," he said, looking directly at Lolly, "when you stood up and gave the judge that note, I was so angry. My God,

I could barely breathe. I remember feeling like I was falling away, all of me thinning into useless sheets of yellowed-paged briefs. My life seemed pointless. I was being laid waste."

Lolly began to feel that maybe it had been the mad bear that had died and left her father here in its place.

He drew himself up on his elbows. "And then something changed. I was drawn back."

"It was Sophie," Lolly told him, taking a step closer.

"The blue sarong?"

"There was no one like that here, Regan," her mother said. "Please, lay back and rest."

"It doesn't matter," he said. "What's important is this moment. Only this moment."

Lolly's throat ached.

"Come here," he said to her, but she didn't move. "Come on. I'm not going to bite."

She inched forward. With a show of strength she did not think he had to call on, he reached out and pinched the cap off her head and flung it across toward her grandfather, who caught it and stuffed it in his back pocket. Her father's dark eyes snapped and a faint smile broke the grimness of his face.

Lolly ran her hand over the patches on her head that had filled in with soft short hair. "Daddy," she said. "I'm sorry for what I did in court."

Tell the truth.

"I mean, I'm sorry that I hurt you. But I knew that Sam wasn't the one that killed Moose. I knew it even before I found Bob Bob's note. But I was afraid to give it to you because I knew how much you wanted Sam to be bad and I didn't know what else to do because I knew that Sam wouldn't kill someone and the way things were going I was afraid that Sam was going to be put in jail for life or executed."

Her father exhaled such a shuddering breath that it frightened her and she stopped talking as he sank back into the bed. "I'd better call Doc," her mother said.

"No," he said. His chest rattled. "I'm all right."

"Daddy?"

"I've made so many mistakes," he wheezed. "Been hard on people. On my wife, on my daughter, on Jeb." He spoke about them as if they weren't in the room.

Then he pulled back and looked at Clarissa. "Ridiculous as it may sound, I think I've been given a second chance," he said slowly. "Forgive me, Clarissa."

Her mother cupped her father's face in her hands. Lolly had never seen a show of affection between her parents and it embarrassed her. She looked away.

"Lolly?"

"Here, Daddy. I'm right here."

"I don't want you to change," her father told her. His tongue ran across his cracked lips. "You're a good person, Lolly. I think I finally understand. For years I've taken my anger at my father out on you. If I could go back and talk to that young Regan Candolin, I'd tell him not to carry the past around with him. It's too damn heavy."

He fumbled for her hand and she slipped it into his.

"It's your daddy who needs to be considering the consequences," he said.

She stiffened at the word.

"Do me a favor and open the top drawer of my dresser," he said. "There's something there that belongs to you."

Lying beneath stacks of socks and ironed linen handkerchiefs was Sam's snakeskin belt.

"It's yours," he said. "Sam gave it to you."

Lolly lifted the belt out and ran her hands over the scales

and the silver buckle that formed the head of a snake. She took two turns of the belt around her waist, causing her seersucker pajamas to pleat under its grip. "Thank you."

Her father struggled to get his legs over the side of the bed.

"Regan, you should be resting," her mother said.

"What do you need, Daddy?" Lolly asked him. "I'll get it for you."

"This is something you and I are going to do together," he told her.

Leaning against the bed to get his balance, he began to shuffle across the room.

"I'm not sure you should be doing this, Regan," her mother said as she came up and took one of his arms.

"What's the point if you can't make things right?" her father said.

"Let me help," her grandfather said, taking the other arm.

Lolly led the way, and the three of them followed her down the stairs. Halfway, her father stopped.

"Damn, I'm weak," he said.

"You'll get stronger," Lolly said.

"Come on, Regan," her grandfather said. "Let's keep going."

They made it down and her father led them to the kitchen. When he went to the cupboard and pulled out a bottle of vodka, Lolly's heart squeezed. Her grandfather put an arm around her shoulder.

A horn of corn! He's going to drink a horn of corn?

Her father uncapped the bottle and held it up. "Here's to you, Lolly," he said. Then he upended it and poured the liquor down the sink.

"So, missy," her father said. "You've got yourself a deal. I'll stop drinking, if you won't cut your hair—for a while."

He extended his hand and she took it.

"Deal," she said and laughed.

He drew her to him, wrapping his arms around her. "One more thing. Those people across the levee."

Lolly's breath stopped and she pulled away. "What about them?"

"I've been thinking. Maybe there's something we can do to help them in the wintertime. You know, when the river rises and floods their camp. I think there might be a simple way of diverting the river just enough so Cougarville can remain dry."

Yes, she thought. Now she was sure. The mad bear had died.

"I'm not saying it would be easy. Lot of folks in town aren't so keen on those people who are living on the other side, but I expect if you, your mama, your grandpa, and me work together, we just might get it done."

"Thank you, Daddy! Thank you!" Lolly whipped the snake belt from her waist and cracked it with fierce snaps, and then she reared and pranced around the kitchen.

"Whoa, there little filly," her father said. Her mother laughed so hard tears rolled down her cheeks.

"I've got to tell Tick!" Lolly exclaimed.

"Slow down, princess!" her grandfather said.

"Now?" her father asked.

"Yes! Oh, please, can I go?"

"No," her mother said. "You can't go over there by yourself."

Lolly opened the door to her grandfather's old Ford. "Sure

you don't want to come?" she said to both of her parents. Grandpa turned on the car and it choked before settling into a steady idle.

"Not this time," her mother said, smiling. "I think it's better if just you and your grandpa make this trip."

"Daddy?" Lolly asked.

"You go on," he said warmly and put his arm around her mother's shoulders. "And give our regards to that redheaded girl."

Lolly closed the car door.

"And Lolly," her father called to her. "You're doing the right thing."

Lolly and her grandfather bumped up the levee ramp road and on to the gravel track, stopping near the trailer camp.

"I'll be right back, Grandpa," Lolly said, getting out. She knew she wouldn't have to go far to find Tick as Tick would have heard the motor.

In seconds Tick appeared, her red curls glowing in the late afternoon sun. She walked toward the car and placed her hand on the windshield.

"Hey, Lolly," Tick said. "What're you doing here?" Then she peered into the car. "Grandpa!" she exclaimed.

"I've got great news!" Lolly said. "My daddy's not going to die and he's real sorry for what he did to Sam *and* he's going to try and get people to fix the river so it won't flood you out in the wintertime."

Tick's eyes closed to a squint. "Are you teasin' me?"

"No," Lolly said. "It's true."

She turned to her grandfather who got out of the car and joined them.

"It's true, Tick," Grandpa said. "It doesn't matter who you are or where you live, we all have lessons to learn in our lives.

Lolly's daddy has just learned a couple, as we all have, from you and the other folks in Cougarville."

Tick began to smile, but then her expression darkened. "You still mad?" she asked Lolly.

"No," Lolly said. "I'm not mad anymore."

"You sure?" Tick asked.

"Yes," Lolly said. "The mad's all gone."

"And that means everything's right as rain!" Grandpa said and pulled Lolly's cap from his back pocket and sent it flying over the levee.

A smile broke across Tick's face, then she leaped, her arms flinging over her head, and she whirled into wild contortions. Lolly tossed back her head, and then sprang into her own version of a dance. The two of them held hands as they waltzed in circles over the crown of the levee road, laughing and crowing and chanting: *"Hiram infata cum, Lo epoodo sonesta tum..."*

The End

ABOUT THE AUTHOR

Elizabeth Appell's short stories have placed in national competitions and she has published in Storied Crossings, Scribes Hill, VA, Wilmington Blues, and Snake Nation. She has written four novels and six screenplays, two have placed as finalists in national screenwriting competitions. She has completed three full-length plays that have been given directed readings in New York, Los Angeles, and San Francisco. She recently completed a musical for cabaret.